MW01536500

D.G.R.

Vancity Vampires The Collection

Copyright © 2022 by D.G.R.

All rights reserved. No part of this publication may be reproduced, stored or transmitted in any form or by any means, electronic, mechanical, photocopying, recording, scanning, or otherwise without written permission from the publisher. It is illegal to copy this book, post it to a website, or distribute it by any other means without permission.

This novel is entirely a work of fiction. The names, characters and incidents portrayed in it are the work of the author's imagination. Any resemblance to actual persons, living or dead, events or localities is entirely coincidental.

D.G.R. asserts the moral right to be identified as the author of this work.

First edition

This book was professionally typeset on Reedsy.
Find out more at reedsy.com

Contents

Forward by RW Duder

D amien Richard and I met in 2019. You know the expression, the student becomes the teacher? That's what quickly happened for me as my intended mentorship of him turned into a great mutual respect and admiration for each other. As it turned out, we also were writers. It wasn't what introduced us nor brought us together and yet we both write horror. Horror fanatics are quite a bunch aren't we? We have our own sub-genres that we love and tropes that we chase and weird dark rabbit holes of content we sometimes explore. But we are just regular people... sort of.To find a like-minded, genuine, fiercely emotionally intelligent individual with whom you connect with... over horror... what are the chances? As they say in New York, Forgeddabuddit.

Damien and I began a relationship of reading, editing, promoting, discussing, and building each other's stories. Currently my backlog includes 11 horror novels, 2 series', and a number of projects planned for release in 2023. From my first horror release of Desolation in 2014, it was another four years before I published my second and third novels simultaneously, Amy and The Art of Dying. Just before Damien and I began to mentor each other through the voracious jungle of indie authorship, I released Captive. So 50% of my work I've actually written, released, marketed, and sold in the last three years. I owe much of that prolific content to Mr. Richard.

Make no mistake though, I could not and would not associate myself so closely as an author with someone whose work I did not completely enjoy. As a reader, as a cinephile, as a gatherer of popular culture content, I needed to make sure that in order to give back what he was willing to give my work, I needed to truly enjoy the content.

Vampires. As soon as I say that word you have an image, a perception, an expectation, an experience that you relate to vampires. They are so ingrained in our culture that nearly every person, but especially fans of vampires, have the perfect ideal vampire tale they enjoy.

I was sixteen when the 1994 film Interview with the Vampire came out. My local video store I frequented held every new release for me every Friday. I'd go from school, straight to the video store and gather my treasures. I was such a regular that they always included the R-rated films for me as well. Having led a very sheltered deeply religious life before the age of 14, this was my first experience with a whole new plethora of films.

This is the time I fell in love and became obsessive about horror as I invested hours into the Halloween series, Friday the 13th, Child's Play, Hammer Horror and the completely bizarre horror films like Chopping Mall or Jack Frost.

I don't remember being a vampire fan or really knowing much about vampires prior to 1994. Interview with the vampire blew me away. I was hooked. It started a passionate frenzy down the vampire rabbit hole. First came the novel. In addition to being a total cinephile even at 16, I was a voracious reader. I had recently discovered Stephen King and now Anne Rice. I devoured her series. Anne Rice's vampire world directly influences how I see vampires today. Bram Stoker's Dracula, obviously. You have to see where the lore began (although whenever I read Dracula I'm admittedly underwhelmed.)

Vampires are literally everywhere in popular culture and it's because we love vampires. I love vampires. That being said, I like my vamps a certain way. To each their own, but I like them dark, mysterious, eccentric even.

When it comes to Damien's Vancity Vampire series, I got to see the beginnings and evolution of what it became. I was a reader from the early drafts and have since read the series again at least twice.

I'm sure you can all agree that if you're a fan of the vampire, you have a certain expectation of how they should be portrayed. For most of us, it's a traditional, classic vampire but with allowance for unique traits or abilities or situations. The first in the Vancity series, Newborn, nailed every single thing for me. It's riveting, it's thoughtful in its creation of the world they live in, where vampires very much exist.

What makes Newborn and the subsequent sequels so good for me is the characters. You're literally dropped into these two brothers' lives at various stages. You see the impact of the childhood trauma and how it follows a man his entire life. Jonah is a man of great moral fiber who will go to great depths and risk becoming what he hates the most.

The crux of the entire series for me is Eldon. While the series immerses you in the lives of these two brothers, there is the darker side. Eldon is the personification of a great vampire. The evil is what really gets under your skin and stays with you after you've finished. The darkness that surrounds the vampire in the series is haunting. It's the devil in the details. The way the vampires speak, act, kill, leaves you eagerly anticipating their next move. All the while you're completely invested in the lives of these two brothers over the course of decades and how this completely chance encounter changes their very lives forever.

Listen, if 10,000 hours make you an expert at something, I'm an expert at horror. I've watched at least that in films, not to mention my own writing I've spent years on. I've been an active member of the horror community for many years. Vancity Vampires puts the myths and legends squarely in the streets of Vancouver for a battle over human lives that not all will survive. Not only do the backbone of the stories resonate with horror fans and vampire lovers but the short stories included in the omnibus tie it all together in a perfect blend.

Damien Richard's world is a fantastic, cutthroat, edge-your-seat ride and an absolute gem for horror readers.

Newborn Chapter 1

Jonah had been waiting weeks for this night, just so he could see the look on his brother's face. It had taken a bit of legwork, but that was okay— he and his brother had made it. They. Were. In!

Jonah and his younger brother, Jimmy, followed Chad down a dark employee corridor that was not nearly as well maintained as the theatre's public areas. Unlike the lobby and theatre, there was no carpet back here. Most of the lights were burnt out, and one even flickered like in a bad horror movie. The floors were sticky from spilled pop, though, so at least that was the same. Jimmy had been obviously nervous walking through the unfamiliar halls, and honestly those lights were a bit creepy, but Jonah had given him a pep talk when his brother started to look a little scared. Bolstered, Jimmy beamed with excitement again. After all, it was opening night!

Jonah held on to his little brother's hand. Jimmy could barely contain himself! They were about to skip all the lines and see the last Star Wars, *Return of the Jedi*, in theatres on opening night. People had been camping outside of the theatre for the last two days just to ensure they got in. Jimmy had wanted to be out there with them, to be the first in line with Jonah. Their parents quashed that idea pretty quickly. They thought it would be just fine to rent the VHS when it came out next year, or at least wait until the movie hit the dollar theatre in a few months. Parents didn't understand, but Jonah knew better. Science fiction was Jimmy's life, and Star Wars rated above all other sci-fi worlds. So Jonah came through, because that's what a big brother does.

At fifteen Jonah was in his last year of junior high, while Jimmy was only in grade four. Despite the age difference, the brothers were pretty much inseparable when they weren't in school. They played video games, read comic books, and took piano lessons together. Next year Jimmy would probably start taking guitar lessons alongside Jonah as well. Jonah couldn't wait until Jimmy's hands were big enough to reach around a guitar fretboard. For now, Jimmy practiced piano while Jonah played guitar.

They were best friends. There was no way Jonah was going to let Jimmy miss out on the opening night of the last Star Wars movie if he could help it.

Chad sat next to him in science class and, naturally, was his partner for collaborative assignments. He knew Chad worked at the White Rock theatres, and it had only taken a little bribery to convince Chad to sneak them in. Jonah just had to introduce Chad to the school jazz band's drummer, Melanie. Jonah had even put in a good word for him. They had set a date for next weekend, since Chad didn't have to work.

Chad pushed open a door that let in the light and buzz of a cinema full of excited movie-goers. People had even dressed up for the occasion. Boys wore lightsabers and girls had their hair in tight braided balls on either side of their heads. Where Jimmy had been apprehensive of the grungy corridor, his face lit up with pure joy at the sight of everyone ready to take in the movie. Chad ushered them to a set of three seats where another girl sat in the White Rock Cinema uniform.

"Sylvie," Chad called to her, "This is my friend Jonah, and his little brother Jimmy. Can you make sure they keep these seats?"

Sylvie nodded. That was good enough for Jonah. He took the seat next to the girl, which gave Jimmy the aisle seat.

"Chad must really like you," Sylvie stated flatly.

"Why's that?" Jonah asked.

"This is going to be the biggest movie of the year, if not the decade. These seats are supposed to be reserved for ushers, and I can guarantee every employee in here wants the seats you're sitting in." She said in a matter-of-fact tone. "Some of the guys are stuck watching Chained Heat right now, and I doubt they're happy about it."

"So why let us stay?" he asked. Jonah couldn't help but be a little nervous.

If Sylvie wanted to kick them out, she had every right.

"You're cute." She smiled at him, "And I like that you obviously went through some trouble to get your little brother in here"

Sylvie leaned over Jonah to look at Jimmy, "You a big Star Wars fan?" she asked.

"Yup," he said with a huge grin.

"Who's your favourite character?" she prompted.

"Yoda!"

"Oh yeah?"

"Yeah, cause he knows all the Jedi secrets."

Sylvie let out an adorable laugh, and Jonah joined in.

A great movie, and a cute girl! Jonah was sure tonight was going to be a good night.

* * *

Eldon woke. It had been a long time since he had taken to the ground to sleep. Instinctually, he knew not to open his eyes or mouth. For five nights he had lain with Patrick, feeding the man his own blood. Tonight, his new protégé would rise as vampire. His vampire.

Anticipation filled Eldon. He needed to feed, and he wanted to teach his newborn how to eat as well. A meal had been arranged and was ready and waiting. Had he not been underground, Eldon would have licked his lips with eagerness. He could feel his dead heart thump just once in anticipation. He craved the sensation of it pumping as his teeth sank deep into flesh.

As he had each night when he went to ground with Patrick's human corpse, he had encircled his arms around the body, transferring himself into it, changing it. Yet something did not feel right now. Eldon stretched his hands through the earth, searching, and finding nothing.

Faster and faster, Eldon pushed the dirt away. His vampire strength moved him easily through the earth to the surface. The ground should have compacted overnight, but Eldon could feel that it had just been disturbed moments before. There was no doubt––it had been disrupted by the vampire Eldon himself had just created.

As he breached the surface, his hands ceased their digging and instead hoisted him out of the dirt in one fluid, serpentine movement. At the sight before him, he opened his mouth wide in a hiss of rage. His protégé was gone.

The night before, knowing his newborn vampire would need to feed, Eldon had gone back to his usual hunting grounds on East Hastings. The derelict and destitute are the weakest of mind; the vampire's glamour can easily be pushed on them, bending them to his will. Even the most taxing of demands will be done without a hint of doubt, once properly glamoured. Eldon had done exactly that. The two homeless men had been sharing a homemade cigarette when he found them. The cigarette looked like it was rolled with left-over tobacco emptied out of the butts discarded in the mall's ashtrays.

The task had been easy, the glamour firm. The two men left that night. They had walked the long way from East Hastings, through Vancouver's downtown, and into the neighbouring city of White Rock, where Eldon's protégé had lived. The men had rested above the vampires, waiting in the graveyard for the vampires to rise. Eldon had envisioned that he and his newborn would feed together, Eldon showing his new son his powers and the joys of feeding. That was not to happen.

The two old men still remained, both cold and lifeless. Their throats had been ripped open. Gore covered both bodies. This was not good, and certainly not a good omen for what was to come.

Even some of the bats that constantly followed the vampire were gone. Many remained but some must have joined Patrick when he left.

Eldon needed to find Patrick, but couldn't chance that the bodies of the two men were found, particularly near Patrick's creation site. Some of Patrick's DNA would have been left behind in the ground during the past five nights of Patrick's transformation.

The older vampire handled the two bodies easily. He tossed them into the hole he had created upon awakening, then tossed any belongings in after them. The hole was deep, almost seven feet down. The two men would likely

7

never be found, if anyone even thought to look here as disturbed dirt is a common enough sight in a graveyard.

Despite the mess of the killings, there was not much blood or gore on the ground. Patrick must have greedily ingested every scrap he could before leaving the graveyard. Of what little gore remained, Eldon could do nothing but hope it went without notice until rain washed it into the ground or the graveyard's scavengers claimed their own paltry meals.

Although he possessed the enhanced speed common to his kind, the clean-up had still taken precious time. With the task complete, Eldon was free to hunt. The smell of Patrick's kills was easy to pick up in the night air, and soon Eldon had isolated the trail leading towards White Rock's small city centre.

Eldon launched himself into the night sky.

Newborn Chapter 2

J immy could *not* stop talking about the movie. To his brother's delight, Jimmy bounced on the balls of his feet, chattering away.

"I can't get over how cool that bounty hunter was!" Jimmy exclaimed.

"Yeah, I like his suit, but I wonder how he's supposed to see with that helmet on."

"Because he's an alien! He's got to be."

Jonah laughed at this. His brother was always good at filling in the gaps if something in a science fiction world didn't make sense. Usually this meant Jimmy would just give the blanket statement of "aliens" but that was okay, Jimmy was likely right. Even when they found out otherwise, Jimmy was happy to say that it easily *could* have been aliens.

"You're probably right," Jonah said.

"Do you think it's really over?" Jimmy asked. He stopped walking and looked at his brother very seriously. "I mean, just because the Emperor and Darth Vader have been defeated, doesn't mean the Empire is just going to fall apart, right?"

"Who knows, we'll just have to wait and see," Jonah said and gave his brother a big smile. He knew Jimmy loved the mystery of it.

This was obviously the right answer because Jimmy smiled brightly and started bouncing along again.

Jimmy continued on briefly about what he'd loved about the movie, but before long he moved into more familiar things about Star Wars that he thought were cool. Above all else, Jimmy loved the Star Wars technology, especially the way the X-wing opened and closed its wings, the tools used to repair the ships, and the laser rifles.

Jonah had heard all of this before. Jimmy had certain themes he loved to talk about, and Jonah found his mind drifting. He was thinking about a riff he had been writing on his guitar. He knew what he wanted to do for the rhythm piece, but he was planning a solo to play over it. As he absentmindedly planned out his riff, he also found himself thinking about the cute girl at the theatre. Maybe she'd be impressed if he dedicated his new song to her?

As he walked along, lost in his thoughts, he was looking at the night sky, enjoying the few stars he could see despite the city lights obscuring most of the display. He trotted along with his brother, and his thoughts turned to camping, and how much he enjoyed staring at the night sky when their mom and dad would take them to the mountains. He hadn't noticed when Jimmy had stopped talking. At least, not at first. It seemed to him like there hadn't been a pause. Jimmy was talking, and then all of sudden, he wasn't.

Jonah stopped examining the night and looked around. His brother had been there! When Jimmy's voice cut out...what had he been saying?

Jonah thought back. "It's so gross that he kissed his sister...ugh." That was it, but then nothing.

"Hey, Jimmy?" Jonah called out tentatively. He spun around in a circle, looking in every direction, but his brother was nowhere to be seen. It was like he vanished along with his BMX. Jonah's heart suddenly felt like it was about to explode out of his chest, it was thumping so hard. Adrenaline surged and his fingers started to tingle.

"Jimmy?!" he called louder, frantic now.

"Jimmy, this isn't funny!"

Jimmy didn't answer.

* * *

Eldon had his hands balled into fists so hard his nails broke the skin of his palms. He knew if he were still human, his heart would be pounding, his bloodstream flooding with adrenaline. Even without his body's physical reaction to this stress, he was overcome with the same feelings.

An hour. Patrick had almost an hour on his own as a newly born vampire. New vampires were wild with hunger. Eldon wanted to act so badly it felt like his skin was vibrating. He didn't know what to do, or where to look.

Eldon had flown through the night, directly to Patrick's newly-abandoned home, but Patrick had not been back there. There was no scent of him.

The only reason Eldon had considered making another vampire was because of the council, and he cursed them now. When Eldon had been asked to join the council, it had been a point of pride. At a mere one hundred and fifty-three years, he was the youngest vampire to ever receive the invitation. Eldon had navigated the vampire world well. He had basked in the glory and esteem that came with the request. Not so long as to seem pompous but not so little that the vampire community would not see the significance of the event.

Of course, the request was not a guarantee that he could join the council. When Eldon had appeared before them for consideration, they had told him that, like each of them, he would need an assistant, one that would be bound to him by creation. As a rule, vampires do not create other vampires when they are still so young as he. Creation must be approved by the council. It is one of their many duties. Never before had *they* petitioned a vampire to create another. Yet that's what was asked, so that is what was done. Now it may all be in ruin.

Somewhere, his creation hunts with a hunger known only to the new. Even after a hundred and fifty years, Eldon could remember the intensity of his own hunger. The first taste of vampiric instinct carried a need that would never be rivalled.

Eldon stared across the expanse that was the city of White Rock, a southern suburb of the greater city of Vancouver. Eldon did not know the streets of White Rock the way he did those of Vancouver. It was an error to create his protégé here, in an area Eldon himself did not know. Strong as it had been near the kill site, Patrick's scent had dissipated quickly in the open air, dispersing and mingling with other smells.

Patrick's hunger would still be so strong that his sanity would likely be held by a small, tenuous string, if at all. If Eldon did not find him and help Patrick quell his newborn hunger, then this night would end in utter disaster.

At least White Rock is a small suburb. That was good. He had first spotted Patrick leaving his place of work in a Vancouver high-rise office building. He soon learned that Patrick often worked late from his office on the eighteenth floor. Eldon tailed his prospect for a couple of weeks before deciding that Patrick was certainly the man he wanted. Patrick was an easy target. The man had no friends at work, lived alone, worked late into the night, and always followed the same route home. His life had the same pattern every night. Patrick was both unremarkable and predictable. At least, he had been predictable as a human.

Eldon took another long draught of air through his nose. When he had been a young vampire the sensations provided by his new senses were so overwhelming, but now he could pull them apart without conscious thought. From the rooftop, he knew that the couple in the apartment below him had just made popcorn. The woman still smelled faintly of perfume that had been applied hours earlier, while the man smelled mildly of sweat, deodorant, and the meat and disinfectants of a butcher shop. The pizza restaurant below the apartment had four pizzas in the oven and had cooked sheets of bacon and beef earlier that day for toppings, now stored in fridges.

The street was as quiet as any main street might be. Cars passed, a bus was dropping off an old woman with a walker on the corner. It all seemed normal, boring, but there was something off. Eldon just needed to pinpoint it. There was adrenaline in the air, thin and distant. He inhaled again, trying to find it. It was then he heard the fearful voice calling from below, perhaps a block further south.

Newborn Chapter 3

"Jimmy!?! Jimmy, this isn't funny!"

Jonah spun, then spun again. The street was empty in either direction. His heart pounded, rushing blood through his body while his mind raced to catch up. The flood of adrenaline that had made his fingers tingle before now made his fingers and toes go numb. It felt like he had been sitting on his hands and feet until they had fallen asleep. Jonah had no idea what had happened to his brother. Jimmy had been right beside him only a second ago.

"Come on, Jimmy!" he yelled. Even he couldn't miss the desperation in his voice. The yell that escaped his throat came out high-pitched, shrill. He was fighting back tears and he was sure Jimmy was going to have a good old laugh when he came out of the shadows. The thought made Jonah flush with anger and embarrassment. He strained his voice and called out again.

"Who is it that you call for?" came a slithery voice from the alley behind Jonah. He had just looked down that alley for Jimmy, and he was sure it had been empty. Where had this guy come from? Had he been hiding behind one of the dumpsters in the alley?"

"I'm looking for my brother," Jonah called back after checking down the sidewalk for what felt like the hundredth time. There was something weird about the man in the alley. Jonah didn't want to look at him. The man made his fast-beating heart freeze. Something about the hissing voice, the chill in it, made Jonah's blood nearly crystallize in his veins. He turned his back to the man. He didn't know why, but Jonah was terrified that this stranger had taken his brother. Jimmy's body was likely hidden behind the man. Jonah would be next. Then their eyes met.

"Come into the alley," the snake-like voice crooned. The one thing Jonah knew, with every fiber of his being, was that he did not want to step inside that dark alley with the strange man. They say that when an animal-- any animal, even man--is faced with extreme danger, the animal will either fight or take flight. Flight was Jonah's instinctual response. In his mind he was already running down the sidewalk, because he was certain the thing in the alley had already killed his brother. His legs and arms were pumping, and he was flying away. That thing in the alley, it wasn't a man, it was a demon. It was an eater of children, and now that it had feasted on Jonah's little brother, the demon wanted the rest of the family. Jonah would not let himself be eaten, he would run until he could run no further. He just had to go.

But he didn't go. He pulled with his mind, giving his muscles orders, but they would not listen. Instead, Jonah stepped forward toward the alley.

"No!" Jonah tried to scream, but his lips didn't move. He didn't understand what was happening. His mind was trying to go to sleep, to mask what was happening, but he fought the sensation. Jonah took another step and inhaled deeply, ready to unleash another scream. This time, with his lungs full of air, he felt his chest quiver with effort. His bottom lip started to vibrate along with his chest, but no sound issued from his mouth.

With Jonah's third step, he was in the dark of the alley. The demon's eyes seemed to radiate with a glassy shine in the glow of the street lamps. They made Jonah think of a cat, instead of a snake, and he found he couldn't take his eyes off them.

"You know me," the thing said. "I remind you of someone you love, and trust. Do you love and trust your father?"

"Yes," Jonah replied obediently.

"All the love and trust that you feel for your father, I want you to feel for me. You will be aware that we do not know one another, but the feelings will be present all the same. Do you understand?" it said.

Jonah wanted to spit in the thing's face. This thing was nothing like his father. His father was a good man, and this thing was vile. Its glossy eyes filled him with horror, with discomfort, with... trust? No, that wasn't right. It wasn't human. Did that make it horrid? No. No, it didn't.

"Who do you call for?" the soothing man's voice asked.

"My brother," Jonah said. He was smiling, although he didn't know why. He had felt anxious a second ago, hadn't he? Jimmy was missing, and he had to find him. That was why. He was sure of it. Maybe this man would help.

"I don't know what happened to him, mister, he just disappeared."

"I see," the man said, "and his name is Jimmy?"

"Yes, sir."

"And your name is?" he purred.

"I'm Jonah."

The man let out a chuckle that Jonah found he liked. It was sincere, endearing.

"Jimmy and Jonah," the man repeated almost musically.

"Yeah, Mom loves her J's"

This made the man chuckle again, and Jonah found he loved that sound.

* * *

Eldon examined the young man. His will was extraordinary. It should have been easy to command the teenager to do anything he wanted, but the boy had fought the glamour. Eldon had won, of course. That was not surprising, but that it had taken effort was.

The use of glamour is as instinctual for a vampire as breathing is to the living. Few could resist even as much as this boy. A vampire's will was absolute. Eldon went through some common questions to get to know the boy. He had a script that he often used, and he deviated from it a little for Jonah, since his goal was not to feed. At least, not yet. Even through the glamour, the boy gave answers that showed some fleeting personality behind the glamour's shroud. Jonah was indeed impressive. Most humans found the hypnotic glamour to be all-consuming.

The boy likely tasted succulent. Eldon was tired of feeding on the dregs of humanity on Vancouver's east side. He craved untainted meat. The idea made his tongue dart out of his mouth, tasting Jonah's skin. The forks felt their way from Jonah's chin to the top of his cheek, tasting him. The glamour didn't allow him to move, but, more to Jonah's credit, his eyes darted and his eyebrows lifted with terror. That made Eldon smile ruefully. The boy would truly be feeling terror, had it not been for Eldon's influence.

Eldon's fangs had extended, his long top canines clicking against the bottom ones. He wanted to feed oh so badly.

"Perhaps later, young Jonah," Eldon said more to himself than to the boy.

Instead, he looked deeper into Jonah and pushed his influence harder. He did not push so hard as to destroy the boy's sense of being, but he needed to ensure that answers came fast and true. Jonah's body relaxed further. Though still standing, much of his body went limp. The boy's jaw went slack, and drool began to run down his chin.

"Tell me, Jonah," Eldon said, pushing still harder. "Tell me, why were you yelling for Jimmy?"

"He disappeared," Jonah slurred in his response.

"Think back to the seconds when Jimmy vanished, and tell me every detail you remember," Eldon commanded.

Jonah obliged.

"We were walking back from the movie theatre. Jimmy was talking about the movie, gushing really. He was telling me about two of the characters kissing. I wasn't ignoring him, but I wasn't giving him my full attention either. I was thinking about a girl I had met at the movie and about camping in the mountains, so I wasn't looking at him when he disappeared. I felt a light breeze on the side of me where Jimmy was. When I turned to look at what made the breeze, Jimmy wasn't there."

Eldon needed no more proof than that. Patrick had picked up his next meal, and it was not a fare his protégé would usually be allowed. One must not be permitted to indulge in those who have family that would search for them. The boy would be missed, and Eldon could not have that. He had neither the time nor inclination to conceal such a debacle. At best, a catastrophe such as this would destroy any chance Eldon would have in joining the council. At worst, Eldon would need to ask for assistance from the council. If the council had to get involved, likely both Eldon and Patrick would be *punished.* In the vampire world, that could mean weeks or years of torture and starvation.

Jonah was the key, Eldon was certain. He needed a guide, instead of travelling by guess and whim.

"Jonah, listen very carefully. You are napping right now, but I must ask you to wake. First, when you wake, you will know without a doubt that I am here to help you find your brother. Second, you will understand that I am your master. You will follow any order I give you, even if it puts you in peril. Lastly, you do not want to have the police, or anyone else at all, involved in finding your brother. In fact, you don't even want anyone else to know what you're looking for. Do you understand?"

The boy nodded, and Eldon was satisfied that his glamour and instructions had taken hold.

"Good. Jonah, wake up."

The boy lifted his head and gave Eldon a broad grin.

"Mister, thank you so much for offering to help me find my brother!" he said, and Eldon couldn't help but smile back.

Newborn Chapter 4

T he vampire and teenager walked down the street together, headed in the same direction as the breeze Patrick had caused when kidnapping Jonah's younger brother.

"I am unfamiliar with this area, Jonah. Can you help me by telling me about our surroundings?" Eldon asked calmly.

"Yeah, no problem," Jonah crooned attentively. "We're in the centre of White Rock, but that doesn't mean much. It's only 8 blocks to the ocean to the west and five blocks before you hit farmland and forest to the east."

While Jonah prattled on, Eldon listened and inhaled deeply. He could smell his protégé in the air. The night was overcast and still, so the smells lingered. A storm was brewing, but it had not yet built up enough to break the stillness.

The scent Eldon followed was thick, too much so, making it seem every- where. There was no way to discern a true direction. He had to find Patrick before the night's rain began. If the rain fell too soon, the scent would be hidden in the petrichor, and he would lose the young vampire altogether. It infuriated Eldon, but there was little he could do except depend on this boy. Then something the boy said caught his attention.

"A park, you say," Eldon said.

Jonah brightened at the vampire's prompting.

"Yeah, it's huge. The trees are massive too, I can't reach my arms around some of them. It winds through most of town before meeting up with the native reserve to the south. The paths in the park are awesome. Everyone uses them during the day, and every weekend the kids I go to school with throw parties in the park."

"But on nights like tonight?" Eldon asks.

"In the middle of the week like this, you won't see a soul at night."

The two had been walking east, and Jonah pointed east again.

"The easiest way to get to the park is to head that way about four blocks. All the new neighbourhoods have paved walks that lead into the park. Do you think my brother's there, mister?"

"I do," Eldon responded softly before gesturing into an alley between a video rental store and a pizza restaurant. "Jonah, let's head back there for a minute."

The teenager complied without a thought for his safety, not realizing that heading into a dark space with a vampire could easily be the last mistake he would ever make. Jonah was still needed though, so for now, he would live.

For now.

Once in the darkness, Eldon turned to his little escort.

"Jonah, could you look into my eyes please?" the vampire asked, and Jonah again complied.

The push was easier this time, and Eldon took over the boy as he had done before. The dull expression didn't look right on Jonah. It was the face of the dim-witted.

"Jonah, I want you to close your eyes as hard as you can. You are going to ignore everything that happens around you until I tell you otherwise, do you understand?"

"Yes," Jonah replied. His eyes were already squeezed shut, and he used his hands to cover them up further.

Eldon gripped the teenager under his arms and lifted him off the ground. It took effort, particularly hungry as he was, but he pushed for the speed all vampires could attain. He pushed down the four blocks indicated by his guide. Eldon stopped at the edge of a paved path. Just as Jonah had said, it led into a heavily treed forest.

The delicious stench of blood wafted through the air, and under that sweet aroma was the undeniable scent of the undead. Bats hung on a nearby tree, not many but likely the same animals that had abandoned Eldon when Patrick woke earlier that night. Patrick was near, and would soon be under the control of his master.

Eldon set his guide down and took a confident step down the path. The world spun as he stepped, and the vampire had to stop himself from falling over completely. His body felt like it had no substance, as if all his muscles had turned into clouds and he was about to float away to join the oncoming storm. He had not expected to be so weak. Five nights without feeding, and calling on his abilities all night, had taken too much of a toll. He needed to feed, particularly if he needed to subdue Patrick before taking control of him.

"Jonah, step over here," Eldon commanded, again gesturing toward the dark.

Jonah obeyed, and he used the teenager's shoulder to steady himself as they walked. Eldon pointed, and Jonah led the way, escorting the vampire into the dark shadow of one of the houses on the edge of the park. As soon as they reached the darkness, Eldon let his fangs extend. He said nothing. He spun Jonah around and brought his teeth down. It was soft, tender, and violent, all in one movement.

Strength flowed into him from Jonah. Eldon wanted nothing more than to rip out the boy's throat and take all of Jonah's life-force. Even that much sustenance would not bring him to full strength, but it would certainly help. To feel strong again. To feel powerful, and in control. He could take the boy. It would be so easy. It was so natural to feed. The blood was so clean, untainted, not like the junkies and destitute husks he had become so used to.

Eldon forced his teeth out of the delicious flesh. Thick red blood pooled in the two bowl-like wounds. With a long sigh, Eldon pushed the healing agent out. Clear droplets fell from his fangs onto the two small puncture wounds. The damaged flesh made a squishing noise as the wounds sealed. Eldon licked away the last of the small meal to reveal clean, new flesh. No damage or scar marred the boy's skin.

As the power of Jonah's blood flowed through Eldon's body, the vampire stretched, as if waking from a long sleep. He was not at his full strength, but he was sure that he would have no trouble mastering his protégé now.

Newborn Chapter 5

In Jonah's mind he walked arms outstretched in the fog. The demon, no, the vampire, was out there somewhere. He said he was going to help him find Jimmy, but that couldn't be right. He was a vampire, and vampires were evil. Everyone knew that.

This fog is probably evil, too, *he thought.*

There had to be a way out. The fog was like a maze with no walls. Mazes always have a way out. Jonah walked forward faster. He brushed against a bush on his left and saw another next to it. It stretched out in a line of hedges.

It is just like a maze! Jonah thought, excitement building. 'Good, now I only have to keep turning right, that's how you find your way out of a maze, is it? Or is it left?'

It was then that a giant mosquito flew out of the fog. It rammed into his chest, its proboscis, no, two proboscises, piercing into his neck. Jonah tried to pull the bug from his body, but he was paralyzed. He tried so hard, flexed his muscles, but he was unable to move more than that. Then his fingers twitched, then again.

Suddenly he could move again, and the mosquito was gone. Jonah checked his neck for a wound. Nothing. Whatever that bug had been, it was gone now. Jonah had to get out. He started to follow the hedge line. He had to find the vampire, and Jimmy. There was only one way to do that. He needed to find the centre of the maze.

* * *

"Jonah, in a moment I will tell you to wake. When you wake, you will remember only that we walked to this park. All is good and safe. We still search for your brother, and I am still in control of the situation. All of your trust is in me. Do you understand?"

Jonah nodded.

"Then wake," Eldon commanded.

"Do you really think my brother is in there?" Jonah blurted out.

Eldon stared at the boy. The glamour had been deep, it should have taken at least a moment for Jonah to become coherent. Yet Eldon was still in control, he could feel it. The boy obviously still trusted him.

"He is. Of that I am sure," Eldon said. He could smell the blood of a youngling as well as the cold scent of his own kind. Patrick was there. On land, he knew, well and newly fed, that the new vampire had the advantage over Eldon. The blood siphoned from Jonah would help even the odds. It would have to be enough.

"Jonah, your brother is in those woods," Eldon confirmed again, "but so is the beast that took him. Do you understand what that means?"

"It means he could be hurt," Jonah said. The boy's face, already pale from blood loss, lost more of its colour.

"That also means that going into those woods is dangerous. I believe we can save your brother, but only if we work together. I have a plan."

* * *

"Jimmy! Jimmy, are you in here?"

Jonah stood under the dark canopy of trees. The illumination created by the streetlights at the other end of the path looked so much more inviting. It looked safer. Jonah moved forward into the dark anyway. The plan was simple, and Jonah was determined to do his part to save his brother. He called out Jimmy's name again.

* * *

Eldon watched as his bait moved down the path. It was dark among the trees. Jonah likely could not see much, but Eldon could see everything. The tree where the older vampire hung provided a perfect vantage point. Eldon was downwind of the forest, and he was backlit by the street lamps. Even with his newly enhanced eyesight, Patrick would have trouble spotting his maker.

Jonah walked the path slowly, as he had been instructed.

"Jimmy! Jimmy, are you in here?" the boy called and Eldon tensed, ready for action. Nothing happened. Jonah took another few steps and called again, then took a few more. The boy was going too fast now. If he continued much further, Eldon would have to find another place to hide, and chance being spotted. He was about to look for an alternative perch when a movement caught his eye. A form was stepping out of the shadows just ahead of Jonah on the path.

"Jonah, what are you doing here?" Patrick called out.

"Mr. Steadman?" Jonah replied.

Eldon wanted to curse. The idea that they might know one another had not crossed his mind, and that was a careless mistake. White Rock was not Vancouver. In a small suburb like this, most people probably knew one another. Why hadn't he thought of this? He hoped that their association didn't cause more problems. Eldon had problems enough already.

Both vampires tensed their muscles, Patrick to launch at Jonah and Eldon towards Patrick. Eldon needed Patrick to look him in the eyes. Glamour was the best tool in his current arsenal and, although the trick wouldn't work on most of his kind, it would work on his own creation.

The two vampires launched at the same time. As Patrick flew towards the terrified Jonah, Eldon soared through the dark. He wanted to smash Patrick in the chest, knock him to the ground, and beat him to a pulp. The younger vampire was rushing Jonah and was almost out of Eldon's reach. Eldon shifted towards Jonah, spinning in the air. Patrick had used all of his unnatural speed to lunge at Jonah, arms outstretched and jaws agape, his teeth aiming at the teenager's neck. Had Eldon waited a split-second longer, he would have missed Patrick, and his night would have suddenly gotten much more complicated. Unable to hit Patrick in the chest, he grabbed him by the back of the shirt, and used the momentum of the spin to flip the newborn over his hip and away from Jonah.

Eldon rolled to his feet to face Patrick, his back to Jonah. He had turned into Jonah's protector now, a predator turned nurturer. That made him laugh, loud and crazed. This night could not be any more backwards, but the fight was in him now. All his pent-up frustration finally had a release.

The sound made Jonah fall back and cower on the dirt path. Patrick's reaction was the opposite--the laugh enraged him. The two met, each swinging blows and connecting with their opponent. Patrick, the better fed of the two, recovered first. Before he knew what was happening, Eldon was flying through the air. A white dagger of pain pierced him as the world abruptly stood still again. He was on the ground, his back to a massive cedar. He knew immediately that he was in trouble. Eldon wanted to jump up, to fight, to win, but his legs would not respond to his desire. His spine was broken, along with many of his ribs.

Then Patrick was on him, fists smashing down. Eldon felt more ribs crack and splinter as Patrick rammed closed fists into his solar plexus. Patrick let out a soul-crushing scream and went to work on Eldon's face, breaking his jaw with the first hit and his nose with the second.

This is it, *Eldon thought.* A hundred and fifty years amount to this. I'm going to die by the hand of a one-night-old vampire, a newborn of my own creation.

The world was turning white. He wasn't feeling the blows raining down on him anymore, but in the distance he could hear Patrick yelling at him with each blow.

"Why?" he yelled.

Another hit landed on Eldon's cheek.

"Why did you do this to me? Answer me!"

Patrick hit his maker again, but Eldon didn't feel it at all.

"Just do it," Eldon tried to say, but no sound made it past his broken jaw.

Patrick let out another wail of anger. From the depth of his pain, Eldon registered that he wasn't being hit anymore. He forced his eyes to focus. Thanks to his vampiric nature, his spine was already healing, but it wouldn't heal fast enough. Patrick was returning, a long branch in his hand. The end was sharp.

Newborn Chapter 6

Jonah walked, and when he didn't think he could walk anymore, he continued on anyway. The hedge that he followed seemed endless, but he knew that the centre was out there. He just needed to find it.

The fog never eased, only allowing Jonah to see a metre or two in front of him. The hedge was changing, and Jonah was sure that was a sign he was making progress. When he had first found the line of bushes, they had been green and lush. As he got closer to the centre, they had changed. Now the plants were decaying, oozing and dripping a thick red liquid. The coppery scent in the air was easy to distinguish. Blood.

That had scared him so badly that Jonah had broken into a run, following the hedge, taking right turn after right turn. He ran until his sides hurt, but even then he continued on. As hard as he tried, he could feel this place fighting against him. The air thickened, so that it felt like wading through the ocean. Still he kept going.

Then, for the first time since entering the fog, he heard someone's voice. One word, yelled in the distance.

"Why?"

Jonah froze, then yelled back, "Jimmy! Jimmy, where are you?"

Again he heard the voice and he rushed for it. It had to be coming from the centre, he just had to get there.

* * *

Eldon closed his eyes and waited for his eternal life to end, but the end never came. Instead, Eldon heard a loud thump, but he hadn't felt any pain. When he opened his eyes to see why he wasn't dead, Patrick lay on the ground with blood pouring from a deep gash in his head. Jonah lifted a boulder, its sharp tip already covered in blood, and brought it down on Patrick's head, then again, and again. Patrick didn't stir.

When Jonah was done, he looked at Eldon. At first the older vampire thought he had traded one killer for another, but Jonah dropped the boulder.

"You said you'd help me find my brother. Are you still going to do that?"

Eldon huffed out a ragged, bloody breath. He was so weak, he needed time to heal. He lifted one finger to tell Jonah, his *saviour*, that he needed a minute. Jonah waited, although impatiently, while Eldon concentrated on the healing that was already taking place. He couldn't force himself to heal faster, but with some effort he could affect what part of him was fixed first. After a minute, his jaw clicked back into place, the bone mending. Eldon had watched his newborn the entire time, noticing that Patrick's head was healing. Eldon had to heal first. There was no way Jonah could take Patrick by surprise again.

With his jaw working, he looked at the teenager who had saved the life of a vampire.

"You need to do it again," Eldon said.

"Do what?" Jonah said, unsure.

"Hit him in the head with the rock. If you don't, he will heal before I do, and then we are both dead."

What little blood continued to circulate drained from the boy's face.

"I don't know if I can. I did it before to save you, to save Jimmy, but he's... you know... defenceless now."

"Jonah," Eldon said calmly, "You have to. He'll heal, we only need to buy a little more time."

Eldon wished he could just glamour the boy again, but he didn't dare. He had expended so much energy. The well where that energy sprung had its limit, and Eldon had reached it. The little energy he had left trickled out, healing his wounds, major though they were. Patrick on the other hand, had fed recently and fed well. His reserves were full and although his wounds would have been fatal were he still human, they were not as extensive as Eldon's own.

Jonah didn't argue further. He lifted his makeshift weapon high overhead, and with all of his force, brought it down on the vampire who had likely killed his younger sibling.

Eldon had not thought of Jimmy's health until then. When they were searching for Patrick, Eldon had thought there had been a chance his protégé had not drained the boy completely, but having seen Patrick's strength and speed, there was no doubt. Pain flashed as a rib pushed out of his lung. The flesh sealed immediately, and, as if he were human, Eldon took a deep, soothing breath. He was starting to feel his toes as well.

Jonah lifted the rock again and brought it down. This time Patrick's skull cracked. The gushing sound reminded Eldon of the watermelon his family had farmed so many years ago.

"Thank you, Jonah. That should do," Eldon said. The look of relief on Jonah's face was palpable, even to the likes of Eldon. "I'll need your help again in a minute."

Jonah, who had looked strong and brave only moments before, looked like a scared little boy.

"What do you want me to do?" he asked.

"Despite what I am––" Eldon started, but Jonah cut in.

"You mean a vampire."

"Yes, despite being a vampire, I still have a threshold. Pain still affects me. My spine is broken, Jonah, and if I try to move on my own I am likely to lose consciousness. Once I have healed a little more, I'll need you to move me to Mr. Steadman. When he wakes up, he needs to be looking directly into my eyes. Can you help make that happen?"

"I can do that," Jonah replied. There was no hesitation now, no fear. The boy might be young, but he had backbone.

"Then let's try it," Eldon said, gesturing towards his own feet, "Drag me. Make it fast."

Eldon gritted his teeth and steadied himself. The pain was like nothing he had ever experienced in his undead life. He imagined that being quartered likely felt no different. Time slowed, seconds felt like minutes, but Eldon did not black out. He was present for every instance of agony. Just when he thought he could take no more, Jonah dropped the vampire's legs. He was beside his would-be killer.

Patrick's eyes held no life in them, even as his head stitched itself back together. Jonah sat in the dirt next to the two vampires and said nothing. They sat in silence. The squishing and squelching of closing wounds disrupted the normal sounds of night, making for a macabre juxtaposition.

As more feeling was returned to his toes, Eldon tried to wiggle them in his shoe. To his surprise, some of them moved. He was about to try lifting his leg when he saw life blossom in Patrick's eyes. It was then that Eldon forced every bit of will into his monstrous protégé.

"Patrick Steadman, do not move," Eldon ordered. He pushed all of his will behind the command, but he was weak. He hoped it would be enough.

For a second, he thought he had failed. Patrick would heal faster than he, and then both the boy and Eldon would be dead. Patrick's face screwed up in a look of determined defiance, but as Eldon pushed his command harder, he watched Steadman falter, then fail. His face went slack, and his body tensed, rigid as he lay on the forest floor.

Finally, something had gone the way Eldon had hoped. The rest was easy. It took almost twenty minutes to heal enough that he could stand. He was aware that Patrick had also healed, but Eldon did not want to give his creation the simple dignity of standing up. Not yet. Let him lay there and wallow for a while longer.

"Hey mister, can we find my brother now?" Jonah asked.

Eldon didn't move at first. He could find Jimmy with ease now. Patrick reeked. The blood of a youngster covered his clothing. He could just kill Jonah. It would be good to fully feed, and Jonah had tasted so sweet. There would be some clean-up needed, but he could manage it. The police of this time were still not so proficient that a vampire could not hide a feed when needed. He could destroy Patrick, here and now, and simply turn Jonah instead. The boy was a better choice than Steadman. Patrick had already been a handful, and

Eldon was already unsure about his choice of protégé. Jonah had proven to be courageous and resourceful. It was obvious now that the boy had broken through a deep glamour; that in itself was a feat. Instead of running once the glamour had been broken, he had chosen to save Eldon.

Eldon was weak though. Perhaps too weak to turn another. It would depend on Jimmy, then. If they found Jimmy dead, then Eldon would take his older brother.

"Patrick," Eldon called out, once again pushing his command onto the young vampire, "You will head into Vancouver proper, to East Hastings Street. Do you know where that is?"

"The ghetto," Patrick said lazily.

"Yes, the ghetto," Eldon sneered."You will let no one see you, you will feed on no one. You will find the corner of Edison Street and East Hastings. One block east down Edison, you will find Agatha Mansion. You will go there, and you will stand on the roof. You will not move from that spot until I arrive and tell you to move. Do you understand?"

"Yes," Patrick said, and turned to leave.

Eldon let him go. If Patrick had indeed fed upon Jimmy until the boy died, then Eldon would turn Jonah. While he went to ground with Jonah, Patrick would stand on the roof until the sun peeked over the horizon and cooked him. All of his problems would be solved.

"Let us find your brother," Eldon said, convinced already that the boy was no longer alive.

It took only minutes. Patrick had been feeding only feet from where the battle had taken place. Eldon had asked Jonah to wait on the path while he stepped through some bushes to find Jimmy lying in the dirt.

The boy's neck was ripped open and blood covered his body but, to Eldon's surprise, his chest rose and fell ever so slightly. Patrick had been feeding, of that there was no doubt, but he had either not ripped open any major arteries or he had inadvertently healed the boy when Eldon and Jonah had arrived.

For a second he contemplated snuffing out what little life Jimmy had left and turning his brother anyway. It was then Jonah came through the bushes. Eldon bit back a curse. He hadn't glamoured the boy a second time. He had just expected he would obey.

"Jimmy!" he yelled.

Eldon made a decision then. He was weak, and the boy had saved him. In return, he would save the boy's brother.

"It will take time, but he will live," Eldon said to the boy.

Jonah ignored the vampire and knelt beside his brother. He started to cry. The noise was grating and Eldon grabbed him. Jonah looked up and the vampire pushed his will on the boy again.

"Calm," he said, "I will fix this but you must be calm."

Eldon could feel the boy's need as he pushed his will. Jonah wanted, needed, someone to fix his brother, and that need allowed Eldon's command to be accepted with ease. It was unlikely that Jonah would push through the glamour a second time.

With Jonah in hand, the vampire picked up the injured boy. Eldon allowed his teeth to extend, and he sank them into the young boy's wounded neck. Before his need for blood took over, the vampire started to excrete the healing agent. It would take much more of the healing liquid than was needed for the small punctures that he had fixed on Jonah's neck. Patrick had not been gentle. The boy's skin was ripped in layers, with long tears starting from the back of his neck all the way down to his collarbone.

Before long, Eldon's resources were exhausted. Even when at full strength, Eldon would not be able to heal such extensive damage. He had done enough that the boy would last until the rest of his plan could be enacted.

Newborn Chapter 7

Where the glamour Eldon had pushed on Jonah had been light and easy only a moment ago, he used all the will he could muster now.

"You must carry your brother," he commanded. "The night is clear, so you must stay in the shadows as often as possible. You must be quick, but let no one see you. You will leave as soon as I command it. Do you understand?"

"Yes, I understand."

The boy was impressive. Instead of the lulled look of the glamour, Jonah's face was set in determination. The boy's own will to see his brother safe worked in tandem with the glamour Eldon had pushed on Jonah.

Jonah, with Jimmy wrapped in his arms, stood at attention. His muscles were taught, ready to spring forth to comply with Eldon's order and the boy's own desires, but Eldon could not let them go yet.

Jimmy was still gravely injured, but Eldon had to wake him. He forced an eye open and pushed his will again. Jimmy was on the cusp of consciousness, enough at least that Eldon could wake him fully with the help of the glamour. Once Jimmy was well under the vampire's control, he pushed a story into the boy's mind, rewriting what had happened on this night. In Jimmy's mind, a new history formed Jonah had taken his brother to the movies. There had been an accident while the brothers were on their way home. Jonah on his skateboard and Jimmy on his bicycle. Jonah hit a hole in the sidewalk and fell off his skateboard. In Jimmy's mind he could see his brother flying off of his board right at him, then the world went black.

Eldon moved to Jonah next, pushing the same story into his mind. The vampire added additional instructions, things Jonah must do when he arrived home so that the story Eldon embedded into the brains of the two boys would make sense to others. This level of glamour was hard, and the vampire hoped he had not done any damage to either of their minds. The irony would not be lost on Eldon if he had gone through all this trouble only to destroy the minds of the boys just before sending them off to safety. It did look like it had worked though. They both stood, waiting for additional orders.

"Jonah, you are your brother's protector, always remember that. Go now," Eldon ordered, and the older brother leaped to obey.

Eldon took to the sky to follow the brothers. Jonah did exactly what he was instructed to do. Only once did Eldon have to intervene because the brothers had been seen. Two policemen had been parked in a car looking over a hill alongside the path on which Jonah was carrying his brother. Eldon dropped from the sky. Again, he pushed his will. The two policemen fought it hard, but Eldon prevailed. With only a few minutes lost, he was able to catch up to the brothers and follow them the rest of the way to their home.

In the distance, just off the coast, a storm was coming. Lightning flashed over the sea. Eldon hoped the boys would make it before the weather reached them. He wanted this wretched night over, and that weather would stall Jonah's progress.

The two boys made it home just before the storm reached White Rock. Eldon watched as Jonah put his brother down in the shadow created by the fence and the street lamp. Lightning flashed, making Jimmy's limp body visible, but there was no one there to see him except Eldon. Jonah snuck into the garage next to the house and came out with his skateboard and Jimmy's bicycle. He ran quickly back to the fence. Even in the shadow, Eldon could make out Jonah positioning the skateboard across the handlebars of the bicycle, wedging the bar in place by anchoring the wheels under the lever for the brakes. He then picked up his injured brother and sat him on the board. Jimmy's torso leaned against his brother. Blood seeped out of Jimmy's wounds and down the front of Jonah's Jaws of Life t-shirt. The black of the shirt glistened as the blood seeped in. Eldon was so weak, the urge to eat was too strong. He would need to feed soon, the boy had to hurry.

Hurry, Jonah did. With Jimmy propped against his brother, Jonah drove the bike behind the garage, stopped, and as instructed, cleared the glamour from his mind.

"Don't worry Jimmy, we're almost home!"

Eldon could hear the older boy's cry as he pumped the pedals, rushing to the house. Eldon watched as Jonah opened the door and yelled to his parents for help. In minutes they had all piled into the car and they drove off.

A few seconds later another car drove down the road. Eldon had not yet taken flight, still hiding in the shadow of the house across the street from the brothers' home. The car pulled into the driveway connecting to the house that provided Eldon's hiding spot.

The vampire, weak and hungry, could not resist. The meal strengthened the vampire. The woman, Karen, would be a great asset to Eldon. She could watch the brothers to ensure the glamour he had set upon them held.

Refuelled, Eldon turned his thoughts to the vampire he had sired. Patrick would need to be punished.

* * *

"Mr. and Mrs. Stilton?" called the doctor. Jonah followed his parents and they stood and walked through the crowded room in the emergency ward. The doctor was a young woman, pretty, with her brown hair tied back in a ponytail.

"Is Jimmy okay?" Jonah's mom blurted.

"I'm not sure yet," the doctor responded, "we have him stabilized at the moment, but he lost a lot of blood and has gone into shock. He might be fine, but we'll have to wait until he regains consciousness to know for sure."

Jonah watched both his parents. They just stood there, stunned. Tears flowed down his mother's cheeks, while his dad had his arms wrapped around them both. He didn't say a word.

This was his fault, and he didn't know how to fix it. He was supposed to be his brother's protector, instead he almost got his brother killed because he couldn't watch where he was going on his skateboard. If his parents couldn't talk, he would have to.

"Is there anything we can do while we wait for him to wake up?" he asked.

"No, sweetheart," she said.

"Will he wake up?"

"I think so. He's been through quite a bit tonight, and that's going to take some time to heal," she responded.

One last question to ask, and it was the hardest one.

"You said he's stabilized for now, but what else could happen? I mean, could he get worse?" Jonah asked. He held his breath, looking at her, hoping.

"Are you sure you want an answer?" she said, and when Jonah nodded she looked at his parents who also nodded.

"Organ failure is a big worry when there is this much blood loss, so is heart failure, and brain damage," she said. "But I'm not saying any of these things are going to happen. He might wake up just fine, but those are the three main things we are worried about. Having Jimmy regain consciousness is the first big step."

"Can we see him?" Jonah's dad asked.

They were ushered into a small room with four beds. All were occupied but none except Jimmy had visitors. Jimmy lay on the bed by a window. Curtains acted as barriers between the patients. Jonah sat on the edge of the hospital bed, while his parents took the seats next to the bed. They sat, and waited, and prayed.

Jonah stared out the window most of the time. At some point his hand had found Jimmy's, and he held it.

Just wake up, *he thought feverishly,* Just wake up and be okay.

Outside the storm had finally reached them. Lightning arced across the sky and thunder boomed so loudly it shook the hospital windows. Every time thunder cracked, Jonah thought he felt his brother's fingers twitch. He was about to mention it when Jimmy spoke.

"Jonah?" he asked. His voice was weak, his eyes only slightly open.

"Where's Mr.Steadman? I was dreaming, Jonah. Was Mr. Steadman coming to get me!"

Jonah squeezed his brother's hand. He was obviously delirious.

"No buddy, I crashed into you, remember?" Jonah replied, trying to calm Jimmy.

"Oh yeah, that's right, I remember," Jimmy said, then drifted into unconsciousness again.

Jonah hadn't seen his mom leave the room, but when he looked away from Jimmy she was coming back through the door, the doctor right behind her.

She checked him over, and happily announced, "We're not fully out of the woods, but with Jimmy waking up so soon, it's a really good sign."

Outside the thunder boomed again, and Jonah was sure this time--Jimmy fingers had twitched at the sound.

* * *

To be sure that all had gone to plan, that the glamour would not fail, Eldon spent time each evening with Karen, in the home across the street from the Stilton family. Karen had proven to be an excellent asset in the surveillance of the Stilton boys. Jimmy had returned home only two days after his meeting with Patrick. The boy seemed to be making a full recovery, and there was no evidence that the glamour he had placed on the two of them had broken.

After a week of checking in, Eldon was certain that there would be no trouble forthcoming. Both boys held to their glamour, and Eldon could leave them in peace. Yet, he found himself returning anyway, night after night. He fed on Karen, and told himself that it was the draw of untainted blood, so unlike that of the defiled and drug-addicted of Vancouver's east end. But he asked questions too, about the brothers, about their parents. He issued orders to Karen too. After weeks of constant glamour, most of Karen was gone and only a servant to Eldon truly remained. She no longer went to work, she didn't call her family, she didn't see her friends. She watched, and allowed herself to be food.

A month gone, and Eldon had learned everything he wanted to learn. Karen was a husk of her former self. She lost a considerable amount of weight and had taken on a sickly pallor. Eldon no longer needed a watcher, and Karen's blood had gone sour with her poor health.

It was time for the vampire to leave White Rock well enough alone. Karen had long beams exposed in the cathedral-style ceiling of her living room. He ordered Karen to make a rope of her bedding, and hang herself from one. She hurried to obey. Outside, the vampire watched as the Stilton family pulled into their driveway. The two boys helped their parents carry in groceries. Eldon tried to extend his hearing across the street, but all Eldon could hear was Karen gurgling and thrashing from behind him. It did not matter. The vampire cared not for the younger brother, but Jonah was different, he was special in some way. If Eldon ever had a need for the boy, he would find a way. For now though, it was time for Eldon to go. He had a newborn to watch over, and a council of vampires to put under his thumb. He left by Karen's back door and flew into the night.

The end.

Trainee Cheverie

I t's funny how much nerves can affect heart rate and adrenaline. Nick had spent entire classes studying to become a police officer, but nothing matched actual experience. The truly weird thing was that nothing that was happening should have had his adrenaline amped up. He was only a month away from graduation with only on-the-job training remaining. That's how he found himself sitting in the passenger seat of the police cruiser wearing an RCMP trainee uniform.

Of course, Nick wouldn't join the RCMP upon his graduation. That would have been a dream come true, but he didn't have four years to spend at university. Instead, he opted for the one-year police course. Graduation guaranteed him a job with the Vancouver Police Force, and that was good enough. Maybe he could do night classes and eventually move up. It was possible that he might be able to challenge some of the courses. He had already learned a lot.

"And this, 'Trainee Cheverie', is a big part of being a cop," Constable Willard said from the driver's seat. He handed Nick a paper coffee cup from Tim Hortons.

Nick accepted the cup, but he wasn't sure he could drink it quite yet. This was his first night on the job, and as calm as he tried to look on the outside, his insides were on fire with pent up energy.

"Coffee?" Nick joked.

"Haha," Willard said dryly, "No, coffee and donut jokes aside, waiting is most of a cop's life. Look around us." He gestured with his hands, coffee swinging in front of Nick, while Willard's donut-filled left hand swung out the window. They were atop a hill, houses sprawling all the way to the Pacific ocean.

"It's a Tuesday night, so there won't be much going on. There are four cars on duty, and we each have a section of White Rock to ourselves. From this vantage point, we can easily get anywhere in town. You'll see the same kind of thing in the city. Everyone working your beat will have a station. You guys see a lot more action, and there are always more city cops on duty, so your range will be a lot smaller than this."

Nick nodded. This statement mirrored what he was taught in the academy. This was the first time those teachings would come into use. They sipped their drinks, and Willard continued, "It's almost midnight now, so one of two things are going to happen. We're either going to be really busy for the next couple of hours, or we're going to be ridiculously bored."

Nick was nodding, and looking out over the hill. His coffee had cooled a bit and he was about to take a larger gulp when he saw the shadow of someone skulking down the road. It looked like he was carrying a smaller figure.

"Constable," Nick said, pointing, "what do you think that's about?"

Both cops looked then and watched as a small boy, probably a teenager, came into the light for only a couple of seconds. He was carrying an even smaller body.

"What the hell!" Willard said, and was already undoing his seatbelt to get out of the car. The kids were only two hundred or so metres away. Nick was following suit, undoing his belt, when the car shook as if something had hit it.

A face popped into view. It was upside-down, as if the owner of the face was on the roof of the squad car. But that wasn't possible−− where could this guy have come from?

"Gentlemen," the man on the roof said, and both cops looked at him. The world went blurry then, and Nick wasn't sure what happened after that. He was sure the man had said more, but he couldn't quite remember what it was.

Nick shook his head, everything was so foggy. The feeling started to clear, but only a little. He squeezed his eyes shut and slowed his respiration. He hadn't realized he was breathing so heavily. He was near to hyperventilating.

39

And his heart was pumping. It was as if Nick had just run a marathon.

The driver's side door of the squad car opened, and Willard got out. He too was swallowing air in huge gulps.. Willard looked at his trainee and tried to speak. He had to spit out one word at a time in-between sucking in oxygen. "What...the...fuck?" he exclaimed.

"I dunno," Nick spit out.

"Out," Willard panted," Get...out of the car."

The older cop was grabbing his side, as if he too had run a great distance. Nick felt no better, but his breathing was coming easier now. He opened the door and got out of the car. For some reason he felt the need to look around, to make sure he and Willard were alone. He had the faintest feeling that there had been others around just a moment before, and there was something important about those people.

"What the hell just happened?" Willard asked his trainee.

"What do you think that's about?" Nick whispered. He had just said that a minute ago, hadn't he? But why? Nick had no idea, so instead he answered his partner. "I have no idea. Could the car be leaking carbon monoxide or something?"

"Maybe," Willard said doubtfully, "I don't care what it is, I'm not taking any chances. God, I feel like I'm gonna puke!"

Nick felt the same. He was trying hard to keep that coffee down.

The constable reached for the radio attached to the shoulder of his vest. Nick barely listened while Willard called in to dispatch. Vaguely, Nick heard the other man call for a ride, and order a tow truck for their squad car. Something was just on the edge of his memory. No matter how hard he tried to grasp at the thought, it kept slipping away. An upside-down face? Maybe, but that made no sense at all.

* * *

Eldon had watched as Jonah carried his brother further down the street. They were no longer in sight, but Eldon was sure the boy would do as instructed and keep to the dark as much as he could. The boys were safe. The vampire was safe too, tucked away in the shadows.

He was still close to the police officers though, and could hear them clearly. The glamour had been strong and forceful. Both men were still in shock from the experience. With that much force behind it, it was unlikely that the glamour would fade or break, but Eldon had to be sure. Even if it did break in a day or two, it would be too late for them to do anything. It was doubtful that they could recognize the boy even if they did remember seeing him. Eldon found it almost funny that both men lived. When he had to glamour with that much force, the mind always fought it. The experience is so visceral that the body reacts, and sometimes it reacts so violently that the person just dies. The heart fails. Eldon always found that funny in a way.

The two cops stood outside their vehicle, sputtering and clutching at their stomachs. No heart attacks this time. He heard the older policeman call for more police, but it was only for a ride. The glamour had worked perfectly. Carbon monoxide. Humans could believe anything, so long as it was something of their own world. Eldon shifted and moved further into the shadows. He could catch up to Jonah in a matter of seconds. This crisis had been averted, but there may be more.

The End

The Taking of Patrick Steadman

Patrick Steadman sat at his desk and stared at the clock on his computer. The day was almost over, and he couldn't wait.

Fuck, I hate this job.

It was not the first time he had had the thought, and even in the short time he had left in life, it wouldn't be the last.

Only six minutes to go. Six agonizing minutes and I can go home.

Wednesday nights were one of his favourite nights of the week. Thai Pho, his neighbourhood thai restaurant, had a great special on Wednesdays, and Patrick loved their food. He was thinking of basil chicken and coconut rice as he packed up his satchel. He turned off his computer and left for the elevator. No one spoke to him on the way through the office. He knew he wasn't well liked at Coleman-Gregard, but he didn't care. The accounting firm paid exceptionally well, and Patrick was good at his job. He wasn't one of the company superstars, but he was good enough that they wouldn't want to lose him. Besides, they put up with his eccentricities. For Patrick, that was enough. It paid the bills and that had to be enough too. Still, every day started the same, full of optimism, and ended the same too, full of loathing.

He got in the elevator alone. Most of the guys on his floor were still packing up. Well, they could catch the next one. Being packed into the elevator with other people always made Patrick feel claustrophobic. Touching other people, even his jacket rubbing against someone else's made his skin crawl. Just the thought of it made him queasy.

It's okay, there's no one here. I'm here alone. I'm alone.

His palms started to sweat as the elevator doors closed, and he had to hold his breath until it hit the bottom. For some reason, not breathing--his chest and lungs still, unworking--was soothing.

The doors opened. Patrick let out a whoosh of air and stepped out. The parking lot looked empty, but something felt weird. Patrick looked from side to side, spinning in a circle. His satchel twisted and caught on his tie, pulling it tight against his Adam's apple.

"Hi Patrick," called a woman's voice from near the elevator.

He had been facing the parked cars and jumped when the voice came from behind him.

"Oh, I didn't mean to startle you!" Colleen called. She walked over and Patrick tensed. He didn't know why but he was sure she was about to try to touch him. To his relief, she stopped a pace away.

"Do you have any plans for tonight?" she asked. She was pretty, and hadn't been with Coleman-Gregard long enough to know Patrick didn't really like...well, anyone.

"Uh, yeah, Thai. I'm going to eat Thai food," he stumbled over the words but they made it out of his mouth. He was so shocked that he had spoken at all that he walked away. Patrick looked back at Colleen. She had the weirdest look on her face, not insulted, not shocked. Patrick wasn't sure how to interpret it. He often didn't know how to read people, their expressions were a mystery to him. This made Patrick even more nervous. He fumbled with his keys, opened the door to his car, and pulled out of the parking lot as fast as he could.

The commute to White Rock took almost an hour, but that was okay. Patrick took the time to gather his thoughts. He had made a fool of himself in front of Colleen. He shouldn't have walked away like that.

How am I going to face her tomorrow? Maybe I won't have to. Maybe she'll have gotten the hint. What was she thinking, just talking to me like that?

Deep down, a tiny part of Patrick said that what Colleen had done was actually normal, and that his reaction had been the one that didn't make sense. And what had been the look on her face? Instead of thinking about it any more, Patrick concentrated on the feeling of the steering wheel, smooth but bumpy. Running his thumb along its pattern was soothing. It whittled away the time and calmed him enough that Patrick knew he could go for food.

The couple that ran Thai Pho were lovely. They knew his name, but he didn't know theirs. They understood privacy. They always sat Patrick away from other people and left him alone while he ate.

When he pulled into the driveway, there were five other cars. Thai Pho was busy. It almost made Patrick turn around, but the thought of his empty fridge at home forced him out of his car. The sensation of being watched hit him again so hard he almost jumped back in. The sun had just set, and what light was left was casting shadows all along the building. Patrick tried to calm down but found he was almost hyperventilating.

He made fists with his hands, clenching them tight. The muscles in his shoulders followed suit, and Patrick could feel his head dip as his neck disappeared into his shoulders. He had always had panic attacks as a kid. They had gotten worse for a while after his parents died, but therapy had helped. His therapist had said that repetitive actions, actions that Patrick himself had found soothing, would help. The action that Patrick had found was tapping a rhythm with his feet. A steady tapping, like a snare drum.

Tap, tap, tap, tap, tap, tap, tap, tap.

The noise and the movement did help.

It took minutes of repetitive beats before Patrick's breathing went back to normal, before he could let the tension in his feet subside. The muscles in his hands and fingers hurt from tensing them as hard as he had. His legs were a little better, his calves tight with the exercise.

What is wrong with me?

He still watched the oncoming night warily. It felt wrong, but Patrick didn't know why. Things he didn't know made him uncomfortable. Why the fuck didn't he know them? Subconsciously, he clenched his fist again. All he had to do was make it to the door, open it, and order food.

Originally Patrick had planned to eat in, but he no longer felt comfortable with that idea. He would get takeout. In fact, he would get two orders and have extra basil chicken for tomorrow night's supper. It was a simple decision, and simple things made Patrick feel good. That way there was no deviation. Deviations, like things that Patrick didn't know, made him uncomfortable.

The couple that ran the Thai Pho restaurant must have been able to tell that Patrick was having a bad day because they kept their distance from him after he placed his order. He appreciated it so much that when his order was ready, he left an extravagant tip. They said thank you, but Patrick had expected the praise and that made it okay.

Leaving the restaurant had been challenging though. Patrick was sure something was out there, something was watching him. He had this feeling often. Patrick knew no one was actually watching him, and even with the help of his therapist he was never able to truly overcome the feeling.

Patrick held his breath again and opened the door, rushing from the restaurant to his car. He placed the bag of food on the roof of the car and grabbed his key to unlock the door. Twilight had truly turned into night, and Patrick wanted to be home.

In this rush, the keys fell out of his hand and hit the ground. Patrick looked around again before bending over to retrieve the keys. He stuck the key in the lock and let his breath go when the lock popped up.

He got in the car and started to drive the few blocks to his home.

The drive was short, and Patrick wasn't able to relax while making the few turns toward home. Instead, he focussed on gathering his resolve.

Just the car to the house. Then I'll be home, and this day can be over.

The two orders of basil chicken with coconut rice sat in clam shells on the passenger seat, in a plastic bag to make sure nothing seeped out onto the seat of the car.

The food smelled delicious, but Patrick was having a hard time wanting to eat. He just wanted to be home. He wanted to feel safe.

He pulled into the drive, gathered his courage, and his food. The walk to the house was dark. Patrick didn't like leaving his porch light on during the day. It was wasteful. He had his key in one hand, food in the other. He opened the car door, hit the lock on the door, and slammed it shut. He sucked in his breath and held it to dash to the house.

Patrick was about to run to the door when he found himself upside down. The last thing he remembered was the sound of his food hitting the ground and thinking *well, I can't eat that now.*

Then something hit his head hard, and the world started to go black. Distantly he mourned the loss of the food that wouldn't make it to the fridge, and not seeing Colleen tomorrow at work--she was nice after all. Something inside him already knew that tomorrow wasn't going to come, not anymore.

The end

Paranoia Chapter 1

J im grabbed the Turbo Rocket out of the freezer and headed for the
cashier. The 7-Eleven was empty, but at four in the morning that was
exactly what he had expected. He paid for the popsicle, and the Techboy
magazine he had tucked under his arm before heading back into the night.
The store was only half a block from his place of work, and he could reach
it easily by way of the back alley. He made the trip once or twice each night
he worked. It was a great way to stretch his legs, and the snacks didn't hurt
either.

Looking up, Jim saw that the sky was actually clear. It was a nice change.
Vancouver rarely saw clear nights. More often, the city was covered with
clouds, if it wasn't outright raining. Jim loved the stars, and he took a second
to bask in their glow. He felt free. The oppression and paranoia, a paranoia
those close to him called delusions, seemed tamped down under the glow of
the open night sky. When the city was covered in grey, particularly if a storm
was moving in over the coast, Jim felt constricted, like every vein in his body
was being pulled tight. Sometimes, he had trouble breathing, especially if
there was lightning and thunder. With the clouds gone, Jim could breathe
easily. Still, as he walked through the streets back to work, he had his hand
in the pocket of his windbreaker, gripping a stubby six-shooter. He was very
aware of his hand on the weapon. After all, he felt free, not stupid.

Jim tucked the Techboy magazine in the back pocket of his jeans, then tore
the Turbo Rocket open with his teeth and spit the plastic wrap on the ground.
He stuck the blue bottom of the tricoloured frozen treat in his mouth to lick

off the melt before taking a bite of the cherry flavoured top, just like he had always done as a kid. He kind of felt like a kid. The open sky made the world seem so big and perfect, like it was full of possibilities, adventure, and fun.

A noise down an alley, a can being kicked over, brought Jim back to the present. He froze stock still, popcicle stuck in his mouth, one hand still in the pocket of his jacket. His heart, bumping at a normal happy thump mere seconds before, was now beating out of his chest. Jim's grip on the weapon in his pocket was so tight with tension that his hand cramped, sending shooting pains up his arm. He ignored the sharp sensation and focused, everything zeroed in on the alley, ready for action.

A minute followed and nothing happened. His heart began to calm, and Jim started a slow count to ten. When still nothing happened, he crept away from the mouth of the alley. He kept his knees bent as he walked, ready to spring like a cat. The night didn't seem so forgiving or free anymore.

When he was further down the alley, Jim started a fast walk. There was no way of knowing what had been in there. It could have been a rat, a vagrant, a serial killer, a vampire.

Vampires. Logic told him that vampires didn't exist, had never existed, but logic also told him that chemtrails, alien abduction, and government super-agents were just fiction too, conspiracies for the nutballs of the world. But he was not crazy, nor was he delusional. He knew these things were real, and people were just too complacent--too safe, too comfortable--to see the truth. They didn't want to see, but Jim saw. In fact he didn't just see, he accepted.

He understood that just because you haven't seen something with your own eyes didn't mean it doesn't exist. He had this argument with his brother, Jonah, all the time. Jonah believed in God, yet he's never seen God. Well, Jim believed in vampires, and aliens, even though he'd never seen them. That didn't make him any more crazy than his brother. It did however make him smarter, since Jonah stubbornly refused to see sense.

Jim unlocked the back entrance to Computer-Fix-A-Lot and slipped in, securing the door behind him. With the lock on the door handle engaged and the deadbolt secured into the metal doorframe, Jim turned toward his workspace. The small light clamped to the side of the workbench was still lit. The halogens hung dead from the ceiling throughout the shop, the shelves they typically lit were filled with malfunctioning or broken computer towers, each with a pink work order taped to the front. A wall separated the work area from the retail space, which faced East Hastings street. The front of the store was filled with refurbished computers that were repaired in-house. During the day, Computer-Fix-A-Lot pulled in steady business, both in sales and repair work. Now, with all the lights off besides the workbench lamp, the shop looked dead and empty.

Before sitting down to work, Jim walked through the front of the shop, slipping past the laminated sign on a stand outlining why '*you--yes you!*' should upgrade your 4 megs of RAM to 8 megs. He peered out into the night, checking the street outside to ensure it was devoid of people. East Hastings was known as one of the most crime-stricken areas of Vancouver. Working in the area at night meant being extra cautious. Jim then tested the lock on the shop's main door. Finding it secure, he snuck through the sales floor back to his workbench. Knowing that he was safely locked in allowed some of the tension to leave his body. Muscles he didn't even realize he was activating loosened. The comfort of being safely contained, allowed Jim to relax and focus on the work in front of him once again.

Next to the workbench sat Jim's backpack. He pulled a laptop out of the bag and started to play the list of audioblogs that downloaded all day while he slept. He recently dropped five hundred dollars on a new 28.8 baud modem, and it was so much faster than his old 16.8 baud modem. He could download almost two full hours of audio recordings during the day. He even paid for a second phone line for the modem.

The computer tower in front of him had a pink carbon sheet taped to it, like all the others. After reading the reported issue, '*It just stopped working*', Jim popped the side off. The fan was covered in dust, and it looked like it had caused the fan to short and... yup... there it is, a short on the motherboard. Jim smiled to himself in satisfaction. One problem solved.

There were over a dozen identical computer towers on the shelves behind him and, once again, Jim thought how lucky he was to have landed this gig with Fix-A-Lot. It kicked ass when compared to working on commission, pawning Discmans to snobby teenagers like his last job. Fix-A-Lot had so much work they needed a whole team of computer technicians but they were too cheap to rent a larger building, so instead they had three techs doing alternating eight hour shifts. Before Jim came along, the techs had taken turns doing the graveyard shifts. They couldn't have been happier when Jim only wanted to work nights. It had been three months now, and he loved it, even though his brother was starting to tease Jim about his pale complexion. Jonah didn't seem to understand the appeal, but that was okay. Each computer brought a new problem, a new puzzle to solve, and that enticed Jim. He also enjoyed the work itself. When he was a kid, he used to like tearing apart old broken machines he found in the trash. Figuring out how they were put together was fun, and that fun had translated into figuring out how to fix the trashed electronics. With his education--a bachelor's degree from University of Victoria in their new computer science program--he could basically work anywhere, but he liked Fix-A-Lot. More than anything else, he liked the privacy that Fix-A-Lot afforded him.

The Conspiracy Can started their latest podcast. The sound was tinny coming from the laptop's small speaker but Jim dialed in on the host, David Hosner, and pulled a new motherboard out of a static bag. The night was going smoothly, exactly the way Jim liked it.

* * *

Patrick inhaled deeply. The smell was so sweet. He savoured the aroma in the air. Vampires may not be able to drool, but he certainly felt like his salivatory gland had awakened. With the scent in him, his fangs started to protrude. His typically unbeating heart started to pump the need to feed through his body. Patrick wanted to eat so badly, wanted to taste the man inside the rundown shop. The night Patrick had been made vampire, he had fed on this boy. It had been so many years, but the vampire would never forget. The little boy had tasted so sweet, delectable even. Could the man taste just as sweet? Patrick needed to know. He wanted nothing more than to break down the door of the computer store from whence the smell came and rip off the head of the human who exuded the intoxicating scent. He would drink of him until nothing was left.

The bats that constantly followed Patrick chittered at his excitement, snapping him out of his daze. He shook his head, and scowled at the animals. They seemed to follow all vampire around, but Patrick found their presence grating.

He had other duties to attend to. He sucked in another unneeded breath and concentrated on stopping his pumping heart. If he didn't quell the desire now, his heart would pump so much that he would be forced to feed. But he could not, at least not yet. He would do his master's bidding first. If he were fast, he could return tonight. Patrick had no idea how long Jimmy would be at the store, but it seemed he worked the night shift there.

It was only luck that he had found the young man as it was, a stray scent on the wind had led him here. A scent of fear tickled the back of Patrick's memory in such a way that he had to investigate, and now he was oh so happy he had.

Patrick cocked his head as he caught a new familiar scent on the air and turned to look deeper in the alley. His eyes accustomed to the dark quickly and in it he saw a small shape.

"What are *you* doing here?" Patrick sneered.

The figure in the alley stepped out. He looked around fourteen years of age, and always would. His dark black hair was long, well past his shoulders. His jeans were ripped at the knees and t-shirt was soiled but he walked strong and straight, full of confidence, nothing like the junkie he had been in life.

"I was curious to see what my master was up to," the vampire responded casually, but Patrick heard the mockery of respect in his voice when he said "master."

Patrick had no idea why he could not will Daniel to follow his instruction, the way his master could will him. When Eldon beckoned, Patrick was putty, ready for his master to mold. Daniel, for reasons Patrick could not discern, had no regard for his master and could fight off even the harshest of compulsions that Patrick pushed on him.

"What are you doing here?" Patrick repeated, demanding an answer from his protégé.

"Hunting," the boy-vampire responded offhandedly.

The fury that welled in the older vampire was instantaneous. With a speed unknown to humankind, he flung his arm out and backhanded his insolent spawn.

Daniel flew into the back of the alley. He felt the boy's jaw shatter, unhinging from his skull, as he slid across the garbage-strewn alley. Before Daniel could react, Patrick was over him, pulling Daniel's ruined face close.

"You never go hunting alone, never without me!" he spat in a harsh, dangerous whisper. "You do it again, and I will make you regret it. You will leave now. Your antics will end, or I will end them for you."

A fleeting memory formed in Patrick's mind; he had ripped open young Jimmy's neck on that long ago night, not just small punctures as he usually did now. The blood had sprayed across his face, perfect, innocent blood.

"We will hunt," Patrick decided, "I must complete my task for Eldon but then we will hunt together. You will come with me now."

He would not share Jimmy with his young protégé, that was a meal Patrick intended to have all to himself. He would feed elsewhere with Daniel and return another night for Jimmy. If vampires had anything, they had time.

Patrick watched as Daniel's jaw tied itself back together. Daniel must have just fed recently, for his bones realigned quickly, but the young need food often. Even Patrick himself needed to eat almost every night while his own master needed blood only once every few days. On Daniel's face, the flesh that had ripped open, cut by the once splintered bone, mended almost instantly.

"As you wish... Master," the youngster spat, before he disappeared into the night.

Patrick forced himself to steady. He had turned Daniel in secret. If the others found out, he would be punished, and Daniel likely destroyed. Patrick had never been a calm person before his turning. As a human, he had his own host of problems. How his therapist could have told stories. Much had changed in the past twenty years but Patrick still fought the anger.

The vampire looked back at the little shop and took another deep inhale of Jimmy's scent lingering in the alley. Soon, he would taste that sweet blood again.

Paranoia Chapter 2

Jim had packed his bag and left Fix-A-Lot just after 6:00am. Glenn, another tech, had taken over. Before being coworkers, they had been acquaintances in University, both computer science majors. As where Jim had stayed and graduated, Glenn left the school after completing only two of the four year program. They had met by chance when Jim was out for coffee. Jim was working a retail job selling electronics. He hated the work but jobs were in short supply, even if you had a degree. Glenn mentioned his own place of work, Computer-Fix-A-Lot. It just so happened that they were looking for another repair tech. Jim jumped on the opportunity. With Glenn's help, he didn't even need to give his electronics shop notice. Jim still smiled when he thought of telling his manager how he wouldn't be showing up for the rest of the shifts on the schedule.

With his shift over, Jim only chatted with Glenn a few minutes before heading out to walk home. East Hastings was quiet at this hour, and Jim loved the walk. This time of year it was still dark out, but Jim enjoyed watching the sun rise as he did his daily workout at home. His apartment in Hastings Park was only twenty minutes away by foot. East Hastings street was known for being the shadiest neighbourhood in Vancouver, filled with hookers, drug dealers, and the dealer's clientele, but they were mostly out at night. That's why Jim took the bus to get to work. There was a stop only steps away from his apartment building in Hastings Park, and another right near Fix-A-Lot. The place was different in the early hours. In the morning he liked to walk home after his shift. East Hastings was peaceful in the early morning. The buildings looked worn and decrepit, but Hastings was still charming in its own way.

It was three stories up to Jim's apartment. The stairs were yellow, stained by the smoke of countless cigarettes and other more illicit smoked substances. Jim didn't mind, he actually liked being in what he thought of as "the heart of hell." Hastings Park was two city blocks composed of multiple apartment buildings––half the buildings were brick from top to bottom, the other half were grey stucco, all showed signs of neglect.

Jonah had been begging him to move for months, but Jim really liked his new digs. It sure beat the lifelessness of living near campus.

His Hastings apartment was a top floor unit in an older brick building. It faced east, granting a delightful view of the morning sun, the parking lot, and the building's dumpster. It didn't have an elevator, but the stairs had become a part of Jim's daily workout.

Jim passed a vagrant on the last flight. The homeless man was curled up in a fetal position, half sitting, his face resting against the wall, snoring. Jim bypassed the sleeping man soundlessly. He was good at sneaking quietly, and he reached the top floor without disturbing the man. Jim was not alone in the hallway. Further down the hall, Caitlin was unlocking her door. Jim smiled and gave a shy little wave. She too had obviously snuck past the sleeping man, and he admired her stealth.

She had straight box-blonde hair cut an inch from her shoulders, which she teased to give it the illusion of volume. She was skinny, too skinny really. She waved back at him, her lips curled up to one side in a smirk that made Jim melt. It was teasing, mischievous, and sexy, all in one expression. What he found most endearing was that she wasn't trying to be any of those things, that was just the way she smiled.

That smile had filled out a bit in the last two months. So had the rest of her. Every day that she stayed clean her appearance improved. Still, it would be months before she would look truly healthy.

She wore a pink cut-off tank top so her slightly concave stomach and ribs showed, and a very short denim skirt with check-patterned black hose. She looked like a hooker, which was her job after all.

Jim never cared about her profession. He thought she was beautiful, funny, and sweet. Helping her get off meth had not been easy, but he had been there for her as often as he could. When the landlord had first given Jim the keys, perplexed as to why a "normal looking guy like him" wanted to live in Hastings Park, Caitlin had passed him in the hall. She had the shakes then, and was obviously jonesing for a fix. Two days later he found her in the building stairwell, passed out in the same place the homeless man currently slept. He carried her into his apartment, laid her on the couch and covered her up with a spare blanket. She was startled when she woke up, and hurried off to her own apartment. Jim had woken to the commotion she made leaving but had continued to lie in his bed, listening to her leave. Later that night she had come back though. Jim still could not decide what made Caitlin trust him, or why he trusted her when he usually didn't trust anyone. Yet they *did* trust each other. She said she wanted to stop using meth, that she had been trying but it was too hard to do it alone. Jim knew he had to help, or at least try to help. He had never used hard drugs, but he knew that most people who try to quit failed. Caitlin, however, hadn't failed and now here she was across the hall from him, her baby face smiling at him.

"Hey Jim," she called, waving as shyly as he had. They saw each other often and had spent time together, but ever since she got sober there had been a tension between them.

"Hey Caitlin, you have a safe night?" he asked.

"Safe as any. I did okay though. Kinda funny, but since I got clean I make more money than I ever did before."

"Well that's good," he called back. He asked this often when they met. He worried about her out there. People are freaks after all.

"Hey," she said hesitantly, "some night soon, I'm planning on ordering in from Thanh's, down the road. I remember you saying they were your favourite, right?"

"Yeah, I love their food."

"My treat, okay?" she said, her smirk turning into a hesitant full smile.

"I'm off Saturday and Sunday this week," he said, his hand still on the key in the deadbolt.

"Saturday is one of my big-money nights, so how about Sunday night?" she countered.

"Sounds good."

"It's a date then!" she said.

Caitlin checked her watch, turned the key in her own lock and opened the door. "I gotta go, but see you soon. Night, Jim," she called before stepping inside her apartment.

"Night," he called back.

He shut the door and his face broke into a huge smile. Jim adored his neighbour. Even while holding her as she vomited and cried in the worst throws of withdrawal, he thought she was amazing. Jim had seen Caitlin at her very worst, but he thought no one could be as brave as she was. She fought her greatest demon and won. That made her a hero as far as he was concerned, and now, he had a date with her.

He turned and engaged the lock as soon as he closed the door. It was a large multi-latch lock that he had found online and installed himself. From the outside, it looked like a normal deadbolt but on the inside the lock had four separate bolt mechanisms—-a regular deadbolt latch and three bars which fell into metal holders affixed to the jamb when the lock was engaged. Once the bars fell into place, Jim picked up a metal rod next to the door and slid it into place, locking the bars in. Even if someone had the tools to pick a normal deadbolt, the rod would stop the lock from turning. In his apartment, Jim felt truly safe in large part because of that lock.

The apartment was small but comfortable. The living room was on the east end of the unit and had a large bay window that looked like it was ready to fall out of the building onto the parking lot. The space was large enough to house a TV stand, a coffee table, and a sofa. The west end of the apartment accommodated an eat-in kitchen delineated by cracked yellow linoleum. The kitchen itself lined the back wall with a green stove, a white fridge with a missing handle, a small bit of counter space, and a single sink. There were two doors at the north end of the room, a door to the bathroom off the kitchen, and a door off the living room that led to the only bedroom.

Since moving in, just after he started at Fix-A-Lot, Jim had already installed the lock, and had fixed both the leaking tap in the kitchen and the leaking shower head. He had also bought a door for the bedroom to replace the old one. He was pretty sure it had been kicked in, and he didn't want his brother to see it when he came over to visit, assuming Jonah ever did so.

Jim tossed his bag onto the couch and started up the entertainment console, which was a computer he had built himself and set up for all his TV, podcasts, movies, and the like. Heading into the bedroom, he wriggled out of his jeans and t-shirt and exchanged them for sweatpants. In the empty dining area just off the kitchen, Jim spread out a mat on the floor, tilted the TV to face the mat, and started up his morning workout videos.

After leaning over a desk all night, it felt good to stretch out. The yoga video lasted only fifteen minutes, but it was a great warm-up. The second video had Jim alternating from push-ups to sit-ups, then burpees until his lungs felt like they were going to burst. He stretched out into the plank position and held it for five minutes. The final video was his favourite, a fifteen minute session of Tai Chi.

Jim was not a big guy. He did this same work out after every shift. The hour and a half of exercise kept him lean and solid but he didn't seem to bulk up the way weightlifters did, instead he was slim and toned. At five foot six, he also wasn't tall, so most people dismissed him, assuming because he was short, he was weak. But Jim would not allow himself to be weak.

After the workout, he rolled the mat back up and slid it behind the couch. Even though he had been up all night and had already eaten two meals, Jim wanted to enjoy a hearty breakfast before he slept the day away. He cooked two eggs and three strips of bacon. When the bacon was almost crispy, and the eggs nearly perfect, he pulled the lever down on the toaster he had loaded a minute before. Like the workout, the process possessed the smooth precision that came with repetition.

Jim savoured every bite of the meal. He cracked the yolks of the eggs with a corner of his toast and dipped it into the softness inside. He loved his post-workout protein kick. Life felt pretty much perfect. All that was missing was Caitlin.

* * *

By the time Jim woke, it was dark outside. Since taking the Fix-A-Lot job, he found he needed more sleep. He guessed the quality of sleep he got during the day didn't match that of night sleep, which was fine. He went to sleep around noon each day and rose each night by ten.

He could feel it the second his eyes opened. There was a tightness in his throat and his stomach knotted up like he had just finished five hundred sit-ups. Jim didn't reach under the bed for the weapon he hid underneath, but instead slipped out of the covers and snuck to the window. He swung back the curtain hard, like ripping off a Band-Aid.

The sky was dark and ominous. Vancouver was usually clouded over, but these were not the light grey clouds that would offer rain. They were the dark black and green of a storm.

As Jim watched, lightning shot through the sky. His knees buckled, and he tried not to fall over, but then the thunder boomed. Jim pulled the curtain closed and retreated to the furthest corner of his bedroom. He tried not to whimper, tried not to call out, but his mind was in a far away place, hiding from the chaos outside. He had no idea he was screaming.

* * *

Patrick loved these nights, so similar to the one where he was born–– truly born. After feeding on Jim as a boy, Patrick's master had found him and forced him away. Patrick had spent the rest of his first night as vampire alone on a rooftop watching lightning rain down and listening to the call of thunder.

Patrick waited for Jim. The rain had not started yet but the sky was brilliant with lightning, chorusing with thunder. His heart pounded in anticipation, his fangs extended. He was fully ready to feed, and he waited in the dark alley. The need pulsated hot and deep in his bones. Not just anyone would do, not now that he had found the boy. He would wait until Jimmy returned to his work. It was a public store. Unlike a dwelling, he needed no invitation to enter. The vampire envisioned tearing the metal door at the back of Computer-Fix-A-Lot off its hinges, jumping in, and ripping the throat out of the man working behind the desk.

In the dark of the alley, Patrick knelt on the concrete. His heart boomed in his chest, the need pushing him farther. The garbage bin screeched, the metal giving way, as Patrick held himself back. He would not enter the store yet, not until his prey arrived.

Paranoia Chapter 3

C aitlin woke to thunder. It was such a distinct noise that she rolled over and cocked her head toward the small bedroom window. The little apartment had been her home for over a year. In this ugly neighbourhood, she had grown accustomed to waking to loud noises. Usually the sound was glass breaking as a car got vandalized, or a drunk couple yelling at each other in the parking lot, or the blare of sirens. Every now and then gunshots would ring out. Loud noises always meant danger, except for storms.

A jagged bolt of lightning cut across the night, setting the sky ablaze. The bolt was so close it turned Caitlin's bedroom window into a glowing white box. Another boom of thunder boom of thunder rang out, in perfect time with the light show in the sky. Caitlin closed her eyes as red squares floated in her vision. When she could see clearly, she noticed that the window was dry. The rain had not begun yet. If it did start to rain, she could justify taking the night off, but Ansel wouldn't like that. It rained often in Vancouver, the city was known for it, but rarely did it storm like this. Her pimp rarely let his crew of girls skip a night, but on a night like this, what would be the point?

Ansel was better than most of the pimps on Hastings. The problem was that *better* didn't mean *good*. Most pimps sampled their girls, Ansel was no different, but at least he would step in if a john got too kinky or rough. A lot of pimps would watch their girls get beaten and then add a few hits of their own when the girl couldn't attract customers because her face was too swollen and bruised. Ansel usually didn't hurt his girls. He always said he wouldn't damage his merchandise without reason. The only time Ansel would get violent is if a girl tried to leave his employ, particularly if she was trying to go to another pimp. Girls who tried to leave the sex trade could expect a few broken fingers, or ribs, depending on Ansel's mood. He never touched the face though, "too valuable," he'd say. A lot of people think hooking is all about having a sexy body. It's not. It's about having an attractive face *and* a sexy body.

If a girl started talking to other pimps, that girl might disappear. The cops could never link it to Ansel, but they knew, and they let it slide. Caitlin hated her pimp for that. He thought he owned his girls for life.

She was thankful he'd never beaten her, but he'd pushed her around when she was too high to work. He'd shove, and shove, and yell, and curse until she forced herself onto the corner. The only time she'd ever needed his help, when a john hit her and then tied her to the bed, Ansel had waited until the last second to come to her defence. The john wanted to get kinky with a whip, a long thing that looked like a movie prop, not a sex shop purchase. He was about to use it when Ansel busted open the door to the room at the Sunflower Motel, the grimy by-the-hour joint most hookers used. The john had whipped Ansel across the face before the pimp got a hold of him. Ansel nearly beat the man to death. She thought her pimp was going to turn on her next, the look in his eyes was so fierce. All he did was call to another of the girls who stood in the doorway to come in and untie Caitlin. She had been thankful, but she had also never forgotten that look. It chilled her every time she thought of it.

Once she was off the junk, she had thought Ansel would treat her better. He didn't shove her around anymore because she worked most nights and her customers had doubled. She found that not only was she in higher demand, but she earned more each time she was hired. Hooking, after all, was a game of negotiation. When she was high, johns knew it and knew they could take advantage. She would be lucky to take in fifty bucks per customer. Now, even though she still had the body of a user, she had her mind back. A trick would drive up, and she'd tell him she was two hundred. Usually they talked it out and she'd walk away with a hundred, sometimes more.

To her surprise, the one person who was not happy with Caitlin's sobriety was Ansel. He too made more money with her sober, taking forty percent of every trick who hired her, but he was sure she'd try to leave. He was paranoid, convinced she'd try to move on to a better paying escort service, or out of the sex trade altogether. The idea made him furious, and his anger scared her.

She was brooding, and she knew it. With a sigh, Caitlin tossed off the covers and rolled out of bed. Her shower was warm and soothing. The one thing she liked about the grungy building was that the hot water rarely ever failed. Since getting off the smack, she showered twice a day, once to get clean before work and once to *feel* clean after work. She had always liked being in water, it felt purifying, even in a moldy old bathroom like this.

The storm was raging when she was finished in the bathroom. A heavy wind had rolled in, and the larger living room window was rippling back and forth with the force of the gale. Thunder continued to boom, and lightning constantly lit the sky. If Ansel forced her to work tonight, she knew she would spend her time hiding under one of the shop's awnings, trying to stay warm. The likelihood of a john looking for some company in this weather was virtually nonexistent. The prospect of standing out there all night held no appeal. She had to either make the call to Ansel to tell him she wasn't working, or get dressed to hit the street. But what was worse, dealing with the weather, or dealing with Ansel?

She was in her bedroom trying to choose some warm clothing that Ansel would accept when she heard something. It was faint and thunder had just boomed, but Caitlin was sure she had heard something besides the storm. It sounded like a person. She moved to the bedroom wall that separated her bedroom from Jim's.

There had been a noise, she was sure of it. Caitlin pressed her ear to the plaster and closed her eyes to concentrate. There it was. Sobbing. She snatched up random clothes out of her closet and threw them on. She only stopped once on her way out to grab the keys that hung on a peg by the door.

The doors to each apartment were made of metal and seemed more appropriate for a warehouse than an apartment. Caitlin banged on the door, her knuckles pinging off the steel.

"Jim! Jim, come get the door! Let me in!" she called.

She hit the door again, and her hand stung. When he didn't answer, she reached into her pocket and picked out the key Jim had given her. She had never used the key before. Jim was such a private guy, she never wanted to overstep with him. She felt safe with Jim, and that was a rare thing that she never wanted to lose, not for anything, but something told her that Jim was not alright, that he needed her right now. She forced herself to put the key in the lock, and turned. Nothing happened, the lock was jammed somehow, it wouldn't turn. She took the key out and was about to try again when she heard movement inside the apartment.

Jim opened the door. His knuckles were white on the frame, as he held the door open for her. Caitlin walked in slowly.

"Hi Caitlin. What brings you over?" he asked. He was trying to sound normal, but he was sweating like crazy, and Caitlin could tell he was barely keeping it together. She stepped closer to him, but he took a step back. Jim kept darting his eyes for the open door to the window and then back to the door again.

"I heard you through the walls," she said, stepping closer to him, "I don't know what's wrong, but it's okay."

He backed away again, and Caitlin took the opportunity to close and lock the door. Jim always felt better when the door was locked.

"You don't understand," he said to her, and then lightning flashed again.

Jim fell to the floor, pushing himself backward against the kitchen cabinetry. His arms went around his head and he ducked his face in between his knees, as if bracing for a crash.

Caitlin rushed to kneel next to him. She didn't care what was wrong with Jim, she only cared about helping him.

"Jim, it's okay," she whispered and wrapped her arms around his balled-up form, "it's okay, baby, I'm here."

She had never called him that before, but it felt right. He felt right.

* * *

64

Patrick's heart pounded. He needed to feed. The boy had to be returning to work soon. If not, Patrick would need to seek some other sustenance before returning for Jim. He didn't want that to happen. He wanted to hold out for Jim as long as he could, but the need was so strong.

The back door of the repair shop opened, and a man stepped out, pressing a cellphone to his ear. He pulled a pack of cigarettes out of his shirt pocket, extracted a smoke, and lit up.

"Yeah, I know," he said into the phone, "we have a decent workload right now, but if Glenn is willing to come in for an extra four hours tomorrow, and I put in a couple more tonight we should be able to make it work."

He paused to take another puff on his cigarette. Patrick was coiled up like a spring, listening.

"Yeah," the man said again, "I don't know what's wrong with Jim. Actually, it was his neighbour that called in to say he wouldn't be coming in to work. Hopefully, it's not something catching. I'll tell ya, I don't need to be sick right now too."

Jim wasn't coming in to work. Jim *wasn't coming*! Patrick didn't even try to hold back any longer. His vision turned crimson as he rushed out of the alley.

The man on the phone didn't have time to scream. Patrick wrapped his fingers around the man's neck, instantly locating and tearing his carotid artery through the soft flesh. Over the years, Patrick had learned to be clean and careful when he fed, but the need had filled him so much that he didn't care to be clean. Blood sprayed up Patrick's face. He sealed his mouth over the pumping geyser of blood and gulped it down. When the lifeblood slowed, the vampire pulled away in anger. He was being deprived again! He knelt over the body in a rage, using his finger to rip the flesh.

On the ground, a sound came from the cellphone, "hello?! Stefan?!? Where did you go? Stefan, are you okay?!?"

Paranoia Chapter 4

Jim let the water wash over him. Every muscle in his body hurt, and his head pounded. The shower let him think. The thoughts weren't good thoughts, but he had to work them out. He didn't know what he was going to do. Caitlin was in his living room, and he had made a fool of himself last night, sniveling and crying like that. He had to face her, and Jim didn't know how he was going to do that. The only person that had ever seen him like that was his brother. Jonah barely ever called him now. He didn't blame his brother for that. Who would want to be close to someone so pathetic? He turned the water hotter until it made his skin red-raw.

Finally, when he couldn't stand it any longer, he turned the water off. He would have to face her eventually, but the thought of her looking at him with... with what? He didn't know, and maybe that made it worse.

He toweled off, then grabbed jeans and a t-shirt. He wanted to go hide in his closet, wanted to do anything other than step outside his bedroom. But he couldn't be weak. He tried to step out but Caitlin stuck her head in the doorway first.

"Hey, you look good," she said with a bright smile, "I thought you could use some food. I ordered Thanh's. I hope you don't mind, I also raided your kitchen for plates and cutlery. I didn't know what you liked, so I just guessed. The food got here while you were in the shower. I can dish it out now if you're ready?"

Jim nodded, stunned. She was acting like nothing had happened, and he was just waiting for the other shoe to drop. It made him sad. Her eyes were so bright, and that full smile shone again, not the smirk. He could have drowned in the beauty of her eyes. He felt like he was going to the headsman instead of sharing a meal with the most incredible woman he had ever met. If there had ever been anything between them, he was sure it was dead now. How could anyone love someone so pathetic, so weak? It was a storm, just a storm. Even as he thought of the weather, he wanted to curl back in on himself, hide in the corner of the bathroom, but the storm was over. The night was clouded over and a light rain fell, but that was all. Jim still wanted to hide, just for a different reason now.

There was nowhere to go but forward, so that's what Jim did, no matter how much that terrified him. *Fear only makes us stronger*, he thought. It was a mantra he told himself every day. He had to. It was how he survived with all the crap that messed up his head. *But if fear makes me stronger, what does loss do?*

He realized loss was exactly what he was feeling. Caitlin hadn't said or done anything to pull away from him yet. Besides, they had never actually been together, not even close, but he had hoped. That's what he was mourning--the loss of that hope.

The dishes were spread out on the coffee table. The TV was on, but the screen was black and soft jazz was pouring out of the speakers. It wasn't loud, but it drowned out the sound of the rain still falling outside. Caitlin had already loaded the plates with a couple of spring rolls, almond diced chicken, and a beef dish Jim had never tried before. It all looked good, and he realized just how hungry he was.

"Are you okay?" she asked and looked straight into his eyes. To Jim's surprise, her eyes didn't hold pity in them, or anxiety, or anything bad at all. Instead, they seemed to hold strength and maybe something more.

"I'm...okay. Honestly, much better now. And hungry," he answered while taking the plate Caitlin was handing him.

For the most part, they ate in a comfortable silence. They talked a little about the food. Jim asked what the beef was. They both expressed their delight in Thanh's food, and how it was nice to have a restaurant open late, well into the morning hours. The meal was perfect. Jim hadn't thought anything could make him feel as good as he did in those moments, especially after Caitlin had seen him... like that.

When the meal was done, they cleaned up together. They packed what was left of the food into the fridge. He moved to the sink to do the dishes, and Caitlin, without a word, grabbed the dishcloth to dry everything as he washed it. It felt so normal, as if she were exactly in tune with him.

He couldn't help but glance at her as they worked. He just wanted to look at her. The whole act of cleaning up after their meal felt natural, as though they had been doing it for years. After staying with him as she got sober, she knew where everything belonged. It didn't feel awkward, or expectant, or anything like that. It felt normal, and good, and perfect. It was as if she were exactly in tune with him. He liked that.

"I'm sorry," he said, as they finished the cleaning.

"For what?" she responded, but he could tell she knew.

"For earlier. I don't know why. I don't know why I'm like that... in storms," he finished in a huff. He was spoiling the moment, maybe even the whole evening––the good part at least––but he couldn't hold it in anymore. Not from her.

Caitlin leaned forward and touched his arm. He was acutely aware of her fingertips on his skin, and it was the caring in her eyes that gave him the strength to continue on.

"I don't know what started it, but ever since I was a kid, storms have scared me like that. I've tried so hard to overcome it, to be strong. I've trained myself to be strong. Every time a storm comes, even if I know it's coming... well, you saw," he still expected her to turn on him. To say he was weak, and that she needed someone better, stronger than him.

"Baby, you don't need to always be strong," she whispered. Her other hand had come up to Jim's cheek. He marveled at how good that touch felt. Then she kissed him.

* * *

The red of the blood, the red of his rage, the red of desire, the three shades had melded into a crimson so intense, so vibrant and delicious, it was all Patrick could see. The sirens were near, only a couple of blocks away by the time Patrick heard them.

It had taken all that he was to tear himself away, to stop feeding. He had made a mess of things. Vampires were supposed to work in the shadows. This was not in the shadows, not by a long shot. He didn't care. The body in front of him had no head. The blood that had sprayed with each heartbeat had slowed to a trickle. The blood still dripped from Patrick's body. He was drenched in it.

He reached down to pick up the cellphone. Sounds were still emanating from it, and Patrick had to admit that he was curious to hear what it was. The sirens were getting closer. He put the phone to his ear.

"Stefan," the voice sobbed, "honey, the police are coming. Stefan, please be okay. Please!"

Pathetic––exactly as Patrick figured it would be. He let the phone drop back to the ground and took to the sky just before the police turned into the alley behind Computer Fix-A-Lot.

Paranoia Chapter 5

J im's eyes shot open. The phone was ringing next to him. Even though he knew Caitlin was beside him, it still shocked him to find her in his bed. The room was still dark, so he reached over and turned on the light. She was wrapped up against his body, her head sticking out of the blanket, nestled on his chest. The phone was still ringing.

Caitlin opened her eyes and looked up at him.

"Do you have to get it?" she asked sleepily but with a hint of teasing that made Jim's mouth go dry.

Despite his better judgment, he answered "I probably should."

"Hello," he said into the phone. Carl, the owner of Fix-A-Lot, was on the other end of the line.

"Jim, you have to come in right now." Carl was almost yelling, which was a strange thing to hear. It actually seemed to Jim that his boss purposefully only used the minimum amount of energy required to get a task done, even something as simple as speaking. Carl was old and seriously overweight. He sounded like he had run five city blocks and was about to have a heart attack. His voice was gravelly and strained.

Jim looked at the clock next to his bed. It shone bright red in the dark room--4:30AM. Carl was still speaking.

"Stefan is dead, killed at the shop. The police are here. They need to speak to every employee, and you were scheduled to work Jim. What the fuck are you doing at home?"

Jim didn't answer; he sat bolt upright. Caitlin lifted her head, observing him. He could feel her body go as rigid as his. His adrenaline had spiked, and she had picked up it.

"I'll be there right away," Jim said into the phone and hung up.

Jim sprung out of bed and started getting dressed. His heart pounded in his chest. He remembered Caitlin calling Fix-A-Lot during the storm. She must have spoken to Stefan not long before he was murdered. Jesus, that could have been him, had he gone into work tonight.

Relaying the conversation to Caitlin in quick, clipped sentences, Jim finished getting dressed and ran out the door as quickly as he could.

Busses ran infrequently in the early hours of the morning, but Jim was lucky enough to catch one as soon as he reached Hastings. It was only a short ride, but it gave him some time to let the events of the past few hours catch up to him. It was hard to focus. His mind kept jumping from Caitlin to Stefan. Jim had wished for more than friendship with Caitlin from the moment she was sober. Although gaunt as she was, she was beautiful and became even more so the longer she remained clean. More than that, she had an amazing heart. Even his pathetic display of cowardice last night during the storm hadn't affected her. The thought of touching her bare skin still sent shivers through him. She had said she was going to stick around his place for a bit, but she was insistent that she had to be home by 6 am. The intensity with which she had said that struck him as strange. Maybe she had to check in with Ansel, her pimp. He didn't know why, but that made him think about the cut and bruising he had seen around her thigh. Jim wondered if one of Caitlin's clients had made the mark, or Ansel. God, he hoped she wasn't using again. It didn't look like needle wounds, but Jim wasn't an expert on the subject either. Caitlin seemed her normal self though, and Jim didn't think she was back on the drugs. The thought that she could have relapsed was depressing, but he had faith in her. Then he thought about what he'd told her. About the storms, about his weakness. Just thinking about the light flashing through the dark sky made him shiver, and not in a good way. The shivers triggered thoughts of Stefan.

Caitlin had likely saved his life, but at the cost of Stefan's. Whenever someone called in sick, the other repair techs often extended their own shifts to make sure the shop didn't get too behind on orders. Given the early hour Carl had called, there was no doubt that Stefan had been working into Jim's shift. Carl had not said anything about how Stefan had been killed.

Jim had liked his coworker. Stefan worked the evening shift and often stayed afterward to chat. They had not been close friends, but Stefan had deserved a long life––a good life. The last time they had spoken, Stefan had just saved up enough money to surprise his girlfriend, Katie, with a trip south of the border into Washington. He wanted to take his girlfriend to the San Juan Islands off the coast for her birthday. Poor Stefan, and poor Katie. It was a waste, and it sickened him.

The bus stopped, and Jim got off warily. From the stop, he could already see two police cars parked in front of the alley that led to the Fix-A-Lot back entrance. The alley was blockaded with police tape, and an officer stood sentinel at its mouth. In the movies, there was always a crowd around the tape, and the police would have their arms outstretched to make sure no one crossed. There was no crowd here, just the one lonely cop. It shouldn't have surprised him, not at this hour in this part of Vancouver, but it did. This was his first time at a real crime scene.

He approached the tape, and Jim watched the Policeman's mouth turn down.

"Excuse me officer, I work at Computer Fix-A-Lot. I was asked to come in and speak with someone," Jim stated, spitting the words out as quickly as he could. His heart was pounding hard. Fix-A-Lot had been a sanctuary but now it felt like unknown territory.

The cop nodded, then said, "Wait here," before taking a step back and talking in a low voice into the radio attached to his shoulder. A minute later, another man in uniform walked out of the alley. With no one else near the tape, his eyes focussed directly on Jim.

"You're the employee?" he said, and Jim nodded.

The cop lifted the tape and ushered Jim in.

"I'm officer Cheverie," the cop stated as he led Jim into the shop. Jim froze before the door. Blood coated the back wall of the shop like paint. A puddle was forming on the ground in front of it. The red was splattered everywhere.

The sight of it made Jim stop in his tracks. He couldn't move, his eyes locked on the gore. He felt the blood drain from his face and his knees weaken. Inside his head, questions throbbed with his heartbeat. Who? How? What?

The cop touched his arm, and Jim's eyes shifted away from the darkening pool. Jim followed the officer into the shop. Carl was inside. Sweat poured down the shop owner's face. He too was pale. The sight of his employer in disarray actually strengthened Jim. He had to be strong when others were not. It's what he always wanted to be, and it's how he would be now.

The officer sat him down at the workstation and began asking questions. Explaining why Jim had not come in for work would not be easy, but it could be done. Besides, he had the most wonderful alibi in the world. Caitlin.

* * *

Last night had been one of the best nights of Caitlin's life. Sex had always been an means to an end. Her first time, she had been raped. It was at a party back in high school. Everyone knew it had happened, but no one believed her when she said it was against her will. That was why she had left as soon as she graduated high school. She couldn't stand the looks people gave her. It was then that she decided she would take control of her life, or at least she thought so at the time. Sex was easy. It was something she could use to put a roof over her head, food on her table, and until she got sober, to keep shit in her veins. Before last night she had never had sex because she genuinely cared for the person she was with. The feeling of it was so much more than when she slept with customers. With customers, it was almost mechanical. Yeah, it felt good, but in a detached, unemotional way. It wasn't like that at all with Jim.

It felt so amazing to be able to touch him. He had felt so out of reach. She swung her legs out of Jim's cloud-like bed and grabbed her pants off the floor. She was in such a hurry to check on Jim last night, she hadn't realized she had put on the same pants she had worn the last time she worked. Her beeper was still clipped to the belt loop, its screen glowing a bright green. It said there were four messages. Caitlin was sure they were all from Ansel. She looked at the last one.

'You better be fucking dead, bitch.'

She took a deep breath. He had been looking for a reason to be angry at her, and he had likely just found it. He was not going to be easy to handle.

She took a second look at the beeper, but this time to check the time. 5:58 AM.

Quickly, Caitlin pulled her pants on, not bothering to track down her underwear. Her chest felt tight, but she couldn't think why. The feeling was familiar though. It made her think of her step-dad. Paul had wanted to fuck her as much as he wanted to fuck her mother––maybe more. Sometimes Paul was okay, other times not. He had tells like a poker player, and Caitlin had learned the signs. As she would watch his wretched eyes glide over her body, or see him tap the side of his thigh, like he was jonesing for a hit, her chest would feel tight like it did now.

Her body was covered in goose flesh. She wanted to get a weapon, to hide under the bed, to see Jim walk through the door. With only two minutes to six, she abandoned her bra and slid into her t-shirt. She had to hurry back to her apartment, she had to be there by 6:15am. The apprehension didn't go away, but something was pulling her toward her apartment, and she couldn't stop it. She locked Jim's door as she left.

* * *

The police were swarming the perimeter of the repair shop. From a rooftop a few buildings away, Patrick could see everything easily. In the shadows, he was all but invisible.

The area where Patrick had fed was taped off. It was foolish to feed like that. He never should have let himself lose control. It was that damn boy, and the smell of him. Patrick would need to be smarter. It would do him no good to find the boy but have his maker punish him for being careless. His master's punishments were slow and agonizing. Many years ago he had been ordered to leave the boy alone. New as he was at the time, he had no choice but to obey without question. That order, however, was old, and Patrick could feel its power had dissipated. He was certain he could feed on Jim despite his maker's orders.

The vampire watched as his prey got off a bus and made his way towards the police. Patrick watched, content for now. He still felt the need to feed, but the blood of Jim's coworker quenched that need enough for the time being. For now, Patrick would wait and watch the police. He had to make sure they had no idea what had truly happened to the boy's coworker. In a few days, after things calmed down a little, he'd come back, have his fill, and leave this part of town alone for the next 20 years... until everything was forgotten.

Paranoia Chapter 6

It felt weird to be in her own apartment. There was a sense in the back of her brain that she should be anywhere but here and another sense that told her that her apartment was exactly where she needed to be. There was something important about being in her apartment at 6 AM, but she didn't know what it was.

Caitlin looked at the clock on the wall. It was almost six. She walked over to the dining table and tossed her beeper onto it. She would call Ansel after... after what again? She wished she could remember what was happening at six. Her chest was so tight, and it felt like her throat was ready to seal shut. She glanced down at her hand. She was gripping the back of a chair as tightly as she could. Her legs wanted to move, to run. Her heart was pumping like she was already running. Thoughts kept bubbling and popping in her head. *Run...* pop. *Stay...* pop. *Danger, so much danger...* pop. She had to run, she *had* to, but her feet wouldn't move.

"Hello Caitlin," said a voice from behind her, "where have you been?"

The speaker was someone she knew, and he had called her by name. At the same time, Caitlin was sure that deep down in her marrow, she knew she had heard his voice before many, many times. His voice made her lip quiver, the tone of disapproval in it made her want to scream, but she couldn't open her mouth.

As if of its own accord, her body turned and she looked directly into his eyes. His eyes were so calming. She felt her muscles relax. The voice in her head quieted to nothing. Thoughts of Jim disappeared; the owner of the voice was everything.

Vancouver's east side had a lot of street kids, and Caitlin knew many of them. They shared the same streets, and frequented the same dealers. She had gotten high with Daniel more than once but hadn't seen him in months. At least she was pretty sure she hadn't seen him, something in the back of her mind said that wasn't right. Maybe she was having trouble remembering, she didn't think so though. She normally had a great memory, and it was getting better again now that she was clean.

"I stayed at Jim's place last night," she said. Inside she knew that telling him about Jim was a very bad idea, but she couldn't help it. He had asked, and she needed to answer.

Daniel hopped through the open window. He stepped close. Caitlin's heart pumped violently in her chest, she wanted to take a step back, but it was like there was an immovable board behind her rather than air.

"And who's Jim?" he demanded. The edge in his voice made Caitlin whimper, but she couldn't stop herself from talking.

"He's my neighbour," she replied. She didn't want to say anything else, and he hadn't asked for more than that.

"Did he pay you?" His face almost touched hers. His fangs were out, and his eyes shone with anger. With danger. "Did he pay you to fuck him, Caitlin?"

"No," she said through the haze. She wasn't sure if it was the fear, or the simple truth that she wanted to say out loud, but she continued, "I wanted to sleep with him. He never paid me, he wouldn't even think of it, and I wouldn't accept it. I love him."

Daniel roared. Spittle shot from his mouth, hitting Caitlin in the cheek. His anger broke the spell on her. She was about to run, but Daniel dove forward. She felt his fangs sink into the skin of her neck, and then nothing more.

* * *

The statement Jim gave the police had somehow been difficult and effortless at the same time. He had only lied a little. He did tell them that Caitlin had been with him all night. Hopefully she didn't mind being his alibi, it was the truth, after all. They had taken down his information, and Caitlin's. There was a look when he mentioned what she did for a living, and he had to explain at length that he was not one of her customers. He also had to state a number of times that Stefan had met Caitlin once, and he was also not one of her customers. Stefan was... had been, happily engaged, and as far as Jim knew, Stefan had been faithful.

Jim had only lied about one thing, and that was his own reason for not showing up to work that night. The police had noted right away that Jim was completely healthy. He told the constable that he had called in sick so that he could spend the evening with Caitlin. It was how the night had played out, and it was close enough to the truth.

The questions had come slow and hard, the way cops have to ask them. Since they didn't seem to have a clue who had actually killed Stefan and were feeling everything out. Jim didn't have any more of an idea than the cops did. God, there had been so much blood. Thoughts flitted through his head. He could hear the podcast in his mind...

Vampire, were-beast, creatures of the nightmare. You know they exist.

But did they, did they really? Deep in his marrow, Jim knew they did. He was also sure that nothing else could have done this to Stefan. The question was not only what had done it, but why. Could it be so simple that Stefan was in the wrong place at the wrong time? If that were the case, then that could have easily have been Jim's blood smeared and pooling around the Fix-A-Lot building.

The bus ride home was short, but it felt interminable. It was still night, and Jim didn't feel like taking his usual walk home. His hands shook so badly he couldn't hold still. Questions flooded in and rushed out like waves, and the answers he came up with were eroding the insides of Jim's mind. The bullet he had dodged——Stefan's loss instead of his own demise——weighed on him. If Stefan had not been killed, Jim would have called last night the best night of his life. In many ways, it still was the best night of his life. The same questions kept creeping in. What the fuck was wrong with him? How could the night his coworker was murdered be the best day of his life? What kind of person did that make him?

The bus reached his stop and he got off. His hands were stuffed in his pockets as he approached the apartment building. All he wanted to do was go to Caitlin, but he didn't want to smother her either. Still, she would likely want to know what had happened, and the cops would be calling to confirm his alibi. She would need to know exactly what Jim had told the police.

His door was locked when he arrived. That brought a smile to his face. It was an obvious thing to most people, but she had still done it, and that action meant the world to him. The locked door also likely meant that his apartment was empty. She had to be in her apartment for 6:15 AM she had said. Caitlin never brought customers home. That was a rule for her. Besides, she likely wouldn't be meeting a john at six in the morning.

The apartment looked different somehow. More inviting. The carpets looked vibrant, the window brighter. His bedroom brought a giant smile to his face. The sheets had never looked rumpled like that. He could distinctly see where he had gotten up, and where Caitlin had been. That sight made his pulse accelerate. It sped up even more when he looked down at the bra and panties on the floor next to the bed. They were plain, not like the sexy things he had pictured her wearing in his fantasies, but for some reason, it was better that they were normal, boring. Their simplicity made Caitlin more than she had been in his eyes. Jim didn't know why and didn't care.

He thought about giving them back to her next time he saw her, but he wanted to see her so badly. What if things were different now? They easily could be. What if I wait too long though? Could that make it worse?

Part of him knew he was being stupid. She obviously cared for him. How much, he didn't know. He loved her, he had been sure of that before last night. Now that he had touched her, was inside her, all he wanted to do was be touching her again, loving her again.

He picked up her underthings and left his apartment. Like the bus ride, the walk down the hall seemed to take forever. Those steps carried every fear he had ever felt when it came to his feelings for Caitlin, but every hope too. Jim focused on the hope. It went against every grain in Jim's core, but for Caitlin, the effort was worth it.

Jim pulled out his key for her apartment, which Caitlin had insisted he have. After Jim had insisted the same of her, he couldn't refuse. The result was a key in his possession that he never thought he would have to use.

He slipped the key in the lock, a primitive thing compared to his own, and turned. The door swung open just a little before Jim knocked.

"Cait, it's Jim. You forgot some stuff at my place," he called out.

The blood on the floor made Jim's heart skip a beat. He swung the door wide, and yelled Caitlin's name. Jim's love was on the floor. Her eyes were open, staring at the door, but Jim knew there was no life in them even before he saw the gaping wound in her neck. He rushed in and knelt down, not even noticing his pants soaking up the pool around her body.

"Caitlin! Caitlin, wake up," he sobbed. Jim knew better, he understood that she was gone, but he begged her to come back anyway. She had to come back, his life was empty without Caitlin in it. He reached down to cup her face with his hand. Hands grabbed his hair and Jim felt a yank, then the impact of hitting the wall.

"Hello Jim. I would say it's nice to meet you but that would be a lie."

Jim looked up at a teenager in an ill-fitting, torn t-shirt and dirty jeans. The shirt was covered in blood. The teen's canine teeth were so long, there was no mistaking what he was.

"Vampire," Jim growled.

"Yes, vampire," the teen said and jumped at Jim again. Before he could react, Jim felt his body fly through the air once more. He smashed into Caitlin's tiny dining set before colliding with the wall a second time. Then the vampire was on him, and Jim's neck was ripped open.

Jim wanted to fight, to kill this nightmare before it killed him, but he was frozen. Memories flooded his mind. He saw himself as a child. Jonah had just taken him to see a movie in theatres. It had been *The Empire Strikes Back.* It had been the best night of his life until Patrick Steadman, who had lived down the street from them, took him. Mr. Steadman was a vampire, and he had taken Jim into the woods. The adult Jim cried out, as much from the memory as being fed on now. Jonah had saved him that night, him and another vampire. Jim remembered looking in that vampire's eyes, being told to forget, to forget it all, and Jim had done just that. Until now.

Jim was sure he was going to die, but he couldn't die yet. Someone had to avenge Caitlin. She hadn't deserved this, Jim hadn't deserved what had happened to him either. Someone had to stop this from happening.

Jim could feel his strength ebbing. Soon he wouldn't have enough left for what he had to do. He reached for something, anything he could use as a weapon. Fingers wrapped around wood, and swung it as hard as he could. The table leg hit the vampire in the head but the teen barely flinched. Jim could see his weapon now though, the end sharp and deadly. He spun his grip and stabbed as hard as he could with the sharp end of wood. The vampire screamed as the makeshift weapon sunk into his neck. The wound likely looked similar to Jim's own, a ripped gash in flesh. Jim pulled out the stake and stabbed again. He knew what to aim for. The stake punctured the heart. The vampire didn't scream, didn't bleed, didn't breath, just died.

Jim scrambled across the floor to Caitlin.

"Oh Caitlin!" he sobbed, "Caitlin, I'm so sorry. Baby, they're real. They're really real, and I'll kill them. For what they did to me and to you. I'll fucking kill them."

The erosion of all those waves broke the bank inside Jim's mind. He had lost everything, both his past, thanks to Patrick Steadman, and his future, with the loss of Caitlin. He had one thought and one thought only. Revenge. He rose and stormed out of Caitlin's apartment. He had to hunt, and he wasn't going to stop hunting until he had killed them all.

The End

Ansel

"Where the *fuck* is it!" Ansel growled. Was everything he owned going to fucking disappear? First Caitlin ending up dead, then Kara disappearing, then Jules. At least he was able to find Jules. She wouldn't work for a while after the beating he laid on her for running from him, but he *had* found her. That was key. But the girls were not the only things going missing.

His favourite shirt a few days ago, his hair brush yesterday, and now his keys. Seriously, his fucking keys! He never let them out of his sight. At least he was sure they were here somewhere. Ansel had pushed around everything on his coffee table. Usually they sat next to his smokes. It was part of his ritual before leaving the house. First keys, then smokes. Like he wanted to use right now!

He was about to flip the damn table over to look underneath, when a knock came at the door. Before he could answer, the wood around the door handle splintered with a bang. A second bang forced the door to swing open so hard it hammered into the wall, the handle puncturing the drywall. Ansel dashed toward the bedroom, his hands held high, protecting his face from the flying splinters of the door. There was a gun in the drawer next to the bed, he just had to get to it. Why hadn't he had it on him?

Something hard hit him from behind, knocking him to the ground. His face hit the floor first, sending jolts of pain all the way through his eyes to the back of his head. Blood filled his nose and ran down his throat making him cough and gag.

"Ansel Whitticker, you are under arrest," came a woman's voice from behind him. "You have the right to remain silent. You've the right to an attorney."

"What the fuck!" Ansel screamed. He tried to shove the bitch-cop off him but he couldn't get any leverage. The click of the handcuff told him exactly how fucked he was.

"What is this! I didn't do anything! I didn't DO Anything!" he yelled.

"Tell that to Caitlin Flock's parents," a man's voice said behind Ansel.

"What are you talking about?!?" he growled at the cops.

One cop reached under his kevlar vest and pulled out a plastic bag. The bitch-cop maneuvered Ansel around on the ground until he faced the busted door. He was looking directly at the cop with the bag. A knee came down into the small of Ansel's back, and the bitch-cop put her full weight down. She moved around a bit, then handed another, larger plastic bag to the male cop. Ansel recognized the contents right away.

The male cop put on a plastic glove before opening the two bags. He dumped Ansel's keys from the bag to the floor. Then he took out Ansel's favourite shirt, a smear maring the blue, turning it slightly purple. He could see blood on his keys too.

"What are you doing?" he asked, but he already knew the answer. They were framing him. For what? Caitlin?

"I didn't kill no one!" he whispered, then louder, "I didn't kill no one! You can't do this!"

"But you did, Ansel, you killed Caitlin Flock. The evidence says so," the bitch-cop said. As if coming out of a daze, the male cop shook his head, then bent over to pick up the keys.

"Hey, Shoemaker," he said towards the female cop, "look at what we have here!"

"What the fuck! You just put that there!" Ansel exclaimed, the cops ignored him.

"Looks like blood on it," the bitch-cop, Shoemaker, said.

Ansel couldn't believe what he was hearing. They actually sounded like they were sure they had not just put the things on the floor themselves. They bagged up the keys in the same damn bags they had just used to plant them. Then they moved over the shirt.

"I'll bet you a beer that's Flock's blood," the man exclaimed. "It is, isn't it?"

This time the question was directed at Ansel. He wanted to yell and scream at the two cops. They knew where it had come from, they had put them there. He just stared at them, mouth gaping.

"What the fuck?" he whispered at the cop.

"You don't need to say it. Forensics will tell us the truth, Ansel. I'll bet the hairs we found in Flock's place will match your DNA too, won't they? Then you'll be off to prison, never allowed to hurt another girl again."

Ansel stared blankly. He thought about his missing hairbrush and wondered about the last time he had seen that shirt. There had to be a way out, but he didn't think so. He thought about all the girls he had been forced to beat over the years. Not that many really, but enough. This was karma taking a big bite out of his ass, wasn't it. Well, this fucker bit back.

Ansel lifted his head, pulled up everything he could out of his throat and spit the oyster as hard as he could into the cops face.

"Fuck you, piggy," he sneered.

The cop wiped his face, then looked at bitch-cop over Ansel's shoulder.

"Get this piece of shit outta here, would ya?"

Rex's Diner

Every cop needs a place where they can go to forget about the job. It's a place where even if they are still wearing their uniform, as I often was, they could just sit back and let all the shit that accompanies the job leech out. For me, that place was Rex's Diner. Sometimes it feels like I've sat in one of these booths in the early morning hours after every shift for damn near eight years.

I first found Rex's in 1984, not long after I joined the Vancouver Police Department. It was a dive then, and still is now, but it feels like home to me. I'm not sure if the décor is 1950's original or if a previous owner redid the place to give it that Golden Age look. I didn't care either way; all I cared about was having a place where I knew the coffee was hot and the pie was perfection on a plate.

This early February morning, I was enjoying a slice of good 'ole lemon meringue. At this fine hour, I was the only one in the restaurant, which suited me just fine. The sun wasn't up yet, though it wouldn't be too much longer. In an hour, maybe two, kids would be making their way to school under an orange sky, assuming clouds didn't roll in. At that point, I would be back in my little one-bedroom condo, fast asleep. Even after eight years on the force, I still insisted on working the overnight shift. I know it's why I'm still working the beat instead of making detective, but that's okay. I was born for the beat. I love the beat, and it loves me back. Still, sometimes, I can't help but think if it really loved me so much, I wouldn't need a place like Rex's.

In a lot of ways the diner was just like me. We're both showing our age, both still working the overnight. I had to chuckle at that. I hoped I looked a little better than this old building. I wasn't even that old, but being a cop had a tendency to age you fast. Almost a decade as one of Vancouver's finest would put a strain on anyone. The hours sucked, the pay was okay as far as city cops went but not enough to make up for the pressure of the job. That's why places like Rex's were so special - they helped to vent the pressure.

The diner had changed owners over the years, but right now it was run by Barbara Gordon. Yes, just like Batgirl in the comic books. I was a huge Batman fan as a kid, and I actually own the first issue where Barbara Gordon is introduced as Batgirl. I brought my copy of Detective Comics #359 in to show her not long after she had taken over the diner. Barb looked at it and laughed, she knew she shared the name with the fictional hero but no one had ever shown her the old comic book before. She thought it was sweet, and we'd been friends ever since.

She was a nice lady in her early thirties. When she took over the restaurant, she bought brand new white t-shirts with "Rex's" embossed on the chest. She's done a good job running the place, but after two years those t-shirts are looking as worn as the booths and the leather bench seats at the counter. Still, she was staying afloat, and she made great pie.

"More coffee, Constable Cheverie?"

I was so lost in stupidly comparing myself to the diner I sat in that I hadn't even noticed Barb walk up.

"Oh, yeah. Thanks Barb," I responded, pushing my cup to the end of the table toward her. "When are you going to start calling me Nick?"

"When you stop picturing me in a blue and yellow superhero outfit," she said with a little wink. "I can see it in your eyes every time you say my name."

She went back behind the counter, and the bell above the door rang indicating new customers were walking into the diner. We both looked up, her from the perch behind the counter, me from the corner I occupied most mornings. Three men entered. I didn't know them, but I recognized their type right away. They were the type of guys cops watch with one hand close to their sidearm. They saw me and moved to the other side of the restaurant. They sat in the booth that wrapped around the corner so they could talk, but one of them always kept an eye on me, even when he was addressing his two companions.

Barb made her way over to the thugs' table. Her back was to me. I couldn't tell what she was saying, but her stance told me everything I needed to know. Barb didn't like serving the guys, and although she was nervous, they hadn't said anything to make her truly scared. Still, I figured I could stay awake for another half hour or so. As Barb walked back to the counter, I called out.

"Hey Barb, can I get another slice of that meringue?"

She looked at me with no small amount of relief and affection. Barb nodded, tore the thugs' order off her pad, clipped it to the antique order rack, and gave a soft knock on the frame of the order window. Rex's morning cook was a tiny Aboriginal girl named Desiree. If I had to guess, I'd peg Desiree as a girl who recently dropped out of high school because her parents, if either was still in the picture, couldn't afford to cover the bills. The kid was lucky to get this job. Vancouver didn't hold a lot of options for young Aboriginal girls, particularly in this neighborhood. But she did a good job, and Barb liked her. Now she was looking out the order window at the three punks, the order slip in her hand.

Barb walked around to my table and placed the pie in front of me.

"On the house," she said in a low voice. I didn't have to tell her why I had ordered the second piece; I never ordered more than a slice.

"Say the word," I said back to her, giving her an even stare.

She nodded nervously before answering back, "It will be okay."

I hope so, I thought as I watched her walk to the other side of the diner, coffee pot in one hand, and three mugs gripped by the handle in her other hand. I got off the red leather booth seat and headed to the counter, the three punks watching my every step. I grabbed a copy of *The National Post* off the counter and made my way back to my booth. With the paper open, I could watch the three punks without looking like I was watching them, the same way one punk could watch me while looking like he was just chatting with the others.

The stare-off lasted a good ten minutes. Everyone in the diner jumped when Desiree rang the bell to indicate that food was ready. Barb grabbed the three plates and carried them over to the punks, one plate in each hand, the third resting on her forearm.

The punks seemed to relax once they had food in front of them. One of them still kept an eye on me, but they were much more at ease. I had been so intent on watching the punks that I was surprised when I took the last gulp of my coffee. I set it back down and picked up the fork. They could tuck in, why couldn't I? It seemed like we'd reached a truce, for now anyway.

The problem was, by the time I finished my pie the two cups of coffee had hit my bladder. It had been a long shift with multiple coffees. With nature calling, I now had to listen. I got up for a second time. The bathroom was on the punks' side of the diner. I'd have to walk right by their table on my way to the bathroom. I could've waited a little while, but I had no idea how long the punks planned on staying. Best to get it over with.

I hadn't noticed Barb leave the restaurant floor, but she was nowhere to be seen as I made my way across the floor. The punks were alert now, watching my every step. Since I had no plans on taking action against the three, I kept my eyes averted, watching my feet. When I reached the midpoint, I looked up. I wanted to see if I could check on Barb through the order window. What I saw made me freeze in my tracks.

I could see Desiree back in the kitchen. Her head was tilted up and someone stood behind her, sucking. A tiny trickle of blood ran down her neck. I saw her throat move, which I knew was the teen trying to scream, but not being able to.

"What the fuck," I heard myself say. You see a lot of weird and nasty shit as a cop, but this was so strange, so otherworldly, that at that moment my mind couldn't grasp what I was looking at. The boy sucking on Desiree's neck looked up–– he couldn't be more than sixteen. His fangs, teeth, and lips were covered in blood, but the look on his face, it was so feral, so animal-like, that my hand grabbed my gun like it was muscle reflex.

Somewhere in the back of my mind I heard the crash of the table behind me, but I couldn't pay attention to it now. I was completely focused on Desiree.

You know how sometimes time slows down right at that second where something is going to change your world forever? That's what seemed to happen to me right then. I had my gun raised and was about to squeeze the trigger, but the boy moved so incredibly fast. He dove to the right, where I couldn't see him behind the order window. Desiree continued to stand stalk still with her head tilted to one side, her neck exposed. Blood ran down from two puncture wounds, turning her once-white Rex's t-shirt a deep red. The biter yelled a name, *Patrick*, while he moved out of view. I had gotten one shot off, but it didn't even come close to him.

I had just enough time to register that the freak I had shot at called to an accomplice when a man burst through the door that led to the bathroom, storage room, and kitchen. If it had not been for the two long, sharp teeth and the stretched feral look on his face (a perfect match to his younger companion), I would have sworn this was one of the most normal men I had ever seen. Now, he looked like a monster. A hungry, angry monster.

The three thugs had knocked over their table when I pulled my sidearm, and I saw now that two of them had their own firearms in hand. They had all been looking at me, but they were turning towards the monster who must have been 'Patrick'.

Patrick leapt, with one hand outstretched, towards the closest thug. Blood sprayed across the window and the faces of thugs two and three as Patrick ripped the throat of the closest young man.

I raised my weapon at the new threat, as did punk three. We started firing at the same time. I fired three clear shots into Patrick's chest. In all my years on the force, I had only fired my sidearm once on duty, and it hadn't been a killing shot. All three of these shots were, and I knew it. Punk three was still firing seconds after I had stopped. When Patrick stopped moving, thug three stepped forward and put three bullets into the wacko's head. I didn't object one little bit.

At that second, I didn't give a shit how many times thug three shot the guy as long as he still had bullets left. "There's one more in the back," I called to thug three. Punk two had curled his legs up on the booth, his hands were covering his face, his fingers digging into his cheeks. He just stared at the two bodies lying across the booth and floor in front of him. He would be no use at all. I'd have to count on thug three to back me up. Assuming he didn't run or shoot me in the back instead.

I had turned back to the order window, but there was no sight of the kid who bit Desiree. Desiree was still standing there like a statue. I had no way of knowing what thug three was going to do. I had to hope I could trust him, that the last fucked up thirty seconds had created some kind of bond. "You gonna stick around, or am I gonna take on the other fuck alone?" I finally asked.

"That fucker's as dead as this guy," he growled, then shot Patrick in the head one more time. "You hear that motherfucker? Your buddy killed my brother, and now you're fucking dead!" Thug three let three more shots fire, this time toward the back of the restaurant. Thank God, none of them hit Desiree.

"Hey," I yelled, "save your bullets. There's an innocent person back there. I'm sorry about your brother, but let's just take care of the one guy left and no one else. Okay?"

Truth is, two guys packing heat during breakfast at 5 AM in a roach diner? Punk one likely deserved what he got. Still, I needed his brother, and sympathy was the best way to get it right now. "Look, what's your name?" I asked.

"Jessie."

The fact that he didn't hesitate to give me a name meant his real name almost certainly wasn't "Jessie," but I wasn't going to bring that up at a moment like this.

"Well, Jessie, let's get our shit together and go get this guy. Okay?"

I hadn't taken my eyes off the order window during my little exchange with thug three––Jessie––but there was no movement. I chanced a look at Jessie, and he wasn't looking so good. He had tears rolling down his cheeks, and he was pale––really pale. He was holding a Glock that almost mirrored my own, it was trained on the door to the back where Patrick had come from. Before I could really give any thought to the idea of teaming up with him, he said, "Let's go," and moved toward the door.

For the first time, I thought about my radio. I still had the shoulder mic attached to my uniform, but since I was off shift my radio base was no longer in my belt. Instead, it was sitting in the console of my squad car parked across the street. Nothing could be done about that. I had to concentrate on what I had on my hands right now. I had to look out for the only partner I had available. And once this was all over, I was going to find out what the fuck these freaks thought they were doing. The teeth had looked so real. Prosthetics maybe? Fuck, what was this world coming to.

The back of Rex's was pretty basic. A long hallway led to a back entrance which, at the moment, was slightly ajar. Three more doors lined the left of the hall, leading to a women's bathroom, a men's, and a storage room. Jessie ignored each door. His eyes were completely focused on the archway at the end of the hallway. I wasn't taking any chances. At each door, I took the time to open it and hit the light. After checking the women's restroom, Jessie noticed what I was doing, and while I looked in the men's room, he grabbed the handle of the storage room.

Before Jessie could turn the handle, Desiree's attacker jumped out of the archway. He was so fast I could barely keep track of him. He jumped and used his foot against the wall to launch himself through the air at Jessie. The thug barely had time to react. He started to turn his gun, but before he could aim at the teen vampire--God, that's what it had to be-- it had swung a clawed hand, ripping into Jessie's forearm. The weapon went off, and the shot grazed his attacker's leg. The bullet wound didn't slow him down in the slightest.

The vampire reached out and grabbed Jessie by the collar, but before he could sink his teeth into the thug, I popped off two shots. The first went wide, which shows how much this nightmare had shaken me up. The vampire was only four feet in front of me, there was no way I should have missed. The second shot connected. The bullet pierced through the front of the teen's shoulder and ripped out of his back. He let out the most inhuman scream I had ever heard then, with his blinding speed, disappeared into the kitchen.

If I had been hanging onto any hope that those teeth were fake, that these two freaks were just crazy or high or both, that hope died right then and there. That scream sealed the deal for me. I was fighting the undead.

Jessie was still on the ground, breathing hard. He was staring at the archway into the kitchen like the opening was suddenly going to start moving and swallow him whole. I knelt down and gently leaned forward to put my hand on his shoulder. He looked up and his eyes looked crazy, like a horse that had been spooked and was about to rear.

"Look at me," I said, taking swift glances down to see if he listened. He had, so I continued, "Get your shit together, we are going to go in there and we are going to kill that thing, you hear me?" He didn't look like he got me at all, so I kept going. "These things killed your brother, and they might have Barb and Desiree. They deserve to be avenged. You need to avenge your brother, I've got the other two."

I said all this quick and harsh. I needed Jessie to understand. If he didn't pick himself up, then we were likely both dead, but saying that wouldn't help him. He gave me a quick look. It told me a lot--the look said he was going to follow through with this shit, but he was sure he was about to die. He was terrified, but the decision had been made. He ran into the kitchen.

It wasn't how I would have wanted to do it. I'm used to working with a partner, if not a team, and this wasn't exactly my idea of teamwork. Still, I followed quickly. Punk or not, enough people had died tonight. Jessie didn't need to be added to the list.

I made it to the arch just as the first shot rang out. Vamp-boy had Jessie's wrists. The shot had gone into the ceiling. Jessie was no match, and the teen tossed him carelessly to the side. Jessie let out a scream as his back landed on the hot cooktop. Before the vampire could turn back to me, I fired three shots--pop, pop, pop, just like being on the range--directly into the vampire's head. He fell.

"Jessie, you okay?" I called.

"Yeah," he called back, but I could hear the lie in it. He could barely stand, but he was alive. "What the fuck now?"

"I don't know, find a stake?" I said, making the statement a question.

"I think they're dead, I mean, doesn't cutting their heads off work, too?" he responded. Of course, neither of us actually knew. "The head shots seem to do the same thing. It worked on the guy out there, the one that..." his voice trailed off. He didn't want to say the one who killed his brother.

"Patrick," I said for him. "The little shit called the bigger guy Patrick." I kicked the dead teen for emphasis.

"Whatever," Jessie whispered. He was still thinking of his brother and trying not to cry again. "He's dead."

There was a phone screwed into the wall in the back of the kitchen. I pulled the receiver off the cradle and tapped 911. The operator answered and I was about to speak when something came through the order window so fast I could barely make it out. Patrick moved so fast it reminded me of a blurry photo, except the blood wasn't moving in slow motion. Jessie gurgled as his throat was opened. Blood shot up the oven, landed on the cooktop and started to sizzle on the hot metal.

This was my breaking point. In the academy, we were taught that when your fight or flight instinct kicks in, you fight with everything you've got. Well I had fought, and given everything I had and more. This plummeted me over the edge. I dropped the receiver on the floor of the kitchen and stumbled backwards as I tried to run. I had no idea where I was actually going. My hand found the closed door handle to the storage room. Barb was on the floor, her insides spilling out over the concrete. Her eyes were open. They gazed up at me blankly. I choked back a scream and ran down the hall. I felt the overwhelming urge to be outside, to be away from the coppery stench that permeated the diner. Thug two was on top of a table, his mouth gaping open and dead eyes staring at the ceiling. I ran for the door, and that's when the last shot rang out. I felt a thud against my back, like I'd been tackled by an NFL linebacker. There was a feeling of weightlessness, and I had just enough time to think that I was flying. Then I hit the ground, and the world went dark.

I thought I was dead. There was no possible way I had escaped those things alive, but I had. I'd lived. I tried to laugh. I wanted to shout to the world in a fit of hysteria. I wanted to cry for the insane loss of life. I could see an orange glow now out of the corner of my vision. I forced myself to roll over.

Rex's Diner was engulfed in flames. The vintage letters on top of the little building, once cherry red, burned a bright orange. Then Patrick was on me, one of the thug's weapons in his hand.

"Look at me," the vampire growled, and I did. I couldn't help it. That's when the world went black. I did hear one thing as I lost consciousness. I heard Patrick say, "Forget."

The next few days were pretty hazy. I remember a voice way off in the distance saying, "You'll be okay officer, just hang on." I might have been on a gurney, but maybe not. My heart might have stopped, but maybe not. I was questioned a lot about what had happened in Rex's Diner. The remains of five human beings had been found in the smoldering ruins of the restaurant.

Vancouver's finest had attended thanks to an anonymous phone call to 911 from within the diner. I had been found outside lying on the asphalt parking lot with a gunshot wound in my back. I was told my kevlar vest saved my life. The impact from the shot had broken two of my ribs, and shrapnel from the bullet had pierced the vest and lodged in my back.

I couldn't remember a thing. Anytime I tried to think about what happened in Rex's Diner, my brain would get all fuzzy. I could remember other evenings there. I can remember how silky Barb's lemon pie was. I can remember how we used to joke about her name. But every time I tried to think about the events of that night, I got nothing.

I was put on psych leave after the hospital. They tried to coax it out of me. The best I could give them was the memory of a sizzling sound and a sense of a name. The name always seems to be on the tip of my tongue, but never enough for me to say it out loud.

Five people died that night, and I can't remember a thing.

Hunter Chapter 1

The hunter watched from a building top. Below in an alley away from sight, it appeared a man was kissing a woman on the neck. He wore jeans and a dark red t-shirt. She wore a short skirt and tank-top cut off at the waist to show off her skinny belly. The scope on the hunter's rifle magnified so well that he could see the track marks that ran down the woman's arms, even at a distance.

To passersby, it looked like a hooker with her john. Not an uncommon sight in this area of Vancouver. The hunter knew better. He had seen the bat lounging on the rooftop above the couple. It had been a dead giveaway. Through the scope he watched a tiny trickle of blood run down the hooker's neck, only to be lapped up by the feeding vampire.

The hunter had watched this exchange for the last three nights. He watched and waited. Tonight would be the night. A minute later, the vampire had his fill. He stayed another minute, whispering instructions to his meal. Glamouring her, the hunter knew. He had been the subject of that hypnotic gaze before. He had not been the Hunter then, but a boy named Jim. He had been kidnapped by a vampire and been brutally fed upon until he was saved by his brother and another vampire. It was that second vampire that had glamoured him, and it had worked for years. Then Jim had fallen in love. Caitlin had been an amazing woman, strong, funny, loving. He had walked into her apartment after a vampire had killed her. Jim had staked that vampire, the trauma had broken the glamour, and he had become the hunter. Now the hunter was all that was left.

The vampire turned to leave the alley, and Jim pulled the trigger. The silencer made a *poof* sound. The vampire fell over. Death was immediate. All the while the hooker still stood unmoving in the alley. The hunter had to admit, he was curious to see if the glamour would hold now that the vampire was truly dead, but staying was not an option. The hunter wished to learn everything he could about his prey, the answer to that particular question would have been valuable, but the risk of capture was too great.

Instead, he packed up his rifle as quickly as he could. The weapon came apart into three short pieces with only a couple of latch releases. The action had been timed, and less than a minute later the rifle was stored away in his backpack. On the street, he heard a scream. A quick look showed the vampire's meal standing over the corpse. The scream had been hers. The hunter had to hurry, time was running short.

He flung the backpack over his shoulders and ran to the fire escape. The motorbike was waiting at the bottom. The hunter jumped on, key already in hand. The bike sounded like a go-cart when it started, but it was faster than any go-kart. He sped out of the alley, away from his kill. It had been a successful hunt.

* * *

Again, Eldon questioned the decisions he'd made that led to the creation of Patrick. It seemed the only constant that remained to him. Almost twenty years since Eldon had changed Patrick Steadman from human to vampire, twenty years since Patrick had escaped that first night. That was when Eldon's newborn vampire met Jimmy and Jonah Stilton. Eldon watched Jonah now from a rooftop a building away from Jonah's condo. Eldon's vampire body provided vision unknown to any living being on earth. Jonah's high-rise was mostly all windows which allowed Eldon to follow Jonah's movements with ease.

Even after all these years, Eldon still felt a pull toward Jonah that he couldn't really explain. Before Patrick, Eldon had never created another vampire, but Patrick had been a mistake. Eldon suspected it after that first night. The last twenty years had confirmed it. Patrick's actions over the past few months had solidified it in stone.

His fool offspring had created his own offspring. Patrick was too young to properly control another vampire. To make the matter worse, he had chosen a drug addict teenager, Daniel Martin. Patrick and his teenager together caused the problem that now plagued Eldon, and in truth, plagued all vampires in Vancouver.

Patrick had made the poor decision to hunt Jonah's younger brother, Jimmy. Although Eldon had no idea how Patrick had found Jimmy after all these years. Somehow in Steadman's hunt for the younger Stilton brother, Daniel had been killed in the apartment next to Jimmy's. Since then two more vampires in the city had been killed. Jim's scent had been at each of the kill sites.

The cellphone in Eldon's pocket vibrated. He checked the text message.

Another truly gone. Meet me. P

Eldon had sent Patrick on the hunt every night. If any vampire could find Jimmy Stilton, it would be Patrick. Eldon was not the only one fixated.

The elder vampire looked at the bats that hung suspended, waiting, watching for Eldon to act. He launched himself into the night, a flurry of small wings followed.

Minutes later he was next to Patrick. He had found another vampire dead. Who the vampire had been did not matter. What did matter was the attention that these killings were bringing to the darker realm of Vancouver. That was a problem that needed to be dealt with, and since Patrick had caused the problem, it had to be dealt with by Eldon. Patrick's blundering idiocy reflected on Eldon himself, and that was something he could not have.

Little was found where the latest vampire had died. Eldon and Patrick connected Jim's scent to a rooftop where he had presumably shot from and followed the scent down the fire escape. Then it was gone. The bullets themselves had a wooden tip, something either homemade or specialty made.

"Find him Patrick, and when you find him, you let me know. Do you understand?" Eldon growled.

Patrick nodded and disappeared into the night.

With the idiot gone, Eldon brought his thoughts back to Jonah. Since Patrick continued to fail, perhaps it was time to bring in some reinforcements.

Hunter Chapter 2

The east side of Vancouver is one of Canada's least hospitable neighbourhoods. This was a well-known fact, at least in British Columbia, the Canadian province in which Vancouver resides. Hunter loved the dankness, the darkness of the area. Even before he had become Hunter he had loved it. It felt like home in a way that White Rock, the ritzy suburb where he had grown up, never could. White Rock was more his brother, Jonah's, domain.

When Jim had been rebirthed as the Hunter, and later morphing again to simply Hunter, he knew he needed a base of operations. This place would be a nest where he could escape, recoup, and breed his skills. The ideal place would not be easy to find. He had found it though and Hunter could only equate it to destiny. The building was boarded up on the outside, tagged heavily with graffiti. Usually, buildings of this type were dens for the homeless that roamed this end of the city. Not this one. It had once been an office and small warehouse, complete with a bay door. It was abandoned. It was perfection. When Jim became no more, he took every dollar he could muster. It was enough to allow him supplies and weaponry. Now his nest reminded him of a superhero hideout, just like the heroes that Jim had grown up worshiping like The Punisher, and Blade. Jim had dawned a name, just as they had done and had a base of operations.

Truth be, he thought of 'Jim' as the past. Hunter was now. Hunter was everything.

The sniper rifle needed to be cleaned and ready for Hunter's next target.

Hunter could not use regular rounds, they wouldn't kill a vampire. The special ceramic bullets Hunter had ordered worked wonderfully though. The ceramic tip exploded on impact and the wooden centre pierced skin all the way to the heart. Staking by bullet. It was perfect, except the bullets could cause gun-lock or malfunction. Hunter had a routine to ensure his equipment continued to work when he needed it. Fire the rifle, clean the rifle, hunt. Fire the rifle, clean the rifle, hunt. Fire the rifle, clean the rifle, hunt.

As he set to the task, he reflected on the last kill. It had been a clean execution. This was his third rifle kill, his fourth vampire kill. The time between kills was getting shorter, that was excellent. Hunter had a journal that he kept with notes about each mark. Every detail regarding the hunt, and the stakeout was in that journal. The journal was on his only table, along with the cleaning kit for the rifle, a small selection of knives, two Beretta handguns, a second rifle and a samurai sword.

This was not the life Hunter had expected. Behind all the weapons was a pedestal. Upon it was the item that had destroyed Jim, and created him. The broken table leg sat on display, a constant reminder of what he had lost and what he had gained.

Gained. Did he really *gain* anything? It was a question Hunter had asked often, always followed by *was the price too high?* Truth was, Hunter knew the price had been too high. The price had been Caitlin. The price had been Jim. The price had been sanity. The price had been more than anyone should ever have to pay. That was why Jim had become Hunter because those who should pay are those who inflicted the pain in the first place. Vampires.

They had tortured Jim as a child, they had killed Caitlin as an adult, and destroyed Jim in the process. The vampires who had inflicted all that pain did so without thought or regard for those they hurt. They were learning that pain was on loan, and Hunter was demanding to be paid with interest.

Hunter grabbed his journal and started to scribble the day's report.

* * *

The phone rang, then rang again, and again. Jonah counted each ring, not expecting his brother to pick up, but still hoping that maybe this time he would be wrong. Maybe this time, Jim would answer. Instead, at the sixth ring, a recording started to play.

'You have reached 604-555-5460, please leave a message after the tone'

"Jim, please call me. Please." Jonah hit the end button on his Nokia cell phone and dropped it on the couch before sitting down. Calling Jim was getting harder each time he did it. Every time he had to count out the rings and listen to the automated voicemail, it was like listening to a nail being hammered into his brother's coffin. His brother was obviously listening to the messages as the voicemail box never filled.

Jonah took another deep breath and picked his phone back up. A couple of quick thumbs movements and he was making another call. The gruff voice Jonah expected to answer, did.

"Detective Cheverie."

"Hi detective," Jonah said into the phone, "It's Jonah Stilton..."

The detective didn't let him get any further, cutting him off with just two words.

"No news."

Jonah sighed. "Nothing?"

"I'm sorry Jonah, not a thing. I would call you if there was even a scrap." If Jonah's desperation and the detective's frustration were in a foot race, Jonah's desperation would win, but only by a hair. That's part of the reason why Jonah kept calling Detective Cheverie. Not only did it keep him thinking about Jonah's missing brother, but it kept the detective's level of frustration high. Jonah understood that frustration all too well, and he needed to spread it out to others. He wasn't sure he could hold it together if he had to bottle up all of his frustration and desperation inside himself.

In the kingdom at Jonah's core, with walls built of desperation and frustration, failure wore the king's crown. He had failed his brother. Big brothers were supposed to watch over their younger siblings, that's the primary job of any big brother, that's what big brothers do. Jim had never exactly been normal, but things had gotten back on track. He had a job, even if it was in a dumpy part of town, and an apartment on his own, again in a dumpy area, but Jim had been building a life. Then that guy at Jim's work got killed, and Jim's neighbour too, all in the same damn night.

Jim had a hard time as a kid. At around age seven, he had an accident. Jonah was riding his skateboard, and he had tumbled into Jimmy who had been on his bike. They had fallen, and Jimmy had been hurt really bad. He had hit his head, his neck had been ripped open. Everything had fallen apart for Jimmy after that. The change had been almost immediate, and Jonah watched as his brother turned in on himself. His younger brother had been scared of everything, he had trouble leaving the house, had trouble trusting anyone. Jimmy had seen shrinks, been put on meds, had even been locked up for a while, but he had gotten over it, as much as he could have. Then he got the job at Computer Fix-a-lot. Jonah hadn't liked his brother working the grave shift, or living on the east side. It was a recipe for disaster, but at the same time, he had been so proud of Jim. It seemed like such a simple thing, having a job and an apartment, but there had been a time when Jonah wasn't sure Jim would ever have these things.

After the two killings around Jim, he had disappeared. He probably had a complete breakdown. Jonah wouldn't have blamed him, anyone would have had trouble dealing with a coworker getting killed, and a neighbour getting killed the next night. That could send anyone over the edge, but Jim lived on that edge already. Jonah had to find him. He couldn't fail his brother again.

Hunter Chapter 3

The knock at the door startled Jonah out of his thoughts. The more he considered what happened to Stefan Champagne and Caitlin Flock, the more he sunk into himself. In the pit of his stomach, he always worried that Jim hadn't disappeared, but that he had also been a victim that night. Or even worse, the killer. Sure, Caitlin had been a hooker. The cops had pegged her pimp as the murderer, but Jonah didn't buy it. Neither did Detective Cheverie. All the evidence pointed that way, but neither Jonah, nor the detective could get it out of their heads. It didn't feel right, not at all.

Jonah opened the door to a man in his mid-thirties. The guy wore jeans and a t-shirt that would have looked perfect in an upscale nightclub. The strange thing was he had a bat sitting on his shoulder like a pirate's parrot. All the hair on the back of Jonah's neck stood straight up. He didn't know why, but the guy automatically made Jonah want to slam the door. Then he looked into the visitor's eyes. He wanted to tell the man to leave, leave and never come back.

The world went mushy around the sides. Jonah had never done any recreational drugs before, but if he had been able to analyze how he felt, he would have guessed the sensations were similar.

"Hello Jonah," the man said with an air of familiarity, "Would you please invite me in."

"Yes," Jonah heard himself say, "Please, do come in Eldon."

Eldon, how had Jonah known to address the man so? Then the man smiled, and Jonah's eyes popped. Long, sharp canines protruded from the man's mouth. All the times Jim had claimed vampires were real, all the podcasts Jim asked him to listen to, the books he begged Jonah to read, all to make him believe in the impossible. Now, Jonah knew the impossible was possible. It stood at his door, and Jonah had just invited it in.

Jonah felt the fog and tried to fight it, find a way through it. He had to find a way to think, to reason. Then the vampire spoke again.

Jonah moved out of the doorway, allowing Eldon to enter. Jonah didn't *want* to shut the door, yet he did it without a pause. He didn't *want* to be locked in his home with this thing, but he had done exactly that.

"You were always strong of will, Jonah, but I have a long memory. If I must truly push my will on you, I will not be lenient this time."

Jonah tried to puzzle out what the vampire meant, there had never been a first time, at least not one that Jonah knew about. Could the vampire make him forget previous meetings as easily as he had forced Jonah to invite him in? The thought made his flesh break out in bumps.

"I am going to release my hold on you, Jonah, but if you do not remain calm and compliant of your own free will, I will take all choice from you. Do you believe you are capable of following my instructions without my intervention?"

Jonah felt his head slowly bob up and down.

"Good," the vampire said nodding. His expression was a smug smile. Like the vampire held the key to a secret that Jonah couldn't understand.

A wind seemed to blow away the fog that was Jonah's mind. The ability to think clearly came back in a rush, but Jonah's first words didn't reflect his returned intelligence.

"What are you?"

"You know damn well what I am, Jonah," the vampire replied, "You know what I am, but you only know a tiny corner of what I am capable of."

Jonah was sure it was meant as a threat, it certainly sounded like a threat, but there was something lacking in it. Force, maybe? He wasn't sure. Either way, Jonah had no trust for the thing in front of him. His mind seemed to think of Jim when he looked at the vampire. He thought of when he and Jim were kids, and how had he known the vampire's name.

"I can feel your brain trying to puzzle it out," the vampire said, but Jonah wasn't sure what he was actually trying to figure out. His brain kept denying what was in front of him, at the same time it wanted to remember his childhood. Why?

"Did you kill Jim?" Jonah demanded. If he had, Jonah would kill him. One way or the other, Jonah would find a way to destroy this vampire.

"No," Eldon said with a dismissive wave of his hand, "as far as I know your brother is alive, and that is why I'm here, Jonah. I need your help. Little Jimmy needs to be found, and you're going to help me find him."

"Find him! That's all I've been trying to do, and I haven't had any luck at all," Jonah exclaimed, but he couldn't keep the despair from his own voice. He knew better. He hadn't tried as hard as he could have. *As hard as he should have.* Just another failure in a line of failures that was his relationship with Jim.

"Your brain is still trying to fix itself. Being so close to you, I can feel it clicking like a clock. Your mind is acting like a thief trying to crack a safe, but I have the combination. Would you like it, Jonah?"

Jonah had no idea what the vampire was talking about, but before he had time to answer, Eldon grabbed Jonah by the hair pulling them face to face, eye to eye. Eldon didn't say anything, didn't do anything else, at least not that Jonah could see, but memories flooded his mind. Everything rushed in.

Jonah was young, a teenager. He had his 'Jaws of Life' shirt on. God, he had loved that shirt. He was bringing Jimmy to the movies, Empire Strikes Back, opening night. It was the night Jonah fell off his skateboard and crashed into his brother.

Jonah watched in what seemed like a dream, but a dream running at the speed of light. Jimmy disappeared in the street after the movie was over. Eldon walked out of an alley. He and Jonah searched for Jimmy together. They found him in the woods, in the middle of a thunderstorm. Mr. Steadman, who lived just down the street, was a vampire too. He had taken Jimmy. Eldon and Mr. Steadman fought. Eldon was going to lose, they were all going to die. Jonah picked up a rock and he beat Mr. Steadman from behind. He hit the vampire in the head again and again until Mr. Steadman stopped moving.

Jonah was sure he had killed the vampire, but Eldon had been ready for Mr. Steadman to awaken again. Eldon gained control of the other vampire and sent him away. Then he found Jimmy with a massive wound on his neck. Blood soaked his t-shirt, front and back. Even his jeans looked dark, covered in the sticky red. Eldon did something around Jimmy's neck, helped him, healed him. Then he coerced the brothers into going home, lying to their parents, and forgetting. He made them forget it all.

It had all worked too, Jonah had believed the injuries were from a bike crash, a crash that Jonah had blamed himself for. His younger brother had started acting erratic after the accident, even crazy. Jimmy had spent much of his teen years in therapy. On three separate occasions, Jimmy had been committed to psychiatric facilities. Jonah had always blamed himself. He had always thought it was the crash that had caused some sort of brain damage. Jonah never doubted that Jimmy's belief in vampires, werewolves, aliens, and God knows what else, was all damage to his brain. And all caused by Jonah crashing into him. It was all a lie. All his guilt, all his life in fact, had been a lie planted by this vampire, all for what? Why hadn't Eldon just killed both of them? *Why tell me now?*

"Why now?" Jonah asked.

"Why now indeed," Eldon sighed and explained.

* * *

Outside, on the very ledge where Eldon stood earlier in the night, was Patrick Steadman. Steadman knew that his maker visited the older Stilton boy from time to time, but he didn't know they interacted. Now he did, and that was something he could use.

Steadman recognized the sagging, dazed expression on Jonah Stilton's face. Glamour is a vampire's most effective, readily available tool when it came to dealing with humans, with food.

The scene in the high-rise condo confused Steadman. Eldon, actually all the vampire that Steadman had ever met, felt nothing but contempt for the living. Patrick felt the same. He had been a poor excuse of a man, weak in mind, weak in soul, weak in body. That was no longer the case.

Vampire did not fraternize with food, but Steadman watched as the glamour slid from Jonah's face. Within minutes, Stilton's arms were flailing about. His maker sat calmly as the food raged at him.

Steadman hated his maker, but the idea of anything as lowly as a person yelling at a vampire made a deep growl emanate from his throat. How could Eldon just sit there?

"You know what? Fuck him," Patrick growled. If Eldon wanted to croon over Jonah Stilton, Patrick could find his own Stilton. Except Patrick wouldn't be all doe-eyed when he found Jim.

Patrick grabbed his cell phone from his back pocket. It was his main line of communication with Eldon. He crushed the device easily, dropping the plastic crumbs on the rooftop. It was time to hunt for himself, not for his maker.

Hunter Chapter 4

Jonah was exhausted. He wasn't used to being up all night. A nine-to-five job didn't allow for it. Sure, he had the occasional late night at a pub with the guys from work, but nothing like this. Besides, learning the truth about what really happened with Jim, hell, with Eldon and Patrick too, all that had its own type of stress. It all took its turn wearing Jonah down.

He sat down on the bench near the front door to his condo. He was so tired. They had looked all night. Jim had been a busy man. Eldon had first taken him to each place where a vampire had been murdered, if killing a vampire could be called murder. They were already dead after all. Eldon had called it murder, he obviously believed it so, but Jonah wasn't so sure. According to Eldon, Jim's scent had been at each location at the time of the killing.

He was too tired to think much on it, and he knew the following night would be no better. The sun wasn't up yet, but Eldon called off the search with almost two hours to spare. The vampire hadn't said anything, but Jonah had thought Eldon was going off to feed. He had no way of knowing how long vampires could go without eating. At least Eldon hadn't tried to feed off him. That was a good thing.

Jonah took off each shoe with a deep sigh of relief. He wasn't a runner or a gym rat. Although every shoe he owned was comfortable, they were ultimately made for fashion, not function. The two had covered a lot of ground.

Eldon said he would return as soon as the sun set. Jonah wasn't sure he was up for another night like the last one. Everything he wore felt rumpled and worn. He felt the same. Stripping it all off, he ran a hot bath, soaked and thought.

Surely with the powers of an undead and decades upon decades of knowledge, Eldon would be able to find Jim without Jonah's help. Yet he had made a point of bringing in Jonah, and not just as a puppet. Not like last time. Through all the exhaustion, knowledge of Eldon's control over him all those years ago still made Jonah's blood boil. He didn't want to be anyone's puppet. For what felt like the hundredth time, he wondered if he was still being exactly that. Did it matter if he was being used? Jim needed to be found either way.

He sat in the water until it became tepid, nursing every muscle he could find. Each one had been sore. After he dried off, Jonah made his way to his bed. He picked up the receiver on the phone on the nightstand. MetroMetre would have to survive a day without Jonah Stilton. He would get some sleep, then buy proper running shoes before Eldon arrived that night.

* * *

Patrick had quite a few regular blood donors. Every vampire did, but younger vampires more than most. He had been told that it would be at least four more decades before Patrick's blood lust would slow. The hunt for Jimmy had once again been fruitless. He had hoped not to need to visit a donor tonight, that Jimmy would be his *donor*. That was not to be.

So an hour before sunrise Patrick landed at the door of one such donor. Gregory was a small-time dealer, mostly pot, but his drug dealing allowed him to feed the man's true addiction. Gregory answered the door when Patrick knocked. Patrick didn't need to say anything, the rotund man moved from the door and bowed around his girth to let Patrick through. Lips bent downing a sneer, the vampire entered. He had long since made this man his toy, but the state in which the man lived disgusted Patrick. He waded his way through the garbage that lined the floor, moving the multitude of fast food packages with each step. He had degraded himself to this... filth. The vampire let his teeth show. Gregory, as if on queue, put his hands by his side and tilted his head to expose his neck.

"No," Patrick snarled through gritted fangs, "no, I will comprise no more. I let myself miss Jimmy Stilton twice now, but no more. My next meal will be him."

Patrick moved toward Gregory. He gripped the pudgy man by the neck and twisted, sharp and fast. Gregory seemed to smile a little as Patrick let him slip into the garbage sea on the apartment floor.

"I'm coming for you, little Jimmy," Patrick said to the night, then leapt into the sky. He would have to rest. Then he would hunt again.

* * *

Hunter lay on the military-grade cot and stared at the ceiling. He often did this as morning came on. For a few minutes each morning, Hunter would watch as the sunrise made shapes along the ceiling of his den. As he did so, he would let Hunter go to sleep first, and allow the little bit of him that was still Jim shine through.

It wasn't schizophrenia. Nor did he have the pretend multiple personality syndrome that movies always claimed existed. In the few moments of dawn he just let the vulnerable part of himself, usually shoved into the back of his mind, out to breathe. Hunter had named all the vulnerability left in him Jim, and it had to come out every once and a while. So Hunter picked the safest time of the day, when Vancouver basked in the daily glow. Just for a minute, Jim could think about Jonah, about how he missed his brother, especially now that their parents had passed. For that same minute, he could think of Caitlin, not the death that had transformed Jim into Hunter but Caitlin the woman. He thought about the life he could have had with her, a life denied to both of them. When the moment was gone, Jim would go back into the dark recesses of Hunter.

Hunter Chapter 5

"I'm telling you, there is no reason to bother going out tonight," Jonah said again, his hands outstretched, pleading for the vampire to understand.

"You don't seem to comprehend the severity of the situation," Eldon spat, "Every night we delay is another night where vampire are at risk either of destruction or exposure."

Jonah's hands turned into fists and he faced the vampire.

"Do you think I give a shit about your kind? We wouldn't be in this *situation* if it hadn't been for you and your kind," Jonah spat back. Eldon didn't care about him, or his brother. He should have stuck with the police, and let them find Jim.

The thought made Detective Cheverie's voice echo in Jonah's brain: *No news. I'm sorry, not a thing.* At least as it was Jonah knew what his brother was doing, and why Jim was hiding.

Then another thought entered Jonah's mind.

"Jim had grown up terrified of storms. Lightning and thunder make it even worse. As a child, I used to find him curled up in his closet any time it stormed. I just thought he was being a baby, but that was never it." Jonah put every ounce of anger and loathing he could into the words. The vampire had to understand.

"So?"

Of course he didn't understand, there was no human left in Eldon.

"The night Patrick Steadman took my brother, it was storming like it is tonight. Everything he suffered was because of Patrick Steadman, and because of you, because you couldn't handle the vampire you made."

"I glamoured him, it worked," Eldon said. Jonah detected no guilt, no remorse in Eldon's words. "Remember, Jonah, every night we are looking for your brother, my kind are not the only ones in danger. If Jim is caught by someone other than us, he will be killed without hesitation."

Jonah nodded. He had just been thinking the same thing.

Then Eldon took two steps closer, forcing Jonah to step back, his shoulders running against the wall.

"Remember this too," the vampire hissed through his fangs. "You are yourself because I allow it. I could easily consume your mind and make you my puppet. I could make you beg to give me all the secrets I need to find your brother, then suck you dry. You are alive because it is my whim. Press me in that manner again, and you may not find yourself in as many pieces as you do now."

Jonah tried to swallow, but his mouth was too dry. He couldn't speak. Instead, he nodded in short movements.

"Good," Eldon said and stepped away. "If we do not search, then we will do something else of value. We cannot allow time to be wasted."

Jonah nodded and was glad they could at least agree on that.

"I think we need to set up an ambush," Jonah suggested.

"What kind of ambush can we set that does not attract the attention of others besides your brother?" Eldon said.

"That's the rub, isn't it? I have no idea. I was hoping that you might."

Ambushes were things hunters were good at, and vampires hunted like no others. Planning didn't take long. Jonah didn't trust the vampire, but he claimed his plan meant no one would die. Deep down, Jonah knew it didn't matter. He would sacrifice others if it meant he could have his brother back.

* * *

The military cot was overturned. Behind it, Jimmy huddled against the wall. His blankets were tented over the cot and held against the wall so Jimmy could hide. The air underneath was stale and moist from his heavy breathing. Outside another lightning strike flashed, its light booming through the window and penetrating Jimmy's flimsy barrier. He rocked back and forth, tapping his hand against his arms. The movement's sole purpose was to expend energy. It wasn't enough, but Jimmy couldn't bring himself to do more.

"I am Hunter," he whispered, "I am strong. I am Hunter. I am Hunter."

Jim curled deeper. He closed his eyes and pressed the bedding against his face. He had to keep the storm out. He had to keep the fear out.

"I am not weak!" He cried as loud as he could. The sound barely penetrated the blanket. "I am Hunter!"

* * *

Eldon surveyed the street below, then the buildings above. This would be an ideal location. There were a lot of buildings that provided viewpoints that could be used by a sniper, but he could easily make one, the Garacy Building, look more appealing than the rest. One alley made Garacy the best choice.

Despite the rain, working girls were out in full force. Half a dozen girls walked the block Eldon had chosen. Eldon dropped into a dark alley and stepped out into the light of the streetlamps. One of the girls looked in his direction. He pushed his will forth. It was time to get to work.

Hunter Chapter 6

Hunter opened his eyes and tried to move. His muscles screamed but he stretched out anyway, kicking the cot with his foot. The air under the blanket was so humid and hot that Hunter could barely breathe. Light flooded his eyes when he pulled the blanket off. He had to squeeze them shut, dust motes playing across his red vision.

When his eyes adjusted, Hunter went directly to his computer and hit the power button. The machine booted up, the Windows 95 flag seeming to flap in the pixelated wind on the screen. As soon as the machine was ready, he headed to the website for the Vancouver Journal. The paper didn't post many stories on its website, but Hunter could see the most important news in his city.

In big letters read "East Hastings closed as police remove bodies". The text underneath told Hunter much. Three bodies, yet to be identified, all hookers. The cause of death was not released. Hunter can see the stain on the sheets in the photos though. Neck wounds, all three. Hunter remarked on the address. He would scope it out on foot during the day, then when night fell, he would start the hunt.

* * *

It was nice to actually feel rested. Jonah had spent most of the day in bed. A small part of him felt guilty for calling in another sick day. Still, he knew he would call in again tomorrow, and every day after that if he needed to. Time to recoup was good. The nights of searching had been long, fruitless, and stressful. Jonah was getting used to the vampire's presence, but even so, his skin constantly crawled. Being in Eldon's company made Jonah feel like a slug being eyed by a crow.

He showered in ridiculously hot water, staying in longer than he usually would. Spending the time clearing his mind, hardening it for the upcoming night that he would spend with the vampire.

Maybe tonight would be the night. Maybe tonight they would find Jimmy. The problem was that Eldon refused to mention what would happen after that. Jonah figured that the vampire would attempt a glamour again. If not, well, Jonah had planned for that too.

Once out of the shower, he brewed coffee and made some eggs for breakfast. He'd need the protein to help get him through another long night. There were still a few hours before nightfall. Jonah hoped this trap worked. He took the elevator to the main floor and grabbed the newspaper in the cradle next to the building's mailboxes.

The bold type on the front page made Jonah's heart freeze.

EAST HASTINGS CLOSED, POLICE REMOVE THREE BODIES

He almost dropped the paper. The walk back to the elevator felt like a dream. Eldon had agreed that there should be no killing. People would be hurt, but no killing. Jonah thought he had convinced himself that if someone died, he could live with it, that the price would be worth it if they found Jim.

The number on the elevator lit up when Jonah hit it. The elevator light burned into Jonah's vision while the upward momentum made him feel smaller. His world had fundamentally changed thanks to that headline. Jonah had never been a party to anything that broke the law. There had only been one exception, beating Patrick Steadman with a rock. That act had been self-defence but it had also been assault. At least, that's how Jonah thought of the newly obtained memory. This was different. He'd been a knowing accomplice, and part of him didn't care. Those women had lives, families, wants and desires. All that snuffed out, all for Jimmy. None of that mattered, it had to be done.

Jonah would take the guilt and eat it. He would do it because he had to.

* * *

Eldon's eyes popped. One second dead, the next, not. His lips turned upward as his consciousness returned. All the pieces were in place. It would soon be time to play the game.

Hunter Chapter 7

T he sun set over the ocean as Jonah watched. It was the view that convinced him to buy this condo even though it was a little smaller and more expensive than some of the other options he had looked at. Vancouver was so often drowned in overcast skies that he wanted to be able to watch the sun go down into the ocean every time the sky was clear.

Jonah couldn't feel any of the contentment he usually felt when looking at the view. The onset of night brought with it everything he didn't want to think about. There would be no choice though. Night would come. He doubted even a vampire could stop time.

The newspaper lay on the dining table next to an untouched cup of coffee long gone cold. After reading the article multiple times, he flipped the publication over. It was too hard to look at. Like the paper, his emotions kept flipping up and down. One moment, he was accepting of his part in the death of three women, the next moment he was a wash in guilt and shame. Not that he hadn't known it already, but Jonah had truly made a deal with the devil.

Not long after the sun dipped over the horizon, Eldon entered Jonah's home. Jonah gritted his teeth at the sight of the vampire. Eldon showed no signs of inner turmoil, not for the killing illustrated on the front page of the paper, not for the lies he had told Jonah the night before, not for the loss of life.

Jonah turned the paper back over, and upon reading the headlines, Eldon actually smiled. The smug, satisfied upturn of the vampire's lips made the short hairs on the back of Jonah's neck stand on end. He wanted to growl, to scream at the vampire, but he choked it all back.

Eldon appeared not to notice or at least ignored his companion's anger. Instead of addressing the issue, he said, "It is time for us to go. I doubt your brother would pass on investigating such obvious signs of my kind."

This statement made Jonah's anger boil over.

"You don't think my brother will see through the ploy, and figure it's a trap? Jim is paranoid, always has been, and I'd bet my life that his paranoid precautions have tripled since he started killing vampires."

Eldon only looked at Jonah, but the dangerous gleam made Jonah back down.

"Let us hope that your brother does not see through our little setup. Let us go."

The vampire walked out the door. Jonah slipped on his new running shoes and followed. Eldon hadn't said it, but Jonah could read between the lines. Jonah was sure his own life, not just his brother's was at stake. The bet was on the table, as he had so aptly put it.

* * *

Hunter walked the length of the street. First five blocks east to west, then back west to east on the opposite side of the road. Police tape still ran across one of the alleys but the Vancouver police force had long since packed up and left the area.

Not even the cops wanted to get caught open in the streets on this end of the city once night fell. No, instead they kept to the safety of their cars. If they needed to attend a crime scene, five cars would arrive together for the simplest of call-outs. Pathetic.

Like you when the lightning comes?

Shut up, he cried to the voice in his head. His own voice, he knew, but it was no less...true. That made the statement no easier to take. He was weak. Not only because he sometimes let Jim come back and take over, but because Jim was also weak. Hunter was not so blind to think that Jim and Hunter were two different beings occupying the same body, but more that Hunter was Jim's strength, and Jim was weakness. Jim was simply something for Hunter to overcome. It was something Hunter constantly considered and strived towards achieving. One day Jim would truly be no longer, and only Hunter would remain.

Hunter saw no signs of vampire activity while he walked. That was to be expected. He had never seen anything from street level. Vampires hide themselves well unless seen from a height. When examining a crowd, Hunter could point them out easily. They also reacted poorly when they were the prey. After all, they were used to being the hunters.

Hunter took a quick scan of the buildings. One building in particular provided a perfect view into the taped-off alley. No other building had an equal line of sight. Did that matter though? What vampire would return after causing such an uproar in the city? The whole scenario felt off. Vampires live in the shadows. To their core, that's who they were.

Hunter wondered if last night could have been something akin to his own first experience with vampire kind. Could a newly made vampire have run amok, killing without the restraint of his master? Hunter would likely never know, but it was something to consider. It would be good to kill a new vampire. Kill it before it had the chance to do substantial damage to the human world.

He looked again at the rooftops. It still didn't feel right. If any vampire were to return to the scene tonight, they wouldn't likely be hunting in the same alley they had killed in the night before. Vampires weren't that stupid. So that one building, the one that looked directly at the taped-off alley was out. He would find a different perch for the night.

Of course, the other option was that this had been a setup. That the vampires knew he was hunting them down, killing them. That they had set this up as a trap to lure him in. The idea made Hunter's hands close into fists. He was no prey, no easy meat. Not anymore.

When he looked at the buildings again, he noticed how closed in it all was. The street was tight. Most of the buildings were four or five stories. There were many places to hide among the rooftops.

He would find the darkest of them and wait. They would learn that he was the hunter, and they were the prey.

* * *

Eldon had spent much of the ride from Jonah's condominium holding back a smile. Sometimes he even held back full-blown laughter. His plan was moving along exactly as he wished. Meanwhile, Jonah sat in the driver's seat, hands tight on the wheel, face set firm and knuckles white.

His human companion did not like Eldon's methods, nor his deception, but Jonah's brooding felt comical to the vampire.

When they reached the neighbourhood where Eldon had set his trap, the vampire instructed Jonah on where to park. The undead led Jonah into an apartment building, and up three flights of stairs. Eldon knocked on an apartment door, and a woman answered with the glassy eyes and dulled expression of the glamoured.

"You did as I asked?" Eldon said

The woman nodded almost imperceptibly. Eldon stepped inside and motioned for Jonah to follow. The woman put a light jacket on, then shoes, and walked out the door.

"She will not be back until morning," Eldon announced for Jonah's benefit.

"Do you always use people?" Jonah asked, the disgusted tone unmistakable.

Eldon gave a dry chuckle. He walked over to the window and looked to the street below, then up to the rooftop. Ordering the woman to pose as a prostitute on the same corner where he had killed three other working girls the night before had broken the girl. She was his creature now. He didn't need nor want her after tonight. He would likely order her to leave the city, find a place in a forest somewhere, then lay down and sleep until exposure killed her.

"I am what I am, Jonah," he answered. He had instructed his creature to stand under the light of the street lamp where had a good view of her and the Garacy rooftop. "I have been a vampire, an agent of the night, for so long that

I don't remember what it was to be like you. Besides, things have changed so much over the past hundred and fifty years that this world is so beyond what was thought possible when I lived as you. The people of my time would think this world of yours to be wholly alien."

From the apartment, he could clearly see the rooftop where he expected Jim would soon be. His trap was set, there was nothing to do now but wait.

The vampire turned to Jonah to see the look on the man's face. Again, Eldon chuckled.

"There's no need for pity," he told the human, "I will be here watching the world change when all your friend's grandchildren are dead and gone."

"Sounds lonely," Jonah said.

Eldon turned back to the window and smiled to himself, and thought *yes, it is.*

The vampire continued to wait but the woman he glamoured never did take her place in the street.

* * *

Jonah sat at one of the bar-height dining chairs. The little space was surprisingly nice. It was old, but the woman who lived here had obviously wanted to put her mark on it. Eldon stood by the window framed by blackout blinds with large green and cream coloured stripes. The coffee table and TV stand were dark laminate, but the rug under the coffee table matched the blinds although in a different pattern.

He had learned early in their search that the vampire had far superior vision, and his eyes saw every little movement in the street. The window was small, not enough room for two, so Jonah was relegated to waiting in the background.

He checked his watch again. 2 AM. He wasn't even tired at all. Getting back onto a daytime work schedule was going to be difficult. Hopefully, they would find Jim before too much longer and life could get back to normal. No more vampires, no more glamour, no more traps, no more killing. That sounded like bliss.

"I think he saw right through your game, Eldon," Jonah announced. As much as he wanted his brother found and for this craziness to end, there was a small part to him that was giddy at the vampire's failure.

"Perhaps," Eldon conceded, "The occupant of this dwelling did not take her place under the light as I had instructed. Let us go see what happened."

Without another word, the vampire turned away from the window and walked out the door. There was little Jonah could do but follow.

The two made their way to the roof. The night was overcast with a hint of rain in the air. As had become their normal way of travelling from rooftop to rooftop, Eldon stood behind Jonah, gripped him under his arms and launched in the air. Jonah hated the jumps, it felt like a rollercoaster. He had never liked amusement park rides. Unlike roller coasters, his trips with the vampire only took a few seconds with only one real up and down.

Besides Jonah and Eldon, the rooftop on which they had landed was empty of any other person. There was, however, a duffle bag. The bag was leaning against the edge of the building exactly where Eldon had figured Jim would have been.

The vampire took a few steps towards the duffle.

It's possible that Jim had set up here, but had since left. That's certainly what it was meant to look like. If he had set up here, Eldon would have seen him. That means Jim snuck across the roof, but never looked over the side of the building. Jim had known the building was being watched.

"Wait," Jonah called out urgently, and the vampire stopped and turned questioningly. "It's a bomb."

Hunter Chapter 8

Hunter watched the rooftop closely. The present he had lain against the ledge of the roof waited for a vampire to open it. Two figures dropped out of the night sky. The green tint of the night-vision scope at that distance made it hard to pick out features of the two walking towards his duffle bag, but the stance of the second man, the way he walked, Hunter was sure he knew who it was.

"Oh, Jonah," he choked.

He must have been turned into the vampire's imp. That meant they likely knew who he was. If Jonah was an imp, then everything that was Jonah was gone. The vampire had taken it away.

Hunter used one hand to pivot the rifle to see if there were any more vampires on the roof, but the two figures were alone. In Hunter's other hand was the radio transmitter. The antenna was up, his thumb rested on the button.

"You're not my brother anymore," he said, watching Jonah's figure through the scope. To firm himself, he said it again. "You're not my brother anymore."

He hit the button.

* * *

Patrick watched as his sire and the older brother landed on the roof. He had been with Eldon the night before as he fed and killed the three hookers. Patrick wasn't sure at first what his maker had been up to but by the end of the night, Patrick was sure Eldon was laying a trap of some sort. He was also sure the trap was for Jimmy.

Patrick had followed Eldon again upon waking. He had stayed in the shadows as Eldon picked up Jonah, but while Jonah drove to East Hastings, Patrick sped ahead. He watched as Jonah parked and his maker led the human to the same apartment Eldon had visited after they slaughtered the street workers.

Patrick wasn't sure why he had done it. Although he had sworn Jimmy would be his next meal, he could wait no longer. He could have picked any human to feed on that night, but the woman who lived in the apartment that Eldon and Jonah occupied had called to him. As she had left her dwelling Patrick had swooped down. In her glamoured state, she didn't even scream as Patrick tore the skin from her throat. If Eldon ever found out what Patrick was doing, the consequences would be dire. Feeding on this woman, killing her, was like sounding a fog horn. Patrick didn't care. His need for Jimmy was so great, and his anger that Eldon would not allow Patrick to have the boy was all-consuming.

When he was done, and she lay limp in his grasp, he tossed the body aside. The building had a shared dumpster at the edge of the parking area and the body fit easily. Another resident of the building would eventually find her, but that was no matter.

Feeding had strengthened him. It was going to take everything Patrick had to bypass his sire to get to Jimmy. He had chosen another spot to watch, completely hidden from the windows of the apartment where his sire also kept watch.

Time passed slowly. He watched as Jimmy appeared on the rooftop and crept across the building's roof. From his vantage, Patrick was sure he was the only one to see Jimmy on the roof. After Jimmy deposited a bag on the rooftop, Patrick watched as his prey left the roof only to ascend to a different rooftop. It took extra care to ensure that Patrick was not seen by Jimmy and was out of Eldon's view from the apartment window, but he was sure he had been successful.

Then he waited some more. He could feel his master's order prevented the vampire from diving down and gorging on the young man. The order had been issued so many years ago that Patrick was sure he could break free of it if he tried hard enough, but Jimmy had proven himself to be formidable. Patrick would not die trying to fight an order for Eldon. He had to be certain.

As Patrick watched Jimmy take position on a nearby rooftop, he saw Eldon and Jonah land on the rooftop with the duffle bag. Patrick ducked further into the dark. If Eldon saw him now...

The flash of light lit up every rooftop down the entire block. The explosion was grand, loud and destructive. Patrick barely noticed it. He felt freedom, glorious freedom. The constraints Eldon had placed on Patrick were not completely gone but he could feel the weakness in them. It was as if they were ropes so tight around him that they cut skin, and they suddenly slackened so much that Patrick could move of his own accord.

Patrick looked at the rooftop, or what had been a rooftop seconds before. The ledge where Jimmy had set his own trap was gone.

A successful trap. Patrick laughed at the thought and relished in his master's failure.

The back of the building was still intact, but it looked like it might cave into the spaces below at any time. People were already gathering in the streets below, and Patrick could see the building's occupants rushing out the front doors.

Movement on the roof caught Patrick's attention, but it was only a few bricks falling, no longer able to hang on to the structure after the blast. He could not make out any humanoid shapes on the building but he was sure Eldon had not been killed in the blast. If he had, then Patrick would have been completely free instead of just having his bonds loosened.

Patrick sensed movement, someone climbing down a fire escape. It wasn't Eldon, it was Jimmy. The young man was in a hurry, his pack around both shoulders, he slid down the escape as fast as he could. Patrick watched as Jimmy landed on the street and jumped on a motorbike.

Jim drove away as fast as his bike would allow, and Patrick took to the sky. He would follow, and as soon as an opportunity presented itself, he would finally feast on the boy.

Hunter Chapter 9

J onah's ears rang, and his head pounded. He was on his back, but he had no memory of how he got there. Everything hurt. When he brought his hand up to his forehead, it came back wet and slick with blood. Jonah called out to Eldon. Surely the vampire had flown away. He was probably sitting on one of the surrounding rooftops laughing at Jonah's weak human body, and his inability to get away from the blast.

That's what it had been, hadn't it? A bomb? It had to be.

Jonah looked at the missing rooftop. The structure was below, sitting in someone's living room. Seeing that he was on solid ground, he quickly took stock of his injuries. Nothing broken. His ears were bleeding though. When he called out for Eldon his own voice sounded muffled, like he was actually trying to listen to someone else yell from a couple of rooms away.

When he was done, and the vampire had still not materialized, Jonah decided he better get off the roof. The cops were likely already on their way, and he had to be long gone when they arrived. Jonah sighed in relief when he saw the fire escape, still intact and on the undamaged half of the roof.

On the first landing, Jonah found Eldon. The vampire lay still. One of his legs was bent the wrong way. Black blood gushed from injuries on his head and arm.

"Eldon?" Jonah called questioningly. The vampire didn't stir.

Thanks to the undead waking up all the childhood memories, Jonah knew that Eldon would eventually wake and heal. Jonah picked up the vampire and did his best to heft the man over his shoulder.

Descending the fire escape with the vampire's weight on his shoulders made for a slow trip. Sirens sounded, and even though Jonah's damaged hearing, he could tell they were close. Jonah was sure the area would soon be packed with cops, firefighters, and other emergency responders. He needed a place to hide so Eldon could heal.

Or you could just leave him here.

The thought came unbidden, but it also wasn't wrong. The vampire used him as a youth and was using him now. Jonah had been lied to and manipulated. What would happen if Jonah did just leave him and go?

Likely, Eldon would wake and kill anyone who got in his way, then he'd come looking for me.

Jonah was out of breath by the time he landed in the alley below with the still unconscious vampire on his back. Both ends of the alley met with open street. The alley itself was empty except for a big green dumpster. He had nowhere to go. Jonah knew he couldn't carry the vampire out over his shoulder into a busy street. Lights from emergency vehicles flashed on either end of the alley. Although muted through his damaged ears, Jonah could hear the buzz of activity. Neither direction offered any kind of safety. There was a door that led into the neighbouring building, heavy and metal, but when Jonah checked it, he found it locked.

With no options left, he checked the dumpster. The bin was mostly empty, just a few black bags lining the bottom, but the smell was horrible. With no other choices, he tossed Eldon inside, then followed.

Once Jonah was engulfed in the smell, he had to cover his nose and mouth with his shirt to stop from retching.

Eldon, you better wake up soon.

* * *

Jim's bike tipped over when he pulled up to his nest and tried to park. He didn't care. He had killed his own brother.

"I'm so sorry," he whispered in a sob. He needed to get inside, he needed the feeling of safety the interior of the building brought. "I didn't mean to! Jonah, I didn't want to!"

He had been saying the words over and over again ever since he hit the button, ever since he watched the detonation. He couldn't stop himself, and he couldn't stop.

Jim fumbled for the keys. He didn't want to be Hunter anymore. He could have accepted Caitlin's death if he had forced himself to. Jonah would still be alive if he had done that. Instead, that vampire on the roof had obviously taken his brother and turned him into an imp, so Jonah would help hunt Jim down.

He found the right key, stuck it in the lock, and turned. All the air rushed out of Jim's lungs as a blow, something large and heavy, struck him in the back. The door swung open, and Jim fell to the floor of his nest, fingers scraping his neck as he tried desperately to pull in air.

Hands gripped his ankles and pulled him back out the door. Jim was spun around and came face to face with Patrick Steadman. He would have screamed, but his lungs didn't have the air to push out the sound.

* * *

Jonah had no idea how long he waited. Police officers had made a perfunctory search of the alley, but nothing more. With the top closed, the only light in the dumpster came from a small hole in the side of the container. Instead of illuminating his surroundings, the spot of light acted more like a flashlight beam ruining his vision each time he glanced in that direction.

The lack of vision made his other senses sharper. Jonah stayed as still as he could, each time he heard a noise from either end of the alley.

After twenty minutes of waiting, the stench of the bin had seeped into every stitch of clothing, and every pore in his skin. To Jonah's disgust, he was getting used to the smell. The cops had not come down the alley for quite some time.

The vampire still hadn't moved, but Jonah watched as flesh slowly stitched together. Finally, Eldon's hand twitched. A few minutes later, his lips opened and closed. Then again. Finally, he spoke.

"Must... feed..." The words were almost indistinct, but Jonah had made them out through the guttural rasp.

Clenching his teeth, Jonah tried to think of a way to help the vampire, but he could only come up with one solution. The building was surrounded by cops, firefighters, and gawkers. There was no way, even if he didn't reek of landfill, that he was going to convince anyone to follow him into the alley. Besides, if he did, what would Eldon do to them.

"If you feed from me, can you remember that I'm a friend?" Jonah asked, scared of the answer.

"Yes," the vampire croaked.

Jonah closed his eyes and extended his arm. He didn't want to see what was going to happen.

The pain was sharp and numbing at the same time. The shock of it made Jonah's eyes pop open. Within seconds, he couldn't feel his arm at all. It was as if the appendage had been injected with novocaine. Jonah couldn't help himself, he leaned in and examined the vampire feeding. Eldon sucked like a leech, and Jonah felt himself grow cold. The vampire's tee-shirt had been ripped during the blast, and Jonah could see a gaping wound underneath. Eldon only fed for a minute, maybe two. Jonah couldn't be sure. His mind was swimming, and he couldn't focus.

Eldon lifted his head from Jonah's arm and stared at Jonah. Even in his dazed state, the look scared him. He tried to push away from Eldon, but in the tiny dumpster, there was nowhere to go. The vampire had nothing but hunger in his eyes.

Jonah was sure he was about to die. He would be killed, his brother would be killed. The women Eldon had already killed for their failed trap would have died in vain. So much death, and absolutely no use in any of it.

The vampire grabbed Jonah's arms. Then they were both in the air. Clean, fresh, air rushed into Jonah's lungs like a shock. Jonah dangled in Eldon's grip. A scream caught in his throat. When they landed on a rooftop a few blocks away. Jonah's head spun, the world going fuzzy on both sides of his vision. The flight, the blood loss, the explosion, it was all too much.

"Stay," Eldon said, as if to a dog. Then he was gone again.

* * *

The need to feed still hung heavy but Jonah had given Eldon enough for now. He would need to feed well if he wanted any strength at all. It was of no matter for now. He had enough to deal with.

The explosion had taken half the roof. The firefighters had the small blaze under control. The building was mostly concrete and stone anyway. Jonah's brother had to have been near to know when to set off his bomb. Eldon travelled from rooftop to rooftop, until he found the scent he hunted. It was easy to follow down the fire escape to the ground, but then it disappeared again.

Frustrated, Eldon took to the sky again. The night had been another failure.

The vibration from his jeans pocket caught his attention. His phone had survived the blast. Fishing it out of his pocket, Eldon read the text message. I was from a number he did not recognize, but the sender was obvious.

"Found the brother" then an address.

Well then, Patrick seemed to be good for something then.

Eldon returned to collect Jonah. It seemed the night was not over yet.

Hunter Chapter 10

Patrick lay on the floor of the building his prey had reclaimed. Jim's cellphone in his hand. His heart pumped in a way he had never felt before. Jimmy had been delectable, an aged wine without comparison. Never had he felt so whole. By vampire standards, Patrick was still a child, not quite twenty years in his undead life, but he had known ecstasy on his first night as vampire. He had fed on Jimmy as a boy, and no other feed had been the same.

Jimmy had tasted almost the exact same, older for certain, but no less perfect.

His master's hold had loosened just enough thanks to Jimmy's bomb. Patrick could not have asked for more luck than that. The vampire rolled over, and fondly cupped Jimmy's cheek.

"You were always my prey, weren't you," he whispered fondly. Patrick didn't notice the smear of blood he left across Jimmy's cheeks.

Glassy eyes, dead eyes, stared back at Patrick.

"I can only hope to find another meal like you," he said and rolled away from the body.

He still clutched the cellphone in his other hand. There had been just enough time. Patrick had no idea where Eldon was now, but his master had healed. With that healing, the bonds around Patrick had tightened once again. Patrick had just finished with Jimmy. Seconds of pure contentment followed before the bonds clamped themselves around Patrick. He tried to fight it, but Eldon's orders had been explicit. He had found Jimmy's phone in his jeans pocket and typed out the message to his master. When Eldon arrived, Patrick would pay for disobeying. Yet, it was so worth it, no matter the extent of his master's wrath.

* * *

Jonah held on tight as his vampire partner flew through the night. Eldon's mode of transportation was certainly faster than driving, or any other way of getting around the city. For the first time, Jonah kept his eyes open while they flew, watching the city as it passed by.

He couldn't help but be filled with excitement. They had done it! They had found Jim! At least, Patrick had found him, but it all resulted in the same thing.

Buildings whisked by, and in seconds they were landing. Eldon put Jonah down. The vampire did not like carrying Jonah. He got the feeling the vampire felt like a pack mule. After tonight they could go their separate ways. Jonah would never have to deal with creatures of the night again, and Eldon could fly on alone. Jonah couldn't wait. The second they set down Jonah made his way for the building Patrick had indicated in his text to Eldon.

"Wait!"

But Jonah had already opened the door. Even to his human senses, the metallic stench of blood was overwhelming. Jonah tried to rush in, but he was shoved aside by the vampire as Eldon used his undead speed to push into the building first.

Jonah followed but stopped dead when he saw Jim covered in gore on the floor. His eyes were wide. Jim's jaw was missing, red meat exposed on his face, neck and chest. Jonah tried to let out a sob, a scream, anything, but it was all stuck in his throat. Instead, he tumbled to his knees and vomited.

"No, Jim," he whispered, the foul still dripping from his mouth. "I'm so sorry."

Woodenly he got to his feet. Behind his brother's corpse was a table covered in weapons, all handguns and swords.

Jonah knew he could never kill a vampire with a blade, they were simply too powerful, and he had never fired a gun before. *Would the safety be on? I don't even know what the safety on a gun looks like. It's a switch, isn't it?*

Jonah could hear the vampires behind him, Eldon screaming, Patrick grunting each time his elder struck him. He ignored the two. In another minute they would remember him, and then he would probably die with his brother.

If he was going to die, he would at least die fighting. His hand fit the pummel of the handgun perfectly. In one swift motion, he spun and pulled the trigger. To his astonishment, the gun fired. Patrick grunted as the bullet pierced the vampire's skull.

Patrick slumped and fell over, landing face-down in Jim's blood. Into the gore Patrick had created.

The gun smoked. Jonah's hand was shaking and he couldn't seem to stop it. His eyes flickered to Eldon. The vampire would likely kill him now, and Jonah didn't have any power left to resist.

He waited for the vampire to spring, to bite, and rip his throat out. He would be the twin to his brother then.

Instead, the vampire gestured to his offspring. "He will heal."

Jonah knew it was true. Some of the wound was already closing up.

"You will need a stake to kill him. It must be plunged into Patrick's heart. Find one, and take your revenge," the vampire said in a calm and dark voice.

Jonah turned back to the table covered in weapons. Sitting in the middle was a pedestal, almost like a shrine, that held a broken piece of wood, sharp on one end.

The older vampire moved toward Patrick Steadman and used his foot to flip Patrick over on his back. Life was starting to spring once more into the younger vampire's eyes. Patrick lifted a hand.

"Do not move," Eldon commanded, and Patrick stopped.

"Put your arm down and do not move a muscle until I command that you do so," Eldon continued, then motioned to Jonah.

Jonah said nothing, he stepped forward lifted his arms and brought them down as hard as he could. The stake dug deep. Jonah pulled it loose then brought it down into Patrick again, then again, and again.

When he was done, when he was sure, he stopped and crumpled over the stake gulping breaths. Suddenly, Eldon was behind Jonah. He had Jonah by the hair. With a quick movement, he slapped away the stake, then leaned in close to Jonah's ear.

"Thank you for getting rid of Patrick, Jonah," he whispered, "I should have killed him all those years ago anyway. It never should have been him, it always should have been you."

Eldon bit.

The end.

The Puzzle

Detective Nick Cheverie unlocked his apartment door. His uniform felt wet, and the gross he had subjected himself to was seeping through. Another dead hooker. Cheverie, his partner, and twelve uniform cops tipped every dumpster in a five-block radius. Nothing. Again.

The forensics team was stumped, Nick was stumped, everyone was fucking stumped. Of course, because all the vics were women from the lower east side the media mostly ignored the deaths. A rich white woman turns up dead, it's front-page news. A native chick, hooking to either pay her dealer or to pay her bills, well who the fuck cared about that. Canada liked to believe that it didn't have a racism problem, but the truth is that Canada just hides its racism a little better than some other places.

One day the people of this planet were going to have to realize that a life is a life. That was part of the reason Cheverie became a cop in the first place. His sister had disappeared from the same streets he now patrolled. Lauren had been five years older than Nick, and Nick was barely ten when his sister ran away from home.

There had been no word from her for over a year, then one day she called out of the blue. She didn't want to come home, but she wanted to let us know she was okay. She said she was in Vancouver, and eventually, after a few more weekly phone calls, she let slip that she was living on the streets. On East Hastings. Well known for drugs, hooking, and worse, and his sister lived there.

It wasn't great news, but Lauren said she was fine. In Nick's mind, that's all that mattered. Then the calls stopped just as suddenly as they had begun. Nick's folks called the cops. The cops pretended to care, but they didn't. Nick's folks didn't live in Vancouver, they weren't rich, and they weren't white.

For most people, if you get brushed off by the people who are supposed to protect you, especially when you're reporting something important, you get bitter. More than bitter, you resent them for not caring. You resent them for treating you like less than you are. For Nick, it was the opposite. He saw the cops as a problem that needed fixing. The best way to do that was to join them. A lot had changed over the past almost twenty years since Lauren had disappeared. Nick had come to help facilitate that change in every way he could. He specifically requested to be in East Hastings. He wanted to be where he would be needed most, but another part, a small part hidden deep in his soul, hoped that one day he would find out what happened to his sister. He daydreamed sometimes about passing her on the street, or even finding a body that turned out to be her. Not knowing was harder than anything else he could imagine.

The problem was, Lauren hadn't been the only girl to disappear from East Hastings, not by a long shot. No one at the force listened. Every time a new girl or boy was reported missing, it was like Lauren disappearing all over again. When Nick pushed, the entire department pushed back. He had been hung up for promotion, friends on the force snubbed him, one even tried to get into a fist fight after a few too many drinks.

Nick grabbed his sidearm, removed his holster and hung it on a peg by the door. The weapon went into a gun safe embedded into the wall by the door. It was a habit he had gotten into when he was still married to Audrey. They agreed to never allow a weapon unlocked in the house after Cassie had been born. Audrey couldn't handle being a cop's wife, and Nick couldn't handle the idea of being anything other than a cop. Now he got Cassie every second weekend, thus the gun safe.

The entryway was tiny. Two steps brought Nick into his combination living room, kitchen, and dining area. Nick went to the east bedroom, the master, and got changed. Cassie had a room on the west end of the condo, next to the only bathroom.

The living room was as basic as the rest of the condo. A TV against one wall, a couch on another, and a coffee table in the middle. The only thing that made the room at all interesting was a giant wooden frame that held three movie posters in it, all in a row. The posters were Fantasia, The Land Before Time, and The Lion King in it. When Nick had built the frame in a buddy's wood shop, he bought it home to show Cassie when she was over next.

"Let's pick out what posters to put in it, but only your favourite movies, okay?" She had been so excited. Posters had come and gone, but she kept all the old posters rolled up in her room. The Lion King had been the latest addition to the frame, replacing the long-standing Beauty and the Beast. Cassie loved animated movies.

The frame was a great talking point for any and all guests, but the frame had a secret. Nick grabbed a beer out of the fridge, cracked the can and walked the two steps to the living room. He had already eaten, Rex's Diner had finally reopened. It had needed to be almost completely rebuilt after the weird shoot-out and fire that had earned him his detective's shield. Rex's had been his favourite greasy spoon before the incident, and he was sure it would be again even though it was under new ownership. He carefully lifted the big frame and slid it off the wall to rest on the couch. Papers and photos were taped to the wall hidden by the frame. Everything from queue cards to newspaper clippings, and photos. The photos Nick had from work files. Dead files. Since tacks wouldn't work behind the frame, tape held string stretching from headline to photo to queue card.

Nick sat on the coffee table to face the wall and sipped his beer. He scanned the queue cards exclusively, seeing if words sprang out at him, seeing if any fruit would fall from the tree.

Bite.

Wound.

Puncture.

The last word always jumped out at Nick. It was circled in red sharpie. Vampires.

Of course, since vampires didn't exist, Nick was back to nothing. It was a puzzle, and one Nick intended to figure out.

The Player

Ian Carraro's fingers were tired, but at least they didn't ache. He had been worried when the aching had started. His set at the Biltmore had been forty-five minutes. Forty-five minutes of running his hands up and down the fretboard of his hollow-bodied Gibson guitar. The instrument had been a classic when he bought it at a pawn shop. He'd been playing that same guitar for almost fifteen years, and it still sounded beautiful.

Unless a musician is lucky enough to see some mainstream success, it's hard to make a living, particularly later in life. Most drop out to find some 9 to 5 bullshit job, but Ian had been doing okay. He was pretty sure he'd continue to do okay as long as his hands held up. At fifty-five, if he wanted to retire he had to hope for a surprise hit single, or to have a few really successful tours.

When his hands started to hurt, it was serious like a heart attack. To Ian life wasn't worth living if he couldn't play. Parkinson's is a bitch, and fifty-five was early to be showing signs. The doctors had tried him on drugs. They had wanted to stem the flow of symptoms. All the meds did was fuzz up Ian's mind, leaving him lightheaded and often confused. He hated the drugs as much as he hated the disease. Neither let him play. He had originally just gone to the doctor because he thought he was getting arthritis. There was some pain after shows and in the mornings. Sometimes he had trouble doing simple things, like holding a cup of coffee. It was like all his strength had left him. It was a death sentence. Ian spent hours watching videos of guys unable to use their hands because they were shaking so much. He wasn't there yet, but his doctors were sure he'd get there. It was just a matter of when. Pain, the lack of strength, and control of his hands was where it was going to start for him. If he was honest with himself, it had already started. It was going to get worse.

The news, the realization that one day sooner rather than later, life as he knew it would be over, hit hard. The funny thing about that was how it affected his playing and his stage show. When he got on stage, Ian focused all of his anger, his frustration, and fear into his show. The crowds loved it. The more his hands hurt, or the less they responded, the harder Ian played, the louder he sang.

When he wasn't plying, Ian had taken to wandering at night. Vancouver is a big city, and Ian knew it well, but on his wanderings, he never cared about where he went. He chose turns at random intersections. His hands would be stuffed in his pockets, his shoulders slumped.

It was on one of these wanderings that salvation came. Ian made his way to the Burrard bridge. It was well past 3 am. The sky was overcast but the night was still. The city lights reflected off the water.

One thing Ian would never admit to another living soul was that on that night, he contemplated jumping off that bridge. He had no idea if the jump would end his life, but that would have been the intention. He stopped there, leaned on the rail, and tried to decide if he was strong enough to live, if he was strong enough to jump.

Then the world went black.

The next morning Ian woke on his bed at home. He was on top of the covers, and he felt amazing. It was as if he'd had the best sleep of his entire life. He bounced off the bed. As had become his habit, he flexed his hands. Hands open with splayed fingers, then hands closed, tightened into fists. He repeated the action five times. There was no pain. In fact, in that moment, he felt like he could shred like Eddie Van Halen. As far as Ian was concerned, his world was at peace.

He got off the bed and took the five steps to his kitchenette. He flicked the red switch on the side of his coffeemaker and it sprung to life. Ian danced around his tiny kitchen, humming a tune. He felt thirty years younger.

The brew had taken fifteen minutes. The coffeemaker gurgled and sputtered to say it was done. Ian had a cup ready and poured the dark brown liquid. He picked up the drink and was about to sit in his apartment's only chair to read, but he felt a sensation on his neck. It felt like he'd been hit with a drop of liquid. He reached up and touched the spot. Nothing, just his dry skin.

That didn't feel right. Ian was expecting something even though he wasn't sure what. There was nothing. It didn't matter, what did matter was how he felt. He took a gulp of his coffee and grabbed his guitar. It felt smooth and familiar. When he plucked the strings, playing his typical blues warm-up routine, the guitar felt alive in his hands. He played, his fingers running up and down the fretboard with ease. His fingers knew where to go, they had been playing these same chords and notes for years. Never had they sounded so good, so clean, his timing so perfect. When he stopped, he was breathing hard. He hadn't sung a word while playing, and that was fine. The music coming from his guitar said everything he wanted.

He took another pull from his coffee and stared at the instrument. He didn't know what had changed, but something had. And it was amazing.

Ian set the guitar aside, finished his cup of caffeine juice, and decided it was time to shower. If he was feeling this good, he wanted to take advantage of it.

* * *

It was night by the time Ian arrived back at his little apartment. Like most who lived in the city, he had to rely on public transit to get around. He had called all his contacts, and to his surprise, he landed a gig for the day playing in a tiny side studio attached to Greenhouse studios. Some kid was putting together her first demo and needed some backing guitar. Ian had played beautifully, so much so that they allowed him to track a solo onto the album. The notes he chose matched the feel of her pop tune perfectly. He was pretty sure that he had played his instrument better today than any other day in his life.

He set his battered guitar case down. It had been a long day, but he was amped up from the day's experience. Ian decided he'd skip supper and head out walking instead. He might not feel this good tomorrow, but he wanted to savour this feeling while he could.

* * *

Ian woke. He was laying on his bed, fully clothed, and with an awful taste in his mouth. Sitting up, he moved to the sink and rinsed his mouth out. He flexed his hands. Stretch and fists, stretch and fists. They felt good. *He* felt good. Last night was another blur, but that was fine. His hands still felt normal!

He remembered leaving his apartment the night before and walking. Like most nights, he took turns at random, and he remembered walking along the Burrard bridge again. That was it, everything else was gone. For some reason that made him reach up to his neck again, as if he was expecting something to be there. In fact, he was sure he was going to feel an injury of some sort, but there was nothing there. It was just his aged skin.

He made his way to the bathroom for his morning piss. The sight in the mirror startled him as he passed by. He was pale. In fact, not just a little pale, he was dead looking. Well, he could still urinate, according to his bladder, so he went. Afterwards, he examined himself in the mirror further.

"You look like shit, Ian," he said to the empty room. There had been a lot of nights of binge drinking when he was new to his career. After one of those nights he had often looked like this. Too much booze, not enough water. A couple of pain pills typically helped, if he wasn't puking his guts up. The problem was that he hadn't done any of that last night, at least he was pretty sure he hadn't. Booze wasn't his thing anymore, neither was drugs, so why was he blacking out. He flexed his hands again. They felt strong as ever.

"Do I care what's happening at night, if I can keep waking up feeling this good?" he asked himself.

* * *

Ian woke. Like every night over the past week, he was on his bed, fully dressed and no memory of the night before. He was startled this time, waking with a jolt. He had been dreaming. It had been a nightmare if he was honest about it. There had been a beast similar to a bat but shaped like a person. It had been the size of a person. It had been eating him. Ian had been laying on the ground, his guitar strapped to his chest playing the solo for "Ever the long road" which had been his first single. The bat-thing was chewing, pulling chunks of flesh out of his thigh under the base of the instrument. The dream had been so vivid that Ian felt he had to check his leg, to make sure it was whole. It was. Ian touched his neck next. Like every morning, he was sure there was going to be an injury there, but like every other morning, there was nothing.

It was then a face flashed in his mind. The face belonged to a young guy, maybe in his late 20s. Ian didn't recognize him, but the face must have come from somewhere. He was sure his brain was trying to tell him something. He flexed his hands, then brought them into fists. The action was smooth, with no pain, no resistance, no shake.

It was time to go to work.

He made a few calls. Ian had worked with Andrew Rain a bunch of times over the years. He was a great producer, and they got along well.

"I got nothing going today," Andrew had said on the phone, "but I'll tell you what. Why don't we put some stock tracks down today? I got nothing better to do, so let's have some fun."

"Yeah man, I'm on my way. See you in an hour," Ian had replied before hanging up the phone.

Stock music wasn't Ian's favourite type of gig. It meant he'd spend the day writing and playing standard, boring guitar pieces with the intention of selling them for use in radio ads, low-budget tv commercials, or at worst, porn flicks. It only paid if the music sold, but it was work. When you didn't have anything else, you went with the best option available. Besides, Andrew was a great drummer along with being a great producer. They would each play their instruments, and with any luck, the next time Andrew needed a session guitarist, Ian would be the first person on Andrew's mind. Ian flexed his hands again. No pain, life was good. He headed to the bathroom, grabbed some vitamins, and popped them into his mouth. He dry-swallowed and headed for the door.

* * *

Ian woke with a start. His heart was pounding fast, and his fingers and toes prickled with pins and needles. He had been dreaming again. The bat thing was eating him, sucking on his neck, chewing on his carotid artery. The dream had been weird because in it, he was watching himself get eaten. Not in his own body, he floated around as the thing ripped open his flesh, licking the gore from the wound it had created.

Ian shook his head, trying to clear the fog from his mind.

"It was just a dream, come on brain, let it go," he said aloud.

He stood up and immediately had to sit back down. The room was spinning, making him so dizzy he thought he might pass out. It took a few deep breaths for the room to slow.

"What is happening to me?" he said before getting up again. This time the world stayed still, and Ian made his way to the coffeemaker. Coffee would fix him up, he was just tired. It had been a long few days, and like all sessions with Andrew, they had started early and played well into the night. Ian had left at 10 pm, he remembered that much. The Skytrain and the bus ride got him home by midnight. By then he felt the need to walk. He had been sitting in the studio all day and night. His mind was tired but his body was awake, ready to go.

That was all Ian could remember. He fought to remember, trying to wrench the memory to put them on display. Nothing.

He flexed his hands. Stretch, then fist. Stretch, then fist. Again, they felt great.

"At least that's something," he muttered.

* * *

It was chewing. Ian was sure he was dreaming because he was watching the thing chew on him again, but he could also hear it as if it were right behind him, suckling the blood from a gash in his flesh. It was as if there were two of him, the watcher and the victim.

"Why?" he asked and stared as the lips of the victim's lips moved, asking the same question.

The bat thing stopped its gory work. Its face scrunched up as if pained.

"I must," it growled. Then the thing bit down harder. What had been a stream of blood turned into a river, gushing over his chest.

"No," watcher Ian yelled, "you're going to kill me!"

* * *

Ian jolted, his body twisting on the bed.

Immediately he reached for his neck. He needed to stem the flow of blood or he would bleed out! His hand grabbed his neck, and he was shocked to find his skin intact.

"Dammit," he growled and dropped his hands. He covered his face with his hands and tried to rub away the dream. Something was seriously wrong with him. The dreams, the blackouts, and if he were honest with himself, something more felt off. Whatever it was, it had been affecting him all week, and the sensation was getting worse.

He got out of bed and took the few steps to his coffeemaker. He flipped the switch and went to the bathroom for his morning relief. The seat was up, but he just stood there. He knew he should need to go, he always needed to relieve himself in the morning. Nothing happened. A minute later, he had gone a bit, but that was all.

"Maybe I'm dehydrated," he said to the room. "I mean, how would I know. I have no clue what I did last night."

Feeling stupid, he checked his arms and legs for needle marks. He had never been a user. He had watched too many other Vancouver musicians succumb to drug use. Ian was too stubborn for that. His love was for the music, not the lifestyle. He would be damned if he was going to blow his chance at a life making music.

Finding nothing, he started his hand exercises. Flex, stretch, flex and stretch, again and again. His fingers still moved without pain. No jitters either. That symptom had yet to manifest. Something was strange though, his fingertips and nails were blue, like he had frostbite. He touched his fingers tips to his face, expecting them to be freezing, but they were fine. He could feel the sensation of his skin on his fingertips. For all intents and purposes, his fingers seemed to be working just fine. Was this the Parkinson's? He hadn't heard that this was a symptom, but he'd have to find out.

His coffee forgotten, Ian changed into some clean clothes and left his apartment. The bus ride downtown felt like it crawled. The blackouts, the dreams, and whatever was happening to his fingers, it was all too much. He tried not to think about it but his mind always rolled back to those three thoughts within minutes.

Seeing his doctor would be the smartest move, but the idea repulsed him for some reason. The doctor was a decent guy, easy to talk to, but as much as Ian knew the doctor hadn't caused Ian's disease, the doctor had still delivered the news. As irrational as it was, he couldn't help but be mad at the other man.

The bus pulled up alongside the library and Ian got off. The main library was a massive circular structure. Ian wasn't a big reader, but he had a library card. They had a great music program, where Ian borrowed lots of CDs and even vinyl LPs. This time, he was there to use the internet. He sat down in front of the machine and used the mouse to double-click the internet icon.

The computer whirred to life. At his command, the modem made its beeping and crashing noise, then he was online. He opened Internet Explorer and typed into the AltaVista search engine.

It was hard not to stare at his finger as he typed. The odd colour was dissipating, but a tinge of blue still ran down his fingernails. He searched "blue fingers" first, and nothing came up. The internet was supposed to be a great source of information but he had never found it so. Instead, he typically found incorrect instructions on how to play songs, and blog posts instead of detailed information.

Next, Ian tried searching "dreaming of being eaten". That brought up lots of results but none that were at all useful. Apparently, to normal people, dreaming of being eaten meant you were addicted to sex or some such thing. Ian knew that wasn't his problem. If all he needed was to get laid, he didn't think he would wake up terrified each morning.

Then he hit pay dirt with the search "vampire feeding in a dream" as the search term. He didn't know why he had put it. The bat thing that was in his dream certainly didn't look human, the way vampires were usually portrayed, but with its long wings, and human-like statute, what else could he call it.

He clicked the first link. The drawing that stared back at him was old, dating back to the 1700s, but there was no mistaking the beast that was feeding on the woman. It was the bat-thing from his dream. Ian read feverishly. Despite the old reference photo, the post was written by a modern-day mom. The woman's daughter had run away from home. When the parent searched the city for her daughter, she started blacking out. She would lose an hour sometimes, other times, she would forget the entire night.

"That's familiar," Ian whispered as he read.

Then she wrote about the dreams.

It was like I was being tortured. This thing was chewing on me, eating my thigh, and breast. It sounds sexual, but it wasn't. The dreams scared me half to death. My daughter came home a few days later. She had been hiding at a friend's place, not in the city. I had called around but the friend had lied to hide my daughter. Even with my daughter home, I felt compelled to go back into the inner city at night.

Ian thought about his own nightly walks. Each time he reached a corner, he felt the need to walk toward the Burrard bridge. There was a pull in his chest that was undeniable. He read on, but the story seemed to end there. The mom continued going into the city for a few more days before the need went away. Ian's spine tingled when she went into more details about the dream. She mentioned looking through books at her library and books in a store that sold stuff about witchcraft.

I think I was fed on by a vampire. I've never told anyone that in person because I'm scared for my family. I'm scared for me. It's the same reason I'm writing this anonymously. I had to tell someone this story. If I'm not crazy, and vampires are real, then I need to keep my daughter safe. She's the only family I have.

Ian didn't have a family, at least not really. He had a sister who lived in Calgary, but they rarely spoke. If he really thought about it, he had no one. All he had was the music. Sure he had lots of friends, but no one close.

"No built-in warning system," he whispered again, then looked around. If anyone was watching him, he probably looked insane. No one was. That wasn't surprising, when he wasn't on stage, Ian was forgettable. It killed him to acknowledge that fact, but he knew it was true. That was part of the reason he loved music so much, it could make even the dullest rock shine in its light.

As he read, he flexed the hand holding the computer mouse. It was still perfect. It was a gift. Then he looked at the screen again, and he was sure he was looking at the price he paid for that gift.

What would he do if he couldn't play music? What if this thing, or something like it, was real? What if it had him in its clutches.

What if what it's doing to me is what's allowing me to play?

Ian had no illusions about his prognosis, that's what had brought him to the bridge that night. Without music, he was done. He had no savings, no retirement plan, and without music, no reason for being. Without it, he didn't want to live. Was he willing to make a deal with the devil to be able to play just a little longer?

After his first success in finding that mom's tale, Ian found story after story, all describing different scenarios of the same thing. There was a certain segment of the world that was either being fed on by something, or they were all having the same continuous group hallucination. It seemed Ian had joined that group.

The lights in the library dimmed. It hadn't felt like he had been in the building that long, but it must have been all day. The librarians dimmed the lights to announce they were closing. Sure enough, when Ian left the building, it was early evening. He hadn't eaten and was starting to feel woozy. He ducked into a pizza joint, bought a slice and stuffed it in his mouth. Thanks to his research, he recognized the light-headed sensation and discoloured fingers for what they were, blood loss. He would have to stay fed, and maybe get some new vitamins to help stay healthy.

In a couple of hours, he would make his way to the bridge. He was sure that he would wake up on his bed the following morning, no memory of the night before, but when he woke, his hands would be okay. As long as he could play, that was all that mattered. The devil might not know it yet but he and Ian had struck a deal.

The end

Night Things Chapter 1

J onah sat motionless, legs crossed on the mossy green of the forest floor. Technically he didn't require breath, but he inhaled slowly anyway. His hands sat palms up on his knees. His hands made little cups with his thumbs and index fingers. Once his lungs were full, he released the air. Slow and even. In then out. He counted the seconds. Each rotation of air took twenty-seven seconds. The number was unimportant, but the process kept his mind busy, kept it from thinking about feeding. Kept it from thinking about blood.

He had been vampire for nearly ten years, and they had been the hardest ten years of his existence. Jonah took another deep inhalation. No need to think about the past, he just needed to concentrate on the now. He was almost there.

A night bird chirped in the trees above. His hunter instincts also knew that a couple of deer were grazing in a small open meadow less than a kilometre away. They were wary because a coyote was hunting mice at the edge of that same meadow.

Deep breath in, slow breath out. An hour later, Jonah's phone let out a little beep, letting him know another 24 hours had passed. He unfurled his legs and reached for his pack. The journal he withdrew had a heavy leather cover. It was rumpled and worn. The book flipped open to the page Jonah wanted without coaxing. The spine was bent to open in this exact spot. Despite the black of night, Jonah could see the book's contents perfectly. He put a little tick next to thirteen others. It had been two weeks since his last feeding. He would not be able to hold out much longer. The longest he had ever listed was sixteen days.

There were few people in the area, which was in large part why he chose to stay here, but there were some homes that were occupied.

That was a line of thinking Jonah could not follow. It would lead to feeding, it would lead to defeat. He set the journal back in the bag and took up his cross-legged position again. This had been his routine for almost two years. During that time he had learned to curb his need for blood. There was no defeating that need in the end. Sooner or later, the hunger would win. It already won time and time again, but Jonah had beaten it in his own way, at least a little. It took everything he was to feed as little as he did. When he did break down and quenched his thirst, he no longer killed. In the beginning, not ripping his victims limb by limb had taken everything he had. Eldon, the vampire that had made Jonah into this monster, had said that it was the way of the newly turned. They became crazed when feeding. That was why sires usually had such a tight rein on those they turned.

That had not been the case for Jonah and Eldon. As a vampire ages, they gain a power of sorts, so when they turn a human into an undead monster like themselves, that power allows them to control the monster they create. But Eldon had created a vampire only a few decades before, and that creation had drained his power. When Eldon had turned Jonah, he had not built that ability back up. Jonah had been free.

In the beginning that had made all of Jonah's nightmares come true. He had been mad with bloodlust. Eldon couldn't keep him in check. Jonah would disappear into the city, raining death. The police thought they had a serial killer, and in a way they did. Eldon had minions among Vancouver's finest, but the scale in which Jonah had killed made it impossible to completely cover up.

As Jonah aged, the bloodlust subsided. At least enough that Jonah could feel somewhat sane. That was when he started training himself, trying to deny what he was, what he had become.

That had pushed him to leave Vancouver. With so many people around, he couldn't last more than a day or two. They were alluring, intoxicating.

Jonah's phone let out three small chirps, then again, and again. Pulling it from his bag, he looked at the display before answering.

"Yes?"

"The pieces are in place. Time to come home," said a familiar human voice. Fear and excitement filled Jonah. It had taken months to reach this point. This was what he had been waiting for. Even as he had made these plans, and started them moving, he wasn't sure he could go through with it. He tapped his phone to end the call.

Jonah looked at the forest. The place had truly become his home, more than that really, it was a sanctuary. He slipped his pack on, and jumped into the air. The flight back to Vancouver wouldn't take long. One of the only benefits of his turning was the ability to fly. The freedom that came with soaring through the night was indescribable as far as Jonah was concerned.

As much as he enjoyed the night, he feared what would happen in the city.

Maybe I should have found a camper in the forest before leaving. At least I know I can control myself there.

He shook his head. The thought was weak...but wasn't he also weak? Weren't all his kind weak when it came to blood.

"Everything has to eat," Eldon had once told him when Jonah admitted his shame over killing. "Humans kill farm stock, we kill humans. It is no different." Jonah had agreed then, at least out loud. He hadn't actually agreed but he was weak. He needed an excuse his conscience would tolerate and allow him to feed. Deep down he knew better. The truth was that it *was* different, because vampires had once been human. That made all the difference in the world.

Night Things Chapter 2

Eldon had felt his young protégé making his way across the province of British Columbia, toward Vancouver. It had been almost two years since Eldon had last seen Jonah. It irked him still that the boy ran from his place. He should have always been by Eldon's side. Returning now would have to do. A couple of years is only a flash in the pan to an immortal. Eldon would make this work, not just to have the assistant the Council of the Dead demanded, but for his pride. He had *made* Jonah. He had turned him from the frail human he had been into a God strolling among the cattle of the world. He would make Jonah see that, no matter what.

The door below creaked open. Eldon's manservant greeted Jonah in the foyer. Steven had been the previous owner of the lavish condo in Vancouver's downtown. Most of the units in the high-rise were occupied by vampires. He could do what he pleased here.

"Thank you Steven," Jonah said from the main floor.

Eldon made his way to the stairs. During Jonah's absence, he had thought often of how to approach the young vampire when he returned. Now that Jonah was back, Eldon found himself full to the brim with a mix of anger, betrayal, and revenge. He stuffed it all down as deep as he could.

"Jonah, nice of you to finally return," Eldon called as he descended the stairs into the foyer. His tone was polite. Jonah only nodded in return, as if to a lesser. Eldon had to fight hard to keep the anger down. Eldon owned the boy, but instead, *he* was treated like a subject?

"I felt the need to return to the city, I don't know how long I will remain," Jonah finally said. Eldon's anger flared beyond what he could contain. He shot forward grabbing Jonah by the shirt and slamming him into the wall. Steven took two steps backwards to remove himself from harm.

"You will stay, Jonah. I allowed your little...vacation, but I am also your maker. You will remain by my side, where you belong from here on. Do you understand?"

Eldon stared directly into his protégé's eyes, looking for any sign of defiance, but Jonah only nodded again. This time Eldon did not see the arrogance. There was no fear either, but he did see acceptance. That was enough for now.

He let go of Jonah and took a step back.

"We will dine together tonight. I am visiting a friend. He was to show me his new house, and you will be there."

Again Jonah nodded, but there was set to his jaw. Eldon understood at once.

"You don't still hope to stave off the need for food, do you?" Eldon scoffed. "It is foolish. If that is still your goal, then I will break you of this fantasy."

* * *

Jonah could feel the murmur of his heart, thankfully not beating, but a mild pop, like a car trying to turn over on an almost dead battery. The city was causing the change. That was a lie, Jonah knew, it wasn't the city, but the people in it. So many people. It was hard to resist, harder than Jonah had ever anticipated.

Eldon had not lingered after his edict that Jonah accompany him to 'dine'. He had figured Eldon would play such games, and Jonah had done his best to mentally prepare. He sat on the floor cross-legged, working through his breathing exercises. The interaction with Eldon, while not truly violent, had awakened instincts that Jonah had fought hard to suppress. He had to calm himself, and force those instincts back into the pit where they had been buried. If he didn't, he would suffer tonight, and whatever victim Eldon's host brought would suffer right along with him.

It took a long time for Jonah to quell the internal storm. He wasn't sure how long it had taken, but it felt as if hours had passed. By the time Steve knocked on the door, Jonah was nearly himself again.

"The master waits in a car in the lower parking," Steve said when Jonah cracked the door. The servant turned and made his way down the hall. His movements were stiff and unnatural. Jonah knew there was nothing of the actual man left inside that body. Steve was a walking, talking coma patient, only moving because Eldon held invisible strings tied to Steve's arms and legs.

The sight of the servant made Jonah want to cry and scream. Steve had been one of the first humans he had ever fed from. At least, the first that had ever lived, but even that had been a close thing. Eldon had made him this puppet as a lesson.

Jonah slipped his shoes back on and made his way to the elevator. The North Vancouver building was truly extravagant, even for a neighbourhood as affluent as this one. Twelve stories, and underground parking. The building contained over a hundred condos but he had no idea how many housed the undead. Jonah already understood that humans would come and go constantly. The building had a contingent of security guards, all puppets like Steve, glamoured until nothing remained of who they were.

Jonah made his way to a limo that waited in the basement. The underground lot had plenty of spaces for vehicles, many filled with luxury cars. Six of the visitor parking spots were full. The other undead of the house must be entertaining. The thought disgusted Jonah and teased the craving inside him. It had been so long since he had fed. He should have known better and fed before leaving the forest. Being near Eldon, the city, it was becoming harder to control his hunger.

Night Things Chapter 3

The car eased its way through the Vancouver traffic. It wasn't surprising that the car wound from north to east. The limo pulled onto East Hastings street, and Jonah watched as they passed the destitute and addicted. The familiarity made him grip the door tight. This was where Eldon had first taken him to feed once turned. This was also where Jonah had helped Eldon hunt Jonah's younger brother, Jim. The area always made Jonah want to scream in anguish, there was nothing but pain for him here. So much death, so much despair. And not only his. This was a place at the end of human existence. That was why vampires fed here. Most of those who lived on this end of the city were hiding, never wanting to be found. The car turned off Hastings, then turned again. Some areas only a block or two off of East Hastings would change drastically, becoming well cared for neighbourhoods. Such was not the case with the area the vampires were entering.

The car pulled up to a dilapidated house. Few of the buildings in the area were well-kept, but this one looked condemned even in comparison. The windows were boarded up on the lower levels, and a metal door sealed the building. It was likely used as a place for the homeless to squat, or so Jonah assumed. Eldon had taught him that vampires used such homes to find those to feed upon.

"This is the home of a friend, Allister. You have yet to meet him. He is a genius, an engineer of sorts. I had been planning to join him this night before you returned, but the timing seems perfect. You have lessons to learn, and Allister's home will be a fine example for you," Eldon said. He opened the door and gave instructions to the driver.

Jonah followed Eldon. The older vampire pulled out a cellphone and made a call.

"I am here, and I have brought my protégé...Yes, he returned on this night. Where should we enter?"

This surprised Jonah. Vampires usually surrounded themselves with opulence. They only entered areas of squalor to find prey. They were monsters of habit, but it seemed Jonah was not the only outlier.

Eldon ended the call and looked at Jonah "We enter through the top window in the back of the home. Touch nothing, go directly into the closet in the room we enter. It has no floor, go down the shaft to the basement. We will meet Allister there.

Jonah nodded and followed Eldon into the shadows, where they could launch into the sky without being seen. As they made the short trip to the house's basement, Jonah thought about how easy it was, how simple, to just obey Eldon. The ease in which Eldon made him comply made the hair on the back of Jonah's neck stand up. Eldon was not just his enemy. Before turning Jonah, he had turned another man named Patrick. The night Eldon had taken Patrick, the new vampire had escaped Eldon and kidnapped Jim. That was the same night Jonah had met Eldon for the first time. Together they had saved Jim. Eldon had made them forget everything, but something of the horror had stayed with Jim. Somehow he had seen through the fog. He realized vampires truly existed, and he began to hunt them. When Jim disappeared, again Eldon sought Jonah's help. Jonah had tried, but they weren't able to save Jim in time. Patrick had killed him. Jonah had killed Patrick, freeing Eldon to create a new vampire. To create Jonah in his current form.

The shaft into the basement was tight but manageable. Soon both vampires were dusting off. A third undead sat at a desk with multiple TV monitors. The screens showed rooms, each in different states of decay.

"You have arrived just in time," the man, presumably Allister, said from the desk. He stared transfixed on the screens, his eyes darting from monitor to monitor.

"Our meal is almost ready. I am prepping her as we speak."

Just then a woman appeared on one of the screens. She was young, Jonah guessed not yet twenty. She had tears streaking a dirty face, and blood seeped from a wound on her shoulder.

Eldon walked to the desk and motioned for Jonah to approach as well. He did so with trepidation, his eyes focused on the screen, on the girl's wound. It had been too long. His heart, usually dead and unmoving, started to thump in his chest.

Jonah licked his lips. He tried to breathe, to use the exercise to calm him, but he found he couldn't. His heart pumped harder, thick blood moving for the first time in over two weeks.

"Jonah, this is Allister Bentley. Allister, this is Jonah Stilton," Eldon announced.

Alister didn't look away from the monitors, and Jonah barely caught Eldon's big smile as he too watched feverishly.

"Nice to meet you, Jonah," Allister said, his voice husky with need. He too was ready to feed. "Our prey is almost ready. You have never been to one of my preparation houses. The girl you see in the video is in actuality above us. Humans are predictable things, and I have made a study of what makes them most delectable. Turns out, my dear Jonah, that fear makes them so succulent that no vampire could deny their savour. You are in for a treat this night."

Jonah didn't want a 'treat', but he couldn't deny the need either. His heart raced as he watched the woman on the screen. She was huddled against the back of the door, trying desperately to be quiet, but her breathing came as rasping gasps easily heard.

"This house is a newer acquisition," Allister continued. "So not fully prepared."

Something banged the door hard, and the woman screamed. Then she saw the window, the glass was broken. The frame was open and large enough for her to fit through. She dove towards the exit, but Allister was so much faster. He tapped on the keyboard the second he realized her intention. The screens changed to cameras positioned outside the home. The street was empty.

"Good," he whispered. He tapped another key just as she put her hands on the sill to climb through. The window dropped, crushing the woman's fingers. She screamed again, this time in pain. The door flew open behind her. A large man stood there wearing a hockey mask, and pointing a vicious knife.

New tears flooded the woman's eyes. She fell backwards and scrambled on her feet and wrists, holding her ruined fingers off the floor. The man with the knife just stood there, brandishing the blade.

"She is ready," Allister announced. "I will return with her in a moment."

Allister left with all the speed his undead power afforded him. Eldon and Jonah watched the screen as their host brushed past the man with the knife to get to the woman. In seconds, he had her glamoured, commanding her not to speak, but to follow, and to remain cognizant of everything that had happened that night. Tears continued down her cheeks, and her eyes darted from side to side, but she made not a sound as Allister escorted her off-screen.

They arrived in the basement control room. Eldon stared at the victim with open desire. Jonah was sure his own face mirrored that of his maker's, even though everything in Jonah that was still human screamed for this not to happen. He knew returning to complete his plan would mean sacrifice, but he had hoped to hold off longer than this.

Allister opened his mouth, exposing long fangs which he sank into the woman's neck. Jonah let out a deep-throated gasp. Need was taking over. He too must feed. Allister released from her neck, his face full of ecstasy. Eldon and Jonah moved forward as one to join in the feeding.

It had been so long. Need filled Jonah the likes he had not felt since early in his turning. Watching her fear had drawn on his desires, pulling the monster out of him. The blood, so full of fear, full of adrenaline. He had never tasted anything like it. He drew more, and more. He could feel the suction as he fed, the blood also being pulled by Allister and Eldon.

He knew he needed to stop. Eldon and Allister intended to drain the woman dry, not caring that she wouldn't live. Jonah wanted no part in her death. He tried, the voice inside screaming for him to stop, but he could not. Seconds later he felt the pump of her heart slow, and stop. Even as she slipped away, Jonah felt his need only grow stronger. The monster so long suppressed begged to be let loose. Frantically he tried to stuff it back down into the dungeon he'd created in his depths.

Eldon seemed to feel his protégé's struggle and turned to Allister. "My friend, it seems my young friend here is hungrier than I thought. Is there any chance you might have another near to feed upon?"

Allister mused for a moment before finally saying, "I have none prepared, but my minion can be spared. He is near used up anyway."

The vampire host disappeared again, only to reappear a moment later with the massive knife wielder.

"He was a nice find," Allister stated "Cruel, a killer among the cattle. He has been with me for nearly two years now. But the constant glamour, what it does to the mind, you know. He is nearly gone altogether. Better for him to go this way."

Eldon approached the still man, removed the knife from his hand, then the mask. Both fell to the floor.

Jonah was still on the floor with the dead woman, licking whatever gore remained. All hope to regain control was like the memory of a dream, impossible to grasp, oh so far away.

Eldon used his fingernail to break the skin on the man's neck, instantly drawing Jonah's attention.

"Yes, my pet. Come feed, he is for you." Eldon said gleefully. The command wasn't needed, but somewhere deep inside Jonah's mind - the part that was still Jonah - he felt that pull and understood that Eldon's hold on him had become stronger since the time he had left to be in seclusion.

Jonah dove for the man with no thought at all for the life he was about to take. He had to satiate his need, nothing else mattered.

Night Things Chapter 4

J onah stood by the window, staring outside at the Vancouver night. He and Eldon had returned from Allister's home once they were done killing the two anonymous people. Both vampires drunk on their meals. Jonah couldn't believe what he had done, what he had become in those minutes. All his self-discipline had been useless. He had tried so hard to unravel the monster in him, and reshape it into something more civilized. But civility was not in it, mercy was not in it. A monster is all he ever would ever be.

He had drunk so much that his mind had fogged over. His body felt uncontrolled and wobbly. It reminded him of being alive in his teenage years, going with friends into the local forests to get drunk off stolen booze. Those had been more innocent times, so unlike his current existence.

He thought about the plans he had made, and that were well underway. They were the only thing that made sense, the events of the night proved it, and he could stall no longer. Something new was happening to him, and Jonah could not explain it. Why Eldon suddenly had more control over him, he had no idea, but it terrified Jonah. If his maker's will continued to assert itself, soon Jonah would be as much Eldon's puppet as Steven.

A knock came at the door. Jonah sighed, then moved to answer the door. He didn't want visitors, and he was sure no one in the building would have anything to say that would interest Jonah. He answered anyway.

Eldon stood, a sly smile on his face. There was no doubt that Eldon revelled in Jonah's failure, the smug look told volumes.

"I am leaving tomorrow evening," Eldon said with no other preamble.

"Okay," Jonah replied stiffly.

"I am flying to the UK. I wish for you to join me," the elder vampire added.

It was an effort for Jonah to keep his face still, to show nothing in his eyes. There were many vampires in the United Kingdom, along with other things of the night. With so much history, many chose to call the country home, but the timing was uncanny. Jonah had only returned to watch over his maker, while Jonah's partner secured the item they needed. An item located in the United Kingdom. Jonah had little choice though. He had to go where Eldon wanted if he was to ensure his maker did not foil the plan Jonah was acting out.

"Okay," he said again and he felt a shiver run down his spine. Again, it had been too easy to aqueous. Eldon's smile grew wider, as if he knew.

"Good!" his voice cracked like a whip. "We leave at first night. Steven has arranged a jet and accommodations upon our arrival. We will only be there a single night."

Eldon turned to leave, but paused, looking back.

"It is... good... to have you home, Jonah. Particularly at this time. I am in need of help from someone I can trust. We have not always been amicable, but I hope that will change as time moves on. As you accept what you are. Once we return we will have power unlike any other. You will be pleased."

Then he left, striding down the hall with purpose.

Jonah closed the door. Power. That seemed all Eldon ever seeks to attain. Jonah had felt himself be lulled by his maker, while Eldon spoke. It wasn't exactly a sense of subservience, but a true feeling of contentedness at the thought of Eldon being in power. It had been strengthened when Eldon had spoken about Jonah being back by his side. Thankfully, the sensation dissipated the second Eldon had gone.

But for how long? That had never happened before. It used to rankle Eldon that he could not control me the way he had Patrick. Why now?

It would not matter soon enough. The deaths in Allister's home, by Jonah's own hands, and Eldon's growing power over him, proved that he was on the correct course. It would be a ship he would sail all the way to its destination.

Jonah moved back to the window and gazed into the night. From the high vantage point, he could already see the black of night giving way to the ongoing day. Soon he would be forced into slumber, far away from the killing rays of the sun.

* * *

Jonah's eyes popped open. He lay atop the bed. The bedding barely disturbed by his weight. He sat up and immediately looked at the folded paper on his nightstand. He had forgotten about this habit. While Jonah had rested, Eldon had Steven doing his bidding. One such command must have been to leave Jonah instructions to carry out once he woke for the night. Eldon had always been a planner. Even when asleep, his machinations pushed on. Jonah's maker was always so enthralled with his schemes, he often didn't notice - or care - about the schemes of others around him.

The instructions were simple. 'We leave for our flight at 7:30 pm. The flight is booked for 8 pm. Do not be late.'

It was clipped, to the point, and held a complete expectation of being obeyed. Regardless of who wrote the instructions, the words were Eldon's. Jonah packed his few belongings. This hadn't been part of his plan, but Jonah had to play it out now. Either Eldon had discovered Jonah's plan, or he hadn't. If Eldon was still in the dark, then Jonah had to keep him there.

With everything in his bag once again, he set it by the door and unlocked his phone. He spent a moment looking at the photo he used as a background. The photo was old, Jonah in his teens with an arm around his younger brother. The virtual version of the image was a flawless copy of the print photo, but the photo itself was old, tattered. Jonah coveted it nonetheless. He opened the text app and started to type.

'I'm heading to London tonight, I'll be there just before morning.'

The reply came right away.

'That was not part of the plan. What's changed?'

Jonah frowned at the phone. What had changed? That was the question of the night.

'Eldon is making the trip and has asked me to accompany him. Everything is still on track. If we get the chance, we should meet. I will text if available.'

Again, the response was almost immediate. 'Hopefully, that vampire of yours doesn't fuck things up.'

'Agreed. I'll keep you as informed as possible.'

* * *

Jonah tried not to be nervous. Sunlight was a vampire's worst enemy. Getting caught by the sun was made near impossible as the undead instinctually fled for safety and rest the second day began, but he had heard of instances where vampires had been burned. The injuries did not heal the way they should, they took longer, even more so than burns to humans. They were also extremely painful for the afflicted vampire.

The plane was large for a private jet, but could still hold no more than a dozen people. The idea of being in a plane, above the clouds, with the sun just over the horizon made Jonah's skin crawl. The emotion must have shown on his face because Eldon gave a beaming, sardonic smile.

"Do not fear," he said, "the pilots are mine. We arrive at near light. Once we land, the plane will remain in the hangar until dark."

A fuelling truck disconnected from the plane, and two men in uniform walked from the plane toward the vampires. They saluted and stood stock-still.

"Your in-flight accommodations are aboard, and we are prepared to depart, sir." One of the pilots said.

The vampires were ushered into the back of the plane, where two caskets sat open and empty.

"You're kidding?" Jonah scoffed.

"Not in the slightest," Eldon retorted, "You know what sunlight does to our kind. It is unlikely that we would be harmed if we flew in the cabin of the plane, but knowing the consequences, this is a safer option. Besides, it is somewhat traditional, is it not?"

The old vampire was enjoying watching Jonah squirm. They climbed into the caskets. Jonah felt the casket rumble around as the pilot secured it in the plane's hold. Minutes later, the plane began to roll down the runway, and finally, it took off.

Night Things Chapter 5

Flying in a plane as a vampire was one of the strangest experiences of Jonah's existence. Above the clouds, and travelling east, they flew towards the sun, the vampires could not escape the punishment of the orb. Even tucked away in the cargo, sealed in the coffin Eldon had provided, he still felt its rays.

Jonah was only conscious for part of the trip. There had always been a deep uncontrollable urge that pushed him to hide from the sun. For the past couple of years, he had literally gone to ground, digging himself a hole where he would rest for the day. No matter how long he tried to hold out, to see the sun, to feel its heat on his skin, instinct forced him to shelter.

The inside of the plane offered no true shelter. Although completely hidden from the destructive light outside the plane, Jonah felt like he was being set on fire, burning from within. His body was still unmoving, no different than any other human casket-dweller, but inside he burned! It felt as if fire engulfed his every pore. There were no flames, but every synapse in his brain claimed there were.

Had it not been for the voice in his head, Jonah was sure he would have gone mad. It whispered soothing words, which somehow dulled the pain. Jonah knew it for Eldon's voice. He also knew with a deep certainty that Eldon suffered the same way he did, yet his maker pushed these words, caring words of solace and peace, toward him. They took away some of the pain, they kept Jonah sane.

It was hours before the flight was over, but it had the feel of centuries. When it was over, both undead rose from their coffins, and they looked at one another.

"It is never easy. You handled it well," Eldon stated, and Jonah felt something that surprised him. He felt pride.

* * *

A car picked them up at the private hanger where they had landed. Jonah could see the city in the distance. The driver ushered them over rolling hills and then into the dense city of London. They eventually arrived at an aged, gaudy building that was obviously their hotel.

The structure felt like an extension of Eldon himself, elitist, over-the-top, old. The older vampire must have felt Jonah's disdain.

Excitement radiated off the Eldon, so much so that Jonah wanted to back away. He had to force himself to stand his ground. To cover his own discomfort, he spoke, trying to lead the conversation.

"So why are we here?"

It was straight to the point. Eldon gave him an almost playful look, he had seen right through the deflection.

"We are here, my young protégé, because I will it," he replied. "I am here to retrieve something of great value. I thought to retrieve it myself but it will be much easier with you by my side."

Jonah could feel his maker's excitement, his need. Eldon had tried to push his will on Jonah many times in the past, but it had never worked. It was the reason that Jonah had been able to leave Vancouver in the first place, though Eldon tried his best to think it a gift from him instead of rebellion.

This feeling was different. It pulled at Jonah's core, he could feel how he wanted this item. He could feel that same intense desire he knew his maker felt. He tried to force it away, tamp it down like hunger. *You don't even know what this item even is!*

Given the pull inside Jonah's chest, it must be powerful indeed for Eldon's desire to tug so tightly on him.

"What does this thing do?"

"That, my young protégé, you will have to witness for yourself!," Eldon said. The grin he gave Jonah was both mischievous and terrifying. "Tonight I will be out. I will scout where we are to go tomorrow. This, among many other items of power, is held by a cult known as the Paladins of the Sun. They have hunted us, and we them, for ages."

This was interesting but not new to Jonah. Between the blood lust and Eldon's constant attempt to control his *new pet*, he had heard little of vampire history and culture. He found himself leaning in, listening. He kept his own excitement tamped down. That Jonah had knowledge of the Paladins of the Sun was one secret he could not allow his maker to find out.

"Centuries ago, the Paladins were religious fanatics. They were a cult with hundreds of members in every major city of the time. They found ways to stay hidden from us, and eventually, they started hunting our kind as well."

Eldon shared stories as they walked from the car into the hotel. It was the kind of place Jonah figured Eldon grew up in. The two vampires strolled through the lobby, past a packed restaurant that made Eldon smile. Feeding and crowds both always amused Eldon. He said it was because of the parallel between *them* and *us* but also because they were all boxed in, ready for those two parallel lines to meet. The older vampire had remarked on it so many times that Jonah could still hear the comment as if Eldon had said it aloud.

The staff greeted them, and they were ushered into their rooms. Eldon moved quickly then, readying to leave. Within seconds, he was opening the window to exit into the night. At the last second, he paused and turned.

"You, my young Jonah, will not leave the hotel, nor feed this night." Then he was gone.

Jonah was surprised by the order. He was not surprised that Eldon wanted to retain control, but that he thought doing so would work. Eldon was nothing if not persistent, but straight orders had never worked in the past. Still, Jonah had no reason to leave, nor *feed*. The idea of feeding in the city felt almost ludicrous, even though he could feel the need, small but sharp in the pit of his being. And what Jonah truly needed could come to him.

Jonah pulled his cellphone out of his pocket and made a call.

* * *

Nick flipped his phone closed. The phone was a burner he picked up in the country not long after Jonah had sent him here. His hands shook. They always shook after speaking with the vampire. Four years working together and he still quaked in his boots every time he had to interact with the undead. This time had been no different.

He was getting too old for this shit and knew it. He was in this for life though, and he knew that too. Even when he considered giving all this up, enjoying retirement from the police force, and trying to mend his relationship with Cassie before he was gone, his body would tingle all over. It would get worse the longer he considered it. If he tried to actively disobey Jonah, the pain he felt in his chest was sharp and severe. Nick had never suffered a heart attack before, but he thought he could share war stories with guys who had. Besides, he wanted to see this through. Didn't he?

"Fuck it."

Grabbing his keys, and left his apartment to dine with the undead.

Night Things Chapter 6

Twenty-nine years as a police officer and almost the same amount of time trying to prove the existence of vampires had not prepared Nick for the reality. Not even a little bit.

When Jonah had landed, literally landed, on Nick's fourth-floor patio, Nick had thought he had hit pay dirt. Jonah had not only proven that vampires were walking among us, but that Nick himself had been used by them for years. Jonah had picked apart dozens and dozens of glamours placed on Nick's mind. The process had driven him mad to the point that Jonah had to place a new glamour over Nick. This new glamour was meant to hold him together.

Where the other vampires, Jonah's maker among them, had blocked memories of things Nick had seen, things he had been made to do, Jonah had helped put the pieces in place. The glamour did more than that though, Nick could always feel it there. The glamour slowed the anxiety, the fear, the destruction of his mind, but not the hate. Jonah wanted to keep that, Nick was sure. Nick knew Jonah would use him, and Nick would be used. He had come to terms with that.

Nick had learned that night exactly how weak his will truly was. Jonah said the opposite, that Nick could be glamoured over and over again without going mad was a mark of his constitution. Nick knew weakness and fear when he smelled it, and he had reeked of it.

Twenty-nine years was a long time to search. It was a long time to be an unwilling, unknowing servant. He was still a servant, but at least now he knew what he was and who he served.

That didn't stop his heart rate from increasing. As much as Jonah's glamour helped stop the fear, it couldn't stem the full flow.

Nick made his way into the opulent hotel. There was gold paint and arched furniture everywhere. Even from the lobby, he felt like a popper visiting a king.

Within seconds a man in a fancy suit, a maitre d he supposed, approached him with an arrogant poignant stare.

"Sir, do you have a reservation or a room booking?" the man asked, already sure of the answer.

"I do, actually," Nick replied smugly, copying the man's arrogant poise, just for fun. No one fucks with Nick Cheverie and gets away with it. "The reservation is under Stilton, for two."

* * *

Of course the vampire left him waiting in the restaurant. That wasn't a bad thing in itself, but he wanted to get this shit over with. He just had to let the glamour do its thing. It just needed to keep him calm. His fucking hands were shaking like he was a God-damned junky.

Just as Nick thought his hands were about still, Jonah was there. Nick tried to stand, to say hello, to show the respect that was instinct to him. Jonah waved his hand low in a motion of dismissal which made Nick sit and nod. His hands were shaking again. He hoped it wouldn't get too bad.

A waitress arrived then, her hair long and in a tight bow. She wore a white shirt and apron that reminded Nick of slave garments from colonial movies. He couldn't help but think they should swap outfits. He would bet money that when she wasn't in this snotty, nose-in-the-air gig she dressed a lot like him. Meanwhile, he was more a slave than she by far.

"I will take wine, red, whatever the house suggests," Jonah said without missing a beat.

The waitress looked at Nick. "Uh, nothing. Actually beer, I don't care what kind."

"Nick," Jonah cut in, "Relax, eat something. You are my guest."

Immediately Nick relaxed. *Oh, thank God*, he thought, *that's so much better.* His heart slowed, and his hands rested firmly, easily on the table. Somewhere in the back of his mind, Nick understood that Jonah had glamoured him again and that his body was reacting exactly like a junky who had injected a fix, but he didn't care. It felt beautiful to feel normal even if it was a fake normal.

"I'm sorry. You're right Jonah, thank you," Nick said before turning to the waitress. He could see from her eyes that Jonah had pushed his will on her as well. Nick ordered a streak, blue rare, greens, and of course, his beer.

They talked little at first. Nick drank his glass and ordered another while Jonah pretended to sip at his overpriced wine. The steak was delicious, it was nice of Jonah to make him eat. It was probably a hundred pounds for the damn thing, and that was like $150 back in Canada.

When he finished Jonah leaned in, the pleasantries were over. Nick started talking right away, already knowing what Jonah wanted to hear.

"I found the compound about a week ago. I would have told you sooner, but I wanted to be sure if I was going to call you in. I spent a few days watching, playing the tourist in the area to get a good feel for it."

On the surface it was an old restored castle that is used as a church. The main area of the compound was likely under the main castle. Sermons were held twice during the week and twice on Sundays. Nick had even attended and taken notes. This seemed absurd to Jonah, and he said so.

"Why?" Nick had asked.

"That people would worship in the same place that they to actively hunt things like me. I always thought of a place of worship as a place of happiness."

"That shouldn't surprise you too much. History is peppered with stories of vanquishing the evil devil."

"Yes, well..."

Nick's heart sank, and he tried to make up for what he had said.

"You haven't lost all your humanity though," he prompted.

Jonah's eyes were distant when he answered, "We'll see, my friend. We shall see."

Before they parted ways, Nick produced a folded-up piece of paper and handed it to Jonah. It was a map.

"One thing about this part of the world, they have a lot of history and they love to preserve it. This is what the layout under the castle used to be. I don't know how much has changed since it was converted into a church."

Jonah studied it for a moment, then handed it back to Nick. Jonah had done this before and never forgot a detail. It was how they communicated best. Nick kept all the physical data, while Jonah had it all in his head.

"Thank you. Hopefully, this will be all over soon," Jonah said, and Nick couldn't agree more.

Night Things Chapter 7

When Eldon returned to the hotel it was only an hour before daybreak. Jonah waited patiently, cross legged, coming as close to a meditative state as he could muster. Returning to Eldon's side had not been as he had expected. Dealing with the change in their dynamic had been challenging thus far. It was shocking how much power Eldon had gained over him, and he had to admit it was quickly getting worse.

Having the night to contemplate the situation, and clear his head, Jonah liked to think the time had fortified him, but given how the last 48 had gone, he knew that hope to be empty. If he relied on that faith, he would break. Instead, he would deal with each minute as it came. He would stay strong as long as he could, and if he had to, he had a backup plan in Nick.

There was no doubt that Eldon was pleased, Jonah could feel it oozing off him, infecting Jonah. The sensation was so strong it threatened to break the feeling of calm he had worked toward all night. Jonah had prepared to be taxed mentally by Eldon when he returned to Vancouver. He had expected anger, persuasion, sheer willpower, but not *happiness.*

"I have indeed found what I seek," the older vampire exclaimed, his maw stretched in an unfamiliar smile. "Tomorrow night we shall attack together!"

"Who exactly are we attacking, the Paladins you mentioned?" The idea tamped down the feeling emanating from Eldon, so that Jonah felt more himself. He tried not to feel his own fear. He needed his own item from that compound. He had no idea how he was to obtain the item he needed if he was to be at his master's side.

"Exactly that, my young friend." Eldon was still all smiles, not noticing

Jonah's own feelings. That was good, he would hopefully only have to play this game for a short time more.

"We will infiltrate their stronghold, for underneath there are a host of rooms that are in fact safes, well guarded and protected. Since I turned you, you have avoided what you are, but I can feel it in you. I can feel the lust. The need is strong, and tomorrow night you must let it be free. We must succeed. You must obey me."

Eldon's words hit strong. Jonah had thought them himself many times over, but never in the context that Eldon gave them now. He had always wanted Jonah to give in, to be the monster. That was never the path Jonah wanted. The lust was always there, just as Eldon had said. He was right about one other thing too. For Jonah to be free, there would have to be sacrifice. To obtain the freedom he needed so badly, he would indeed need to let the monster within him out. He had to keep his mind on his own prize, not Eldon's.

Jonah hadn't noticed but Eldon was waiting for an acknowledgement. Never before had his sire done so. He had always expected obedience, so had never asked for it.

Once again it proves how much he wants this goblet. We certainly have that in common, if nothing else, Jonah thought. Then he did something he would have previously thought impossible. Jonah nodded, accepting Eldon's request.

* * *

"Our goal can be reached via a tunnel under the homes there," Eldon said, pointing to the townhomes,

"Not the actual church?" Jonah said. He was surprised, Nick had been certain the only way to the safe rooms was through the basement of the church. He had searched for long hours and days, trying to find schematics of the basement, never thinking to look at the home across the road even though both Nick and Jonah knew it housed many of the cult's guards.

Jonah and Eldon flew from rooftop to rooftop, building to building. It was deep into the night. The streets were empty, and Jonah could smell the canal as the water flowed, the tress and the earth that they were rooted in, and the scent of the city.

The streets were empty at such a late hour, save for four men. Each of them were guards, although not dressed that way. They were all dressed casually as if enjoying a night out. Jonah knew better. He could smell their intent. There was no fear in the air, no hate, no love, no happiness. Just duty. Jonah had never experienced the feeling so fully, but he knew without a doubt that these men were dedicated completely to their cause.

His undead senses also told him their locations too. A pair walked the perimeter slowly, another pair watched the church from an alley next to the townhomes where they all lived. The other two men each sat in a car situated at opposite sides of the church.

Jonah and Eldon watched for a while, both waiting for the right moment to strike. The anticipation and the need had Jonah. His fangs were extended, his heart pumping so loudly he could hear inside his head. Never had he hunted like this before.

Then Jonah felt a slight tug inside his mind. Eldon was looking at him. Wordlessly, he pointed his head towards the guard watching the building from a vehicle on the far side of the church from the townhomes. The meaning was clear. They jumped together.

In seconds, the man had been taken. Eldon struck fast, with Jonah trailing just behind. Eldon pulled the man from the car through the open driver's side window and yanked him into the sky. Eldon had ripped open his neck in flight, then let him go to drop to the ground. When he landed on the roof the man was already dead. Both vampires landed next to the body, high above the street, and fed. Each took all they could, lost in the thrill of the feed. Blood sprayed, and gore squelshed as they worked on the man. Both vampires were wild and frenzied, lavish in the spoils of their kill.

The two men walking the perimeter turned the corner, coming closer to where their now dead colleague had been. Jonah was the first to react, but he felt his maker's presence just behind him this time.

VANCITY VAMPIRES THE COLLECTION

Jonah knocked the closest guard to the ground in an instant. His actions were instinctual, his hand covered his victim's mouth, while his fangs bit deep. His victim let out a tiny gurgle, too stunned by the pain to scream. Jonah raised the man into the air, bringing him down along the hedge that surrounded the church.

Eldon landed beside him, the other man still alive and struggling in his maker's arms. Jonah lifted his head and swallowed. His face dripped the gore that gave him life, and he looked at the man Eldon held. There was fear in the man, so much that it was intoxicating.

Eldon bit down and cut the carotid artery, spraying blood on the grass of the church grounds. Jonah dove forward, biting into the other side of the man's neck. The guard's fear was irrepressible, the perfect cocktail, and Jonah drank deeply.

When the guard was drained and lifeless, Eldon dropped the body to the ground. Jonah felt his master's intent, and they both leapt into the sky. Eldon moved to the dark part of the alley while Jonah perched on a rooftop, eyeing the final guard in his vehicle. He was reading a paperback, which Jonah thought was odd.

You should have been more attentive. Not that it would have mattered, *he thought.*

At Eldon's mental signal, they both attacked. Like the last guard, his window was open. Before the guard could react, Jonah had reached in, as if to kiss the other man. He used his index finger and thumb to grab and squeeze the man's throat and Adam's apple. The man looked at Jonah, and the vampire pushed his will hard into the guard. He used his mental power to erase everything in the man. In an instant, the person inside the body was gone. All that remained were eyes that stared dumbly at the vampire.

Jonah could've left him like that, but he didn't want to. With a quick glance to make sure the street was still empty, Jonah bent into the car and fed. The guard didn't fight or scream. The former guard was oblivious as Jonah bled him dry.

178

Night Things Chapter 8

J onah only stopped feeding when he felt the tug on his mind, Eldon was calling him. Obediently, he let the guard drop. The man tumbled from the driver's seat, his body crumpling to the floor of the car across the two front seats. The guard was just tucked out of sight, he would not be seen unless someone stepped close to peer inside.

Again, Jonah used his speed, moving quickly to his master's call from the alley. Eldon waited, the final guard lay dead in the dark farther down the alley.

Killing the four guards felt like it had taken an eternity when in reality only a few minutes had passed. With the frenzy of feeding over, Jonah could feel the truth of his actions. Did these men have families? What kind of lives could they have had if he had not killed them?

He pushed the thoughts away, pushed the guilt away. There was a prize, and he needed it. No matter how much he hated what he had to do, who he had to become, he would do it all to accomplish this one goal.

Eldon motioned toward a door in the alley leading into the townhomes. Jonah could feel his sire's intention. He knew from what he could feel from Eldon that the row homes had connecting doors built-in. He knew without a doubt that he was about to help Eldon kill everyone in the whole row of homes.

Jonah didn't break stride. If he were still human, he would have vomited at the idea of what he was about to do. But he wasn't.

Part of him was drunk on the blood he had devoured, while the hunter in him stayed sharp and ready. To his surprise, the unwavering desire was no longer there. The guards must have satiated him. The sensation of not needing blood was so foreign that Jonah couldn't place the last time he had felt this way, if ever.

His heart no longer pounded, but he felt *warm*. That had never happened before either. Jonah had always thought the coldness was a part of being what he had become. It felt good. Normal. It was no wonder vampires fed so often.

Eldon didn't knock on the door. He reached out, grabbed the handle and turned. Jonah could hear the internal mechanisms of the door grown as it was twisted and bent. Finally, the door handle snapped off, but the door remained barred. Jonah could feel his master's frustration and he tried not to laugh at the vampire.

The older vampire reached out in frustration. He put two fingers inside the hole left from the handle and pulled the whole mechanism out of the door. The action had made noise, lots of it, and both vampires could hear the movements of alarm in the home. The vampires went to work.

Jonah fed only once more while in the homes. He had hoped that the row homes would only house men, guards like those watching the perimeter of the cult compound. That had not been the case. Families lived here. Jonah tried to kill them quickly, snapping the necks of the woman and children. He didn't want them to suffer.

When the gruesome work was done, Eldon led Jonah to the basement level, straight to a trap door in the floor. Jonah was sure Nick would have been giddy over seeing this door after searching so long to find a way into the compound.

Eldon flung the door open and jumped below the house. Jonah assumed that the tunnel connected to sewers or something similar but what he found was a hallway made of stone construction. The walls looked like a medieval castle, except in this castle, the walls were lit with oval-shaped light bulbs protected by metal cages. The lights left no corner dark, no shadows to hide in. The smell caught Jonah by surprise. The dank moisture of being underground was normal, but the smell of bodies, of constant human traffic, unnerved him. Jonah knew what tonight would bring, knew he would have to let the monster out, but it scared him to think how many he might be forced to slaughter.

There had already been so many.

"Have you tried to glamour any of the cult members?" Eldon said softly.

Jonah shook his head. Shame hit him hard. Had he glamoured them, they might have lived. He hadn't tried because he thought Eldon wanted them dead, and he needed to keep up this facade, at least for now. But he had delighted in feeding, in being a monster. He felt free, more than he had ever felt in actual life.

"Don't bother, I don't know why, but it does not work. I tried to glamour one of the guards before entering the home above, and something blocked my attempts entirely. We must continue to be stealthy. Do not maim, kill when seen, but try not to be seen at all. These halls are well travelled and there are few places to hide bodies."

Jonah nodded, but even as he did so, he could feel the disappointment in him well up. The monster in him didn't want to stop, didn't want to be relegated back to its cage built of Jonah's willpower. The bars of that cage had bent, making a hole where the monster had escaped. Jonah didn't know if he could rebuild that prison, and deep down, he was no longer sure he wanted to.

The two vampires moved down the corridor. When they hit an intersection Eldon turned left without hesitation. Jonah was glad for his master's intel. It was obviously better than what Nick had been able to gather.

The problem is that Eldon goes only for his own goal. How will I find what I seek?

They moved quickly through the lower level of the compound, making their way underneath the church proper. Jonah could feel the anticipation, both because he was so close to his own goal, but Eldon's need, as powerful as his own, dripped off the older vampire. It infected Jonah, driving him forward.

To both Jonah's disgust and delight, it was only seconds before they ran into opposition. The halls were so wide Jonah would have to lay down and reach his arms above his head as far as he could to touch both ends, but there were no places to hide when people came.

Four men in clergyman's robes walked down the corridor. The two vampire saw the four at the same time and rushed forward. Like with the guards, the vampires had the advantage of surprise, but this time there were too many of them to stop an alarm from sounding.

As Jonah and Eldon ripped through the first two clergymen, one of the remaining two pulled a dagger while the last yelled down the hall, "Vampires in the Church! Vampires in the Church!'

Jonah, having snapped the first man's neck like kindling, silenced the yelling man by sinking his fangs into the man's throat, ripping out his jugular. He fell limp to the ground, the spurting blood from his torn vein pumping thick blood all over the stone flooring. The damage had been done though. Alarms sounded.

Jonah looked over to see Eldon dispatch the last clergyman, but he had taken an injury to his left arm. Eldon was old and well-fed, the injury should have already been healing, if not already sealed up, but instead dark, dead ooze leaked out of the wound. It was not closing up. Eldon looked at the wound dismissively.

"It seems they have weapons that can harm us. We must hurry."

Night Things Chapter 9

J onah and Eldon made their way quickly down the corridor. Two more
men met them around the next turn, but the vampire's speed allowed
them to silence them and move on.

They met multiple intersections, and Eldon turned and turned again,
confident in his direction. Twice they found stairs and descended to a deeper
level. No alarm sounded here, and the vampires were able to evade anyone
roaming the halls by ducking into nearby rooms. Before long, they entered
a room laden with books. Shelves lined the walls. Rows of freestanding
bookshelves filled the open space.

Jonah understood Eldon's need as soon as they entered the room. The
librarian. Eldon wanted the man for something, but Jonah wasn't sure what.
The room was large, but not too large.

Jonah came across the man within seconds. Down this deep, no alarms
sounded, and the man was going about his work without a care. Jonah cupped
his hand over the man's mouth and restrained him. His undead strength
made it so easy. The librarian fought, but it was useless. Jonah had all the
control.

The vampire sent out his feelings of success to his master, telling Eldon
he had found his prey. The air around Jonah and his captive moved as Eldon
sped to them. Jonah had thought Eldon wanted to man alive, but as soon as
Eldon arrived, he sunk his fangs deep into the man.

Jonah let his own fangs extend and he sunk them into the other side of the
man's neck. Both vampires drank the glorious liquid down, each taking more
than their fill. Even when the librarian was clearly drained, Eldon continued

on. Following his maker's example, Jonah continued to drink, the blood getting thick. The viscous life-blood filled Jonah up. He could feel an intense strength welling in him. He imagined this was what speed must be like to a junky. It was the drunk sensation he had felt before, this made him feel invincible.

When the last drops of the librarian's blood stopped flowing, the two vampires dropped their meal. Eldon grabbed the body, hefting it over his shoulder. Jonah already knew the plan, he was hiding the body.

When Eldon had the librarian tucked away into a corner, he grabbed the man's wrist, twisted and squeezed. Bones cracked under the vampire's pressure. He spun the appendage as the shattered bones broke skin. With a quick tug, the hand came free. Eldon, usually composed and regal, must have been feeling the effects of drinking too. He held the severed hand up by his cheek, using the hand to wave at Jonah in hello. The older vampire giggled as he did it, and Jonah couldn't help himself, he laughed right along. The coy gesture was so unnatural for the older vampire.

When Eldon dropped the hand down, he sniffed the air before looking back at Jonah.

"They have followed us into the lower levels. We must hurry! The guards are coming onto this floor. It will not be long before they search the library and find our now one-handed friend." he said.

Jonah had no idea how the older vampire could make out anything through the heavy scent of the dead man. Unlike so many others that night, they had drank cleanly from the man in the library. The act had not left much in the way of smell behind, but all that had changed when Eldon had ripped the man's hand from his body, for reasons Jonah had still did not know.

Jonah was actually surprised the smell was so limited considering the mutilation. Then it hit him, that was why they had drained the man so fully. Eldon's plan included the hand, he had always intended on removing it.

The older vampire was moving again at top speed, with Jonah trailing behind him. The older vampire ran through hallways. Unlike the previous passageways, these halls had cameras in the corners of each archway. Eldon smashed each camera with his left hand as he passed. His right still held the severed hand dangling limp and white. As Jonah was slower, Eldon had time to dart down extra hallways to smash the cameras there as well.

He doesn't want to give them a straight path to us. The more time he spent with his maker, the more he came to understand the undead's cunning.

Finally, Eldon stopped at a dead end. There was a pad on the wall, and a large steel barrier used to stop any unwanted living or dead to pass beyond. Eldon placed the hand on the panel.

Night Things Chapter 10

Nothing happened.

Eldon removed the hand again and dropped it on the scanner. Still nothing. He tried it a third time, then a fourth. Then he started lifting the hand and dropping it on the pad over and over again in quick succession. Jonah understood his master was trying to use the keypad to open the metal door, and the key was obviously the librarian's hand print. Yet the door would not open.

"It must be heat sensitive," Jonah said.

"What?" Eldon called back, the question almost a growl.

"The hand isn't going to work, it must need body heat to activate the pad," he responded.

Eldon threw the hand to the ground and faced the door.

"We do it the hard way then," he said.

He ran back in the hall a short distance, turned and made a running dash at the door, fist cocked back in a punch. The older vampire jumped when only two steps from the door, launching himself at the metal. His fist punctured the door at the corner of the seal.

A loud ringing tore through the space, echoing down the hall. It was likely everyone on that floor of the complex had heard it.

"Watch the hall, kill any who come down it," Eldon growled as he pulled on the exposed steel of the door around his whole. The steel bent only the smallest bit, not giving Eldon any leeway.

With a scream of frustration, he backed away from the door again, and made another run, this time for the door's other top corner. Again there was a deafening *ping* that reverberated through the complex.

Jonah was shocked no one had come to the source of the noise yet.

"Come," Eldon called, "we must pull it open together!"

Eldon grabbed the first corner again and heaved. Jonah joined him, grabbing the metal around the second hole. Eldon placed both feet against the wall, hanging suspended, using every ounce of his undead strength. Jonah had one foot against the door jamb, hands tucked into the hole.

The top started to bend. The top lip of the door curled, showing a tiny gap. The vampires pulled even harder, the crack giving them renewed hope. When a finger's width appeared in the gap, both vampires reached in and grabbed the top of the door. The steel, dense and thick like a safe, continued to curl until finally, a body could fit through.

The room was pitch black. Usually, darkness would be no issue for the vampires, but with no light at all to bounce shadows, even they could not see.

Eldon started to fumble around the room when Jonah pulled his phone out of his pocket, and let the screen light up. Eldon looked at the device with scorn but used its light nonetheless. Like the library, this room was packed with the same style of thick wooden shelving. Unlike the library, these were not covered with books, but instead, they held all manner of items. From jewelry, to cups, to primitive weapons. Eldon and Jonah both scanned the shelves. The room was not that large, it fit only twenty shelves but they all were lined top to bottom with items.

"What are you looking for?" Jonah called to Eldon.

Eldon took a split-second stare at his creation, weighing and judging. Jonah could see the inner turmoil in the other vampire. Eldon trusted no one.

"A ring," he finally said, "it has a thick gold band, embossed with a drop of blood as the sigil in its centre. We must find it quickly and go from here."

They looked together, Jonah searching side to side, up and down. Then he saw it. Like everything in the room, it gave off an aura of sorts. Many Jonah could feel he should not touch, but this one called to him. He reached for it. Cupping the ring in his hand he called to Eldon.

"I have it."

Eldon turned, his features turned down. It took Jonah a moment to recognize the emotion, it was fear. His maker was scared of him in that moment.

"Pass it to me, Jonah," he demanded, but his voice was strained with tension. It was impossible to miss.

Jonah did not care. He had no idea what the ring did, nor how to use it. He took a step forward and placed the ring into his master's hand.

"Good," Eldon said and slipped the ring on his middle finger. "Now, you have been quite resourceful during this trip. More so than I thought possible. Now comes the true reason I had you join me. You, my protégé, will be leaving this compound the way we came in. I have another way out, but I require a distraction."

"More like a sacrifice. If these people hunt vampires, then they know how to kill us. You know that is suicide for me," Jonah snapped back.

"As I said, you've proven yourself to be resourceful. You will have to draw on that skill. Without the distraction, we would be found, and likely both killed. They know that they have been infiltrated, and they likely know it is by vampires. The inhabitants here may only be human, but these humans have adapted and learned over the centuries. They have means of trapping and killing us. Separating all but guarantees that I will escape."

Jonah knew his maker was self-centred but this was amazing. Still, he wanted out of Eldon's presence, even more now that the other vampire detailed his plans.

"Go, I will create the distraction, and I will meet you at our hotel," Jonah said.

"Good boy," Eldon cooed, "In doing this, you protect me like you once protected your brother. We are family now. Make it out of here my protégé, do not let them kill you. We have an exciting future ahead of us."

Jonah felt the power in Eldon's words. It was more than his will, more than a command. Compelled like never before, Jonah *had* to obey. None would stop him, he would escape alive. Eldon's words bore down deep into Jonah's being. It felt like his will was being erased, yet another part of Eldon's words lit a small fire in the pit of Jonah's stomach. That fire burned hot.

Like you once protected your brother.

Eldon left the room. When he was sure his master would not return, Jonah slipped two items from the shelves into his pocket, then turned to do his master's bidding. He would escape, and he would live to return to Eldon's side.

Night Things Chapter 11

Eldon was waiting when Jonah arrived.

"Did you have trouble?" Jonah shook his head. It was the truth. He had been forced to kill fourteen more of the cult and injured at least a dozen more. It had been so easy to do. The need to obey Eldon was intense, gripping his being.

"Good," Eldon said, nodding.

The slight praise made Jonah swell. As much as he didn't want to, his smile beaming.

"Come! Our plane is ready, let's get out of here now. I have no interest in staying around to see if the cult finds us here."

Jonah followed his master, obedient and attentive.

* * *

Nick paced in his one-bedroom condo. It felt strange to be in the small home again. Jonah had not made contact since Nick arrived back in Vancouver, That had not been the plan. Everything they had worked toward was coming to a close, there was supposed to be constant contact.

Being in his home made him think of his daughter. All the photos were off the wall. It made it feel even less like his space. Cassie was still alive, somewhere in the city. Nothing would bring Candice back. Cassie's twin, she had truly been a cop's daughter. All the guys on the forced loved her. Cassie had always been more of an introvert, shy and nose in a book, while her sister was the opposite. Candice was the star of every show.

When she had disappeared, the whole force hunted for her. It was rare an eight-year-old would just disappear without someone else's intervention. It was the trauma of his losing one of his daughters that had snapped him in half. It was then some of the glamours that had been placed on his broke as well. It was then that he started to remember or at least a sense of memory. It was then his obsession was born.

After years of searching, personal unsanctioned investigations, suspensions, psych evals, and in the end, a forced retirement, he had been no closer to proving vampires had taken his daughter. No closer to exposing that vampires existed if he was honest with himself.

Until Jonah showed up on his patio, four stories up, and gave Nick a gift. Not only had Jonah proven his undead state, but he also helped to break through some of the glamours that had been put on him over the years. According to Jonah, vampires constantly needed cops to help cover up the grotesque shit they did, so most of the force had been glamoured at one point or another. In Vancouver, there were certain cops that were easier to manipulate, weaker of will when it came to the vampire's suggestion. They were used over and over again. Nick had been one of those.

Nick had asked about Candice. He was so sure Jonah was going to tell him that they had taken his daughter away from him and Cassie. Jonah didn't know that answer. He said that had happened before he had been turned into a vampire.

Nick knew now more than ever, even if the vampire who flew up to his patio couldn't corroborate the story. He had always known, at least somewhere in the back of his mind. That was why the obsession had truly started. The endless nights of searching. It tore his marriage apart, and Arlene had left him only a year later. She took Cassie with her, but he still got to see her on weekends.

That gave him five days a week to look, to research, to hunt. He was sure that not someone but some*thing* had taken Candice. He didn't know how he was going to prove it, but he was sure he would.

Years passed, and Nick found exactly nothing. Cassie grew up, still had her nose in a book most of the time, but Nick still taught her. He wouldn't have a second daughter disappear. Cassie could fire a weapon. She was competent with a handgun and a rifle. She could hunt, fish, and forage in the forest. When it came to self-defence, she was quick, agile, and strong. He had done the best he could.

When Jonah had broken the glamours from Nick's mind, when he could see in his mind's eye not only how he had been used, but how often he had been used, he wanted to scream. He wanted to unleash the terror inside his belly through his throat and he never wanted it to end. He could see the evidence bags in his hand, time and again. Some things were planted, other things were removed. He saw himself scan missing person reports, BOLOs, and heard himself say to skip people on the list. He watched himself pick up kids, women, junkies. Instead of bringing them home or the station, he would deliver them into the hands of the undead, so they could be fed upon. He had been as much an accomplice as a victim, but an accomplice nonetheless.

Nick walked out to his patio. A tiny tin garbage can sat on the concrete. He tossed the last couple of pictures in the bin, grabbed the liquid fire starter for his barbecue and sprayed. It was hard watching the images burn after he lit the match. Burning the pictures was like burning his love for Candice, like burning the need he had for so many years to find her.

He saw now how selfish that hunt had been. It had cost him his marriage, his relationship with his remaining daughter, his job. Until Jonah showed up on his patio, Nick had nothing to live for. Cassie was still out there somewhere. She still lived in the city, even if she'd have nothing to do with him. Hopefully one day she would understand, and forgive him for what he and Jonah were about to do.

When the images were all ash, Nick opened his phone and sent one text message.

I'm ready, stop in when you can.

Night Things Chapter 12

"Where have you been?" Eldon asked.

Jonah had just returned. Everything he had planned was now in motion. He had followed Nick as the ex-cop drove a cargo van to the high-rise. With some words from Jonah, Nick had slipped right into the parking garage under the building.

"Out. After those flights, I wanted to spend some time in the night. Are you going to tell me what we risked our necks for?" Jonah demanded. The question came out as a bark. He had killed dozens of people last night. The only thing he could hear in his mind was their screams and their pleading.

"No." Eldon replied flatly.

"Then we must talk."

"Then talk."

"Not here, in privacy," Jonah said and walked out the door.

Jonah made his way to the elevator. He tried to hide a smile when Eldon joined him. This needed to work, he needed this to be over.

"If this is about your inexplicable desire to stop yourself from feeding, or the sanctity for those you have preyed upon, I will hear none of it. We are hunters, we hunt and we feed. It is what we are," Eldon said once he was in the elevator.

"No Eldon, it is not that at all."

Jonah hit the number to the top floor, then gave a nod to the camera in the corner of the elevator, letting Eldon know he didn't want to talk in front of the camera. If Jonah were human, his heart would be beating out of his chest in nervousness. This ruse wouldn't have to last long, it did need to last long enough. Despite the anxiety, Jonah felt at peace. He was ready for what had to be done As Eldon had said, Jonah was a hunter and he was indeed hunting. Eldon was the prey now.

The elevator made an audible *ding*, before doors glided open. Jonah exited and turned toward the stairs. This path was well known to both vampires, The inhabitants of the high-rise often used the flat section of roof off the stairwell to fly into the night.

The two vampires exited the stairwell. By this time, Eldon was visibly frustrated. Jonah could feel the emotion seeping out of his maker. It made Jonah want to laugh. They were almost there.

"We are private. What is this about. Speak now, it will be light soon," Eldon snapped. He was right too, the black of night was already shifting to the brilliant blue that came before the sun.

Jonah felt that pull once again, that intense need to obey Eldon. The sensations so strong, Jonah couldn't fight it had he wanted to. Luckily, he didn't want to fight it all.

The younger vampire pulled out two small items from his pocket, They looked like lockets, designed and sculpted to look like something worn by women a hundred or more years ago. He flipped one open and threw it to the ground near Eldon. The older vampire froze, staring at the piece of jewelry in horror. *Good,* Jonah thought, *he recognizes it. Let him feel fear for a change.*

Jonah opened the second one and dropped it at his own feet. The cool breeze that had been stirring stopped abruptly, like a string cut with scissors. Jonah tentatively stuck his hand out, and even though there was no wall to hit, Jonah could barely move his hand forward. It hit upon an invisible barrier.

"I hate you, Eldon," Jonah said to his maker, "I have hated you from the moment you killed my brother and made me into this monster."

Eldon barely heard. He was using his accelerated speed to look for an escape from the barrier. Jonah stood still watching. These devices had claimed to make an inescapable cage, one that would seek out the closest vampire and trap them indefinitely. Jonah had worried that the claims had been farfetched, and he had planned for that eventuality too. Now seeing Eldon truly trapped, he knew his worries were unwarranted. He felt a second of regret for Nick, then set that aside. There was nothing that could be done.

He reached forward and touched his own barrier. It had no real substance, no opacity as Jonah could still see everything, but he could not move his hand much more than a foot in front of him.

Dawn was only twenty minutes away, and he could feel the pull to go indoors, to rest and hide from the sun. He knew Eldon felt it too. A long time ago, Eldon had told him that age gave vampire more power, but the trade-off was that they had to have a place to rest, always. The calling to rest intensified the older the vampire became.

Eldon pounded on the barrier, his fist not making a sound, his hand just stopping mid-air

"Why have you done this?" Eldon asked, staring hard at Jonah.

"You know, I used to spend every night trying to train myself to stand until the sun rose. It cannot be done, can it?" Jonah said in reply.

"No, our nature demands we retreat to the dark. That is why we must go. We must go now!"

Jonah felt the pull then, so undeniable that Jonah also started to search for a way out of this barrier. His hands felt the air, pushing anywhere he thought might be weak. It was like his hands moved of their own accord, and he couldn't stop them.

"You were not the only one who wanted something from the cult. We each got what we so desired."

"So we did," Eldon scoffed, "My prize will do us little good now, thanks to you. We could have been the kings of this world."

The ambitious goal did not surprise Jonah, Eldon had always been power hungry.

"What did we go there for," Jonah prompted again, "You might as well tell me, now that we only have a few minutes left."

Eldon didn't hesitate this time.

"You saw the ring, but it is not some useless trinket. Jonah, this ring allows me to glamour other vampires. I don't need to sire them, I don't need to look them in the eyes, I only need to make my wishes known. I know you've felt the bond between us strengthen since your return, but that is a drop in the bucket when compared to the power of that ring."

Jonah understood then the change that had occurred before their return trip to Canada. Eldon's hold on Jonah had become ever stronger since his return from his forest retreat, but when Eldon had just the ring on, his commands had been absolute. In the past Jonah had been able to resist Eldon's call. He had found it harder on this trip, Eldon was gaining some control over him as they aged, but he had so quickly acquiesced when Eldon had asked they come home. Like being glamoured as a human, it had been like being hypnotized, but this was so much more. Even now, Jonah still searched for a way out of the barrier because Eldon had asked it. He had no control over his actions.

"We could be kings," Eldon said offering his hand out, "You must know a way out of these things, you couldn't have planned on letting yourself die. Let us rule the vampire together, you and I."

Jonah just chuckled. "To die this morning is exactly what I planned."

Night Things Chapter 13

Nick had watched Jonah fly overhead, finding his own way into the vampire's dwelling. He signed in with the security guard Jonah had spoken to then pulled into the underground parking. The fake credentials and Jonah's words passed muster, the guard let Nick in without much fuss. As far as the guard was concerned, Nick was a plumber, he was there to fix a water leak. The big white van with ladders and tools hanging off the top helped frame that story.

Nick sat in the driver's seat, parked in a spot designated for visitors. He checked his cell phone. Six minutes remained before sunrise.

* * *

Eldon was searching feverishly. To Jonah, the older vampire looked like a trapped cat. Even Jonah could no longer hold back, his need to rest, to hide from the sun, was undeniable. The sensation overtook Eldon's command, and Jonah started fighting the barrier in earnest. The feeling of tightness in his chest was almost unbearable, constricting like a snake crushing its victim.

The sky had turned from the dark blue to a light blue of pre-dawn.

It won't be long now, Jonah thought, even as he fought his cage. The thought was desperate, pulling him in two directions. One would end his existence, the other was his fight to survive, an instinct he wasn't sure he could overcome.

Eldon, still moving, still trying to escape, screamed at Jonah.

"Why!?!"

"Why? Have you been a monster so long that all of your humanity is gone? You destroyed my childhood, then you took my life and my brother's. We are an abomination."

Jonah could hold back no longer, the tightness and the need in him dwarfed any compulsion to feed he had ever endured. He smashed against the barrier, screaming. It would not give. He tried to break through the ground and found the barrier there as well. The tension in him ran up his neck and into his brain, making Jonah scream again. He could sense Eldon doing the same, but Jonah couldn't hear anything. It was like a bomb had gone off, making the world silent outside of the ringing in his head. He could feel that he was losing his grip on who he was. He thought of his maker, his brother, that poor woman in the abandoned horror house, then he thought of the ring on Eldon's finger. He with every fibre of his being that had made the right choice. In Eldon's hands, that ring made him unstoppable. Even after the sun kills them, if another vampire found it... he had indeed still made the right choice. As the sun started to peek over the eastern mountains, all sense of self shattered, escape was all that mattered.

Then he burned, his exposed hands, and face ignited when the glow of sunrise touched his skin. He looked over to where Eldon had been trapped and saw his maker's face contort before his entire body caught fire. Jonah let out a cry, he tried to move, to run from the light, but it was too painful. He stood there, stalk still, as the flame ate him.

It's over. It's finally over.

Briefly, Jonah thought about his phone. Nick was the backup plan in case the amulet traps didn't work. He could have called Nick, and told him to back off, to go home. Jonah hadn't even considered it. He really was a monster.

It's over now though.

Jonah crumpled to the ground, his legs burned to ash. He tried to lift a hand to block the sun from burning his face. The pain was too much. His hand was a blazing hot coal, fingers tumbling into ash as he lifted them. Then the darkness came.

From somewhere deep inside his head, he heard a voice, familiar and welcome. It was Jimmy. It was his brother.

"Don't worry, I got you."

* * *

The timer on Nick's phone went off. He had been hiding in the back of the van, staring at the timer as it ticked down the seconds. Finally, it rang. To Nick, it had all the deafening sound of a gong being hit right next to your ear.

He looked at the duffle bag next to him. Nick had volunteered for this task. His vampire friend was willing to glamour a guard for this, but Nick had said no.

What if the guard broke the glamour? It was likely, given the task they would have been asked to do. If Nick had glamoured someone to the point that they were dull enough in the head to complete the task, what would they say if challenged by security?

They'd drool a bit, and then they'd get caught. This would be over, *Nick thought.*

He unzipped the bag and stared at the plastic explosive. The red bricks seemed to be staring back, glaring and accusing. Nick reached past them to the controller box with a big red button.

For the hundredth time, Nick thought about how weird it had been planning with Jonah to gather the explosive. The Vancouver special units have the Semtex explosive on hand in the case they need to blast open a door or for any other explosive needs. Jonah had easily glamoured three officers and had them steel the Semtex under his instruction. Seeing all this from the other side, not being the poor soul under the vampire's spell, made him sick. Would those cops know that the explosive they stole would be used like this? Would they ever remember that they stole it? Nick doubted it.

Nick had to admit, he was glad he was under a glamour. Jonah had offered, trying to be nice. Originally Nick had turned the offer down, but at the last minute, he had changed his mind. What if he couldn't go through with it? The glamour had only been used to bolster his resolve, and he needed it now.

"I love you, Candice," he said aloud and pressed the button. Nick didn't even have time to see the flash as the explosion went off.

Night Things Chapter 14

C assie Cheverie was watching the news again. She couldn't help it. The story was on every screen on every channel. The police have already announced that the explosion is believed to be a terrorist act. And her father was missing.

She hadn't spoken to her dad in years, not since she'd found his crazy detective diary about vampires taking her sister. It had been too much. It also explained so much. The need to teach her survival techniques, and how to fire every manner of weapon. His constant push for her to join martial arts classes. By the age of eighteen, Cassie was pretty sure she could out-cop almost every cop she had grown up with.

The newscast cut to commercials. Cassie still couldn't drop that feeling in the pit of her stomach. She had already called work and told them she wasn't coming in today. Her boss was not happy. Luckily they didn't have any huge cases on the go but they did have a mountain of smaller cases. Ed Gabboid was a fine lawyer, and he needed all hands on deck. That included his legal secretary.

The explosion had first hit the news right at dawn. Cassie was in the middle of her morning Tai Chi routine. The daily ritual helped ground her for the day ahead, but as always, she had her TV on the morning news running in the background. Cassie had called in sick as soon as the news gave a sneak peek of the explosion.

She didn't know how, but she was sure her father was involved in that explosion. Every instinct in her body said so. Cassie had even gone so far as to pick up her phone to call him. But what if she were wrong. She didn't want to talk to him, but she did want to make sure he was okay.

A knock came at the door. The sick feeling in her stomach turned into a quiver. Were there cops at the door, were they delivering conciliatory news? Who would it be? Johnson and Colby maybe. Maybe Amoud and Prouse. They had all been dad's friends before his retirement.

Cassie made her way to the door in a dream-like state. The walls seemed to wobble as she walked, the sides of her vision rounding, making the short hallway to her front door seem miles long.

When she finally opened the door, she was convinced with all of her being that it was the police and they were delivering the worst of news.

It was not cops, but a man in a suit. Even more strange, she knew this man. Garret McNeil had stood on the opposing side of the courtroom from her more than once. He was a good man, but like all lawyers, he always thought he was right. Cassie guessed that made him a good lawyer too.

"McNeil?" she asked, even though she knew full well it was him.

"Yes, Cassie, isn't it?" he replied, "Cassie Cheverie?"

Cassie nodded dumbly, still unsure why McNeil was on her doorstep instead of the police.

"I have a package for you. I was instructed to give it to you today. There is a contract inside that I need you to sign. I'm sorry for your loss," the man said.

"What loss?" Cassie snapped.

"Jonah Stilton," he responded. Mouth open, he took a hesitant step back. "I am the executor of his will, and he has left you a sizable sum."

Even more confused, Cassie apologized and let McNeil in. She had no idea who Jonah Stilton was, but McNeil was too good a lawyer to knock on the wrong door, and he'd asked for her by name. Something else was going on. She still had that sick feeling in her gut, and she didn't like it one bit.

"I don't know who that is," she responded as she let him walk passed her. Cassie led McNeil into her kitchen. Her coffee maker was on a timer and brewed the drink while she had done her Tai Chi session. McNeil refused the cup she offered, which was telling, he didn't expect to stay long.

By the time she was done adding cream and sugar to her drink, the lawyer had laid out a contract across her dining table. Cops and lawyers both used the same trick with drinks. If they wanted to stay, they accepted whatever drink was offered, even if they had no intention of consuming even a sip.

"It doesn't bother you that I don't know this guy?" she asked him.

"Not really," he said, "although it is a pretty cool mystery. I mean, it's clearly your name and address on the will. You were added to it a couple of years ago. I remember you specifically because we'd already faced off in court a couple of times, and your name was on the docket. It's not often I do executor work. In fact, I'm not really sure why I took this guy on. I must have been feeling generous that day. Anyway, he even called me about six months back and had me update your address, so I knew where to find you."

She had just moved into this place. She had been frugal all through college and continued to have two roommates once she graduated. Every spare penny went into her bank account, she wanted her own home desperately and had finally signed the papers only six months ago.

"Okay, what did this mystery man leave me?" she asked.

"The contents of a bank account with just over $800,000, and this sealed letter," he said, holding up an envelope.

Cassie's jaw hit the floor.

"Garret, I can't" she whispered hard, "I don't know this guy, you must have the wrong person"

McNeil smiled and grabbed a small bundle of papers held together with a clip, he flipped a couple of pages and read aloud.

"Know that Cassidy Cheverie and I have never met. She is the daughter of a great friend of mine, and I wish to leave this gift for her upon my passing. If she is anything like her father, she will question, cajole, and rebuke. I expect the executor to deliver this portion of my will nonetheless. This is the most important task in this document."

McNeil set the papers down looking hard at Cassie.

"There's no doubt this is meant for you. Accept it, Cassie. It's a life-changing gift."

Cassie sat stock still, processing the words the lawyer had just read aloud. When she could take it no longer, she nodded and numbly grabbed the pen McNeil held out to her.

* * *

Cassie sat at her dining table with the envelope in her hands. Garret McNeil had left only fifteen minutes earlier. He had seemed so happy for Cassie. She should have been happy too but that feeling in the pit of her stomach wouldn't go away.

She cracked the seal on the letter and unfolded it.

"Dear Cassidy,

My name is Jonah. You don't know me but I knew your father. If you're reading this, we are both dead. The first thing you should know is that your father loved you very much. The second thing is that I was a vampire."

Cassie read on, even as tears flooded her eyes.

The End

Haven

The road ahead was littered with dead leaves. Traffic that would have usually brushed the leaves to the roadside, of course, was non-existent. Everything about society as she had known it was was non-existent.

Cassie Cheverie adjusted the pack on her back and looked at the sign again. She had been following highway 99 north, skirting the coast out of Vancouver for days. Britannia Beach 4km. She tried to step towards the turnoff, but her feet refused to move. She was safe where she stood. The town would be full of the dead. Except instead of being dead, they were roaming the town, seeking the living like her to bite, to tear away flesh, to strip her bones clean. The town would also be full of food.

Her stomach made a noise again, not just a grumble but a hollow roar. It was a stark reminder of her choices. Continue on the highway towards Squamish, and hopefully on to Whistler, or detour. Guaranteed food, and guaranteed threat, versus a small chance of food and an unknown chance of threat. Her stomach made the decision as it roared again. She had to eat. The knowledge made her think of the dead again. They also needed to eat.

She tried desperately not to think of the people she left Vancouver with. Sarah, her eight-year-old frame lumbering around with the rest of the dead in North Vancouver, or of Eric and Don, both dead on the highway now.

Nope, nope nope, don't think about that. Just hold it together.

Her face started to crumple into tears, but she pushed the pain back.

I need food. That's just the way it is.

Her feet moved.

Just like Lions Bay and Oliver's Landing, as houses started to dot the side of the road, cars began piling up, blocking passage for anyone not on foot. Cassie hung her pack loosely on her shoulders, a trick Eric had taught her. It was quick to correct if she needed to run but easy to drop if she needed to fight. She pulled the knife from her belt. The gun would only get pulled if she absolutely had to. Noise attracted the dead, so stealth was key.

Once upon a time, the knife she held was likely used to fillet fish. Cassie had a smaller knife folded up in her pack that she used for food. The filleting knife was for defence, there was no way she would chance eating with the same blade she stuck in those dead things.

The front seats of the first car were empty but she approached the car slowly and crouched to the ground. Once alongside the car, she could see all the windows were closed. If something was in there, it couldn't get to her. She straightened tall enough to look inside. The back seat was empty.

Her hand hurt from the tight grip she had on the knife, and she had to force herself to loosen it. She tried to laugh at herself. All that build-up for nothing. The growl made her jump. Cassie spun, knuckles white on the knife again.

Two cars down, the body in the front seat reached toward the dash, eyes empty and teeth gnashing. The seatbelt kept the thing in place. Even though the noise it made was muted by the vehicle, Cassie looked over the cars, and in th surrounding yards, to make sure the sound didn't attract more of them.

They seemed to be alone, but for how long? She ran to the car and opened the back door. The thing in the front seat tried to turn, but Cassie was faster. She plunged the knife through the body's ear, into the brain. The growling and the constant, relentless push toward Cassie ceased. Whoever they had been, they were truly dead now.

Cassie knew she could have left that one alone. The thing had been trapped in the car, no threat at all. They weren't smart enough to open doors or undo seatbelts, but she had learned firsthand that leaving a threat behind you could literally come back to bite you. The way the world was now, if a threat could be neutralized, it was.

As much as she hated her dad, she was thankful for the skills he had taught her. As a cop, he had seen the worst of the world, at least before the sickness, and he had tried to prepare her for it. Cassie had grown up doing most things sons did with their fathers. Self-defence classes, the gun range, hunting, fishing. By the time she had turned eleven and her parents had long split up, she already resented him for not seeing a daughter. She tried to change. Dressed in the right clothes, became an expert at applying make-up, started taking dance and acting classes alongside martial arts. She had stayed with her father every second weekend throughout her teens. To her surprise, he was always front and centre at dance recitals and plays. He was gone now but what he had taught her, those things kept her alive in this new world.

Cassie made a quick search of the car, but found nothing. All hopes that the dead person in the front seat had been leaving town at all prepared popped after only a quick scan. She was about to leave when she thought about the trunk. With a sigh, she opened the driver's door. Going in to get the keys was not going to be easy.

She held her breath, and kept her eye on the prize. The keychain and fob hung limp, the car key secured in the ignition. Cassie had to remind herself three times that the body in the seat could no longer spring to life to bite her. She leaned in, grabbed the key, twisted and pulled it free.

The trunk popped open and Cassie smiled. A pack similar to her own sat on the trunk floor. There was a tent next to the bag, but it was a large thing, too big to take with her. The sleeping back strapped to the bottom of the pack was a huge score. Her own was dirty and ripped in more than one place. The bag in the trunk was clean and looked new. With no risk came no reward, and this relatively small risk had certainly paid off. She dumped the bag inside down, letting the contents fall to the road. She hoped for a protein bar, or a bag of M&Ms, anything. It was all clothes.

She left the trunk open, the keys sitting on the roof of the car, and continued on down the road. She wanted a store, a gas station would be perfect. It had been about a month since most of the population had gotten sick, three weeks or so since they had all died, a fortnight since they all come back. Since then, for those left, survival was the only goal. That's why Cassie wanted a gas station. The lights went out not long after the sickness struck. Grocery stores were useless now. All the meat on the shelves rotten and stinking. Worse, the stench attracted the dead. Any larger grocery store she had seen had the dead swarming the parking lot and around the contours of the building.

Houses were a little better. When the sickness had run its course, and the victim was about to die, many became euphoric and had an overwhelming need to be outside. Most houses had doors ajar, but Cassie knew better. Not all the dead were outside, some hid. That was a line of thought she needed to tamp down too.

The houses were getting closer together as she walked the road. Hopefully, she'd see what she needed soon. She topped a rise, and down the hill was the town's main street. She could almost see right to the Pacific coast. There were only four real street blocks with larger buildings, most three stories. The centre of town only consisted of forty, maybe fifty homes.

The gas station she had hoped for, wished for really, was on the north end of the main street, only three blocks down the hill. The Petro-Canada station was perfect. Like most Petro-Can stations, it was a convenience store with gas pumps. The entire front of the store was glass with small decals. From the outside, Cassie could see the entire interior. She watched the store from the street to make sure it was completely unoccupied.

After a few minutes passed, she gathered all her nerve and headed to the door. She fully expected it to be locked. When it swung open, she nearly laughed out loud. With no power, the electric ding Cassie was so accustomed to upon entering the store never sounded. She went straight to the counter, grabbed a package of jerky and ripped it open. The meat sticking out of her mouth, she pulled the little handgun out of her belt holster. She only had nine bullets left. The knife was always an option but in such close quarters, she didn't want to take the chance. The one aisle that wasn't visible from the street was empty. The back of the waist-high counter had also been obstructed from the exterior of the building. Again, nothing hid behind it. That left only the back room.

Her dad's voice ran in her mind. *Always take prey out in the open,* he had taught when on their hunting trips into Washington. *Prey can turn dangerous when boxed in.* The back room of the store was certainly a box. As Cassie prepared to open the door to the storage room, she couldn't help but wonder if she was the hunter or the prey in this scenario.

The employee door opened into a dark room. The only noise was Cassie's breathing and the hiss of the hydraulic pump slowly easing the door shut again. Cassie, gun outstretched, waited for the telltale growl of the dead. A minute passed, then two. Nothing. Cassie slipped off her pack, stashing it behind the counter. The mag light she pulled out of the side pocket lit up at the push of the back button. It likely wouldn't be noticeable outside, but she held the beam against her leg anyway, dampening the light. She wasn't about to take any needless chances.

The little light shone against the walls of the back room of the convenience store. Empty, blessedly empty. Boxes lined one wall, Lays and Cheetos labelled on the cardboard. Cassie walked directly to the back door and checked the deadbolt.

Locked, excellent.

If she could lock the front door, then the gas station might be a refuge for a little while. The employee door was thick steel, and also had a deadbolt on it. The room likely doubled as a safe for employees during a theft before the world went to shit. It could be a safe again, this time for her. There was food, strong lockable doors and two points of egress.

Cassie made her way back to the main store and searched the back counter for a key. If she was going to make this store home, for now at least, then the main door had to be locked. The back room was completely dark, with no way to see anything outside. It wouldn't work as a safe room if she had to worry about being eaten every time she wanted to exit the room. She popped open another jerky and munched on it while she searched. Then she found it, a small hook hidden underneath the counter. On the hook was a ring with two keys.

Once the front door was locked, Cassie loaded her pack with more jerky and a few bars of chocolate. She was behind the store's one food aisle, getting a new two-litre of water out of the fridge when she heard the bang of the gun outside.

The instinct to drop found her on the floor. Two more pops rang out, then a male voice yelled out. Cassie peaked around the aisle, her own gun in hand.

Four men stood in the street, rifles pointed west towards the ocean. They fired a few more shots before running down the road Cassie had come in on. Seconds later, the dead stumbled past the store. There were dozens of them, all in one giant swarm, like bees.

Cassie jumped back behind the shelving, but she watched the procession through the perforations in the metal shelves. Her safe place no longer felt like a home, but a cell. She should have known better with so many houses around.

After the last of the swarm had passed out of sight, Cassie gave a full count to two hundred before moving. She grabbed her pack, strapping it tight this time. She wouldn't be staying to fight anything, running was the only real option.

The dead were only a few blocks up the street. She could be gone well before they made their way back to town, if they came back at all. There was no way she was going to wait around to find out. She had to hope that was the only swarm in Britannia Beach. The back door would be a better option, no chance that swarm would see her.

Although Cassie had yet to explore the back alley of the store, the devil she knew was not a devil she wanted to face. If she had to, she could just close and lock the door to the alley and take her chances leaving for the front of the store.

Gun in hand, she swung the door hard and fast. The growling started immediately. She took aim, but seeing only two, put the gun away. They could have once been a mother and daughter. Now their clothes were ripped, the girl's cartoon-printed nightie covered in blackened blood. The woman was missing half her face, her jaw dangling limp off her skull.

Cassie had intended to run, but she could handle two. She dropped the pack, pulled the knife from the belt strap and rushed them. She kicked the woman back, separating the two. The blade slipped past the girl's reach, and up into the head. Cassie tried to pull the knife free, but it was stuck. The hilt had gone right in and got caught on bone. Cassie yanked desperately, but it didn't budge. Dead hands grabbed her shoulder and Cassie whipped her fist, hitting the woman in the head. Pain shot from Cassie's hand all the way up her arm from the blow, but the punch had been effective. The thing was pushed back just enough that Cassie could get her leg up. Her second kick pushed the dead woman even farther away. Knife stuck, and one hand hurt, she had little option left. She pulled out the handgun and fired a single shot into the thing's head.

"Fuck, fuck, fuck," Cassie hissed, "too much noise."

She holstered the weapon and grabbed her pack. It was time to go. Fast. The alley was only ten feet wide, with stores on one side and a six-foot concrete embankment on the other. That other swarm could be doubling back after that gunshot. Cassie grabbed her pack off the ground and ran as fast as she could towards the coast.

Growling already echoed at the end of the street. Two small groups were converging on the mouth of the alley. Cassie pushed two aside and kept running before they boxed her in. The alley ended, and Cassie cut north. Moans and growls came from the south. The only chance she had was to outrun them and hide.

Another two dead started coming towards her from the north, trying to block her run. She was about to dart back towards the highway when a navy blue Chevrolet Caprice squealed out of a side street. The car flew forward, hitting the two approaching dead. The window popped down and a man yelled, "Get in!"

Cassie ran to the back door, grabbed the handle and jumped in the back seat.

Tires squealed again as the car spun up the north road. Cassie watched as lumbering bodies disappeared into the distance.

"Thanks," she said to the driver.

"No problem," he said through a groan of pain. Cassie looked over the seats. He was wearing a dirty grey tee shirt and blue jeans. The jeans had a long rip in the thigh. Blood gushed from a round wound. It was a bite mark. He saw her looking at the bite and gave a hoarse laugh.

"Yup. There were six of us a few minutes ago. We were trying to get find gas, ended up finding a bunch of those dead fuckers instead." He was crying while he talked, but his voice stayed steady, "I'm the only one left, and we both know I'm out of luck too. My plan was actually to use the car to take out as many of them as I could until I ran out of gas. Then I saw you."

Sweat was pouring down his face. The bite was bad. Soon he would likely bleed out, not long after that he would be walking around with the rest of the dead, stalking the living.

"Since your plan changed, what are you thinking now?" Cassie asked hesitantly.

"This road heads up into the hills, before circling northwest back towards the highway. I'm hoping there's enough gas to get me to Kendal's Lookout. You can have the car after that, I'll take a dive over the cliffs there. I won't become one of them."

That last was said in a determined whisper. Cassie understood all too well, she wouldn't want to be one of them either. If her choices were to become one of them or take a bullet in the head, she'd pick the bullet every time.

The gas light on the dash glowed bright orange.

"How far is the lookout, think we'll make it?" she asked

"Dunno, been on empty for a while," he said. As if in answer, the engine sputtered.

At least we're already surrounded by trees. What am I gonna do with this guy though? He's already dead, and he knows it.

"What's your name?" she asked.

"Mark," he answered. His teeth were gritted in pain.

"Mark, I'm Cassie. You likely saved my life back there. I can't thank you enough, but we both know what's going to happen to you," she said, her hand pointing at the bite in Mark's leg. "If we run out of gas before we hit these cliffs of yours, what then?"

Mark reached across to the rifle in the passenger seat, patting it. His lips were creased, and Cassie filled with pity. He pulled a single bullet out of the pocket of his vest, holding it up for her to see.

"We each carried one as an emergency. For this kind of emergency," his voice trailed off. He probably never thought it would actually come down to using the round. Before today, it had likely been only a half-serious joke. With all his friends dead or worse, and his leg ripped up, it wasn't a joke anymore. "I figure," he continued, "if we can make it to the cliff, then you can take my gun and my bullet. You'll need it more than I will."

Cassie was about to thank him again when the car died. There had been no more warnings after the first engine sputter, it choked and seized then gave up completely.

"Well shit," Mark sighed.

"What now," Cassie asked even though she didn't want to know the answer.

"I'm going to try and walk, if I can't then there's the bullet."

"Do you have something to staunch the bleeding?"

"Depends, you got a knife?" he answered.

Cassie automatically thought of the filleting knife, left behind in that alley. "Yes," she said, but it came out reluctantly. The folded pocket blade was her food knife. She didn't want it contaminated, but she wanted to help Mark too. He had likely saved her life. Besides, even in a messed-up world like this, a person should be able to choose how they die if they can.

She dug the knife out of the bag and handed it over. Mark pulled his belt off, and wrapped it tight around his leg, cutting off circulation to the wound. He was already pale, likely from blood loss.

Hopefully not because of whatever turned people into those dead things.

Mark used the knife to make a new hole high on the belt, so that it fit over his thigh. "Okay, let's give this a try. Can you try and find me a stick I can use as a crutch?"

Cassie nodded and got out of the car. As she did with every new location, she stood still for a minute, listening. There was no growling, no sound of bodies fumbling through the trees, just the occasional songbird. When she didn't hear anything that might indicate danger she walked to the roadside. It took a few minutes of searching until Cassie found a branch that would work.

She brought it back to the Caprice. Mark was already out of the car and was hanging on to the side mirror to stay upright. The stick turned out to be a little short, but it worked well enough.

He passed her the rifle harder than she'd expected, the scope dug into her chest.

"The bullet's already in the chamber. I only need to make it a couple of kilometres up the road."

She nodded, but she was sure within a few steps, Mark would be falling over. They started up to walk, and Cassie did her best to keep Mark's mind off the pain as he limped along. Mark had grown up in Britannia Beach. Most of the dead he shot had once been people he knew. The cliffs they were going to was a local hot spot, where he and his friends used to camp in the summer.

For her part, Cassie talked about growing up in Vancouver, her dad the cop, and how she was headed for Whistler. The last report she had heard on the news was that the military had commandeered the resort town as a refuge for those who hadn't gotten sick. All Vancourites who were well were supposed to make their way there. Mark nodded at that.

"Yeah. We saw military trucks headed that way just before everyone started dying, they all had gas masks on. I don't know how much of a difference that made, sooner or later I'm sure they had to take off the masks to eat. No one ever figured out how the thing spread." His comment had quieted them both for a bit, then Mark's face brightened, "Wait a second, I knew I recognized you! Didn't I see you on the news before all this started? Wasn't your dad that bomber, he blew up that high-rise?"

The world ends, and I still can't escape what he did.

"Yeah, that was him," she huffed. She was tired of having this conversation. Before, well, before the end of the world, her dad had blown up a twelve story building. She, hell the country, if not the whole world, thought he was delusional. He had been convinced the building was home to all the city's vampire population. Since it was an act of domestic terrorism, CESIS had been called in. The feds had questioned her for hours. She told them about the letter from Jonah Stilton, but every time she said his name, the agents' eyes would glaze over. It was like they stopped thinking. Like they were zombies. Her father's act was the most horrific act of terrorism on British Columbian soil and in the top ten worst in Canada, and she couldn't tell anyone what had actually happened.

"Figures I had to wait until the apocalypse to meet someone famous," he laughed. Cassie found herself laughing with him.

The last month had done anything, it had made her question everything she thought she knew about the world. Hell, if zombies could exist, then why not vampires? Of course, if they did exist, they must be hurting now with their food source almost completely eradicated.

Mark had pushed through the pain and found a slow stride with the crutch. They had been walking for a while, but his face was draining. He wouldn't be able to go much further. Blood still seeped out of the wound, even with the belt cutting circulation from the limb. Finally, he stopped at a dirt road that headed west.

"It's here," he said flatly, "if you keep going on this road you'll angle back to the highway. You'll hit another town on the way, but it's small, maybe a dozen homes and a corner store. It was where we were going to go, but we ran out of gas too soon."

Mark looked at Cassie, as if waiting for her to leave. Cassie forced herself to take a step backwards. She nodded at Mark, and was about to turn around when he spoke again.

"Cassie," he had held it together the whole drive and the walk from the car, but he faltered now. His face cracked, and he choked back tears. "I don't know if I can do this alone. Can you stay with me until I get to the cliffs?"

Cassie tamped her own tears down. She was so tired, so lonely. Just having Mark to talk to had been the best thing to happen to her in days. She nodded.

"Thank you."

They only made their way down the dirt road a few hundred paces before Mark cut off to the left. The area looked well used. A circle of rocks designated a fire pit and flattened circles in the grass showed where tents had been set up not that long ago. A couple of picnic tables sat worn by weather and use. The campsites were in an oval around an outcrop providing a view of rolling hills all the way to the ocean.

Mark walked to the edge and turned around. His eyes were glassy and flat. A tear trickled down one cheek. "It was nice to meet you, Cassie," he choked.

"Thank you for saving my life, Mark," she answered.

"I can do this," he whispered, forcing the words out.

Then Mark dropped the walking stick and dropped off the side of the cliff.

As Mark fell out of sight, Cassie let the tears come. She collapsed on one of the picnic table seats. She cried for Mark, for his dead friends, for Eric and Don, both dead a week now. She cried for the world, for being alone in it again.

She watched the sun set on the water. Everywhere she went, Cassie watched people die. The sun made the water glow a bright fiery red.

Fire. Now that would be cleansing. It's what the world needs. To wash away all this shit and start over again.

The thoughts were dark and unhealthy. She knew it but couldn't stop them from coming. As night moved in, Cassie wondered how long she would last. Every survivor she had met thus far was gone, dead and not dead. She contemplated Mark's single emergency bullet. Did it have to be an emergency? Couldn't she just use the bullet to end this? End all this bullshit. One bullet to the head and she would be at peace. No more running, no more fear.

In the end, it was Mark that brought Cassie from the brink. At least, it was his last act of kindness that did.

He didn't save my life so I could take it.

She had to repeat the words to herself over and over again, forcing herself to believe them.

Cassie couldn't say how long she sat at the table, but it was full night when she moved again. The moon was bright, casting everything in a purplish light. When she felt she could, she forced herself to eat another stick of jerky and a chocolate bar, washing it down with water.

She took another quick inventory of her pack and weapons. One round in the rifle, and eight in her handgun. Moving at night was not a good idea. It was too hard to see any dead that might be lurking in the shadows. Cassie didn't care, she couldn't stay here any longer. Every time she looked at the view, her mind replayed Mark letting his body topple off the side.

With the bright moon, the road was well lit. That made Cassie nervous. Anything could be hiding on the roadsides. The trees blocked all the moon's glow, making thick black patches she couldn't see into. Progress was slow, inching as quietly as possible along the road.

Time was hard to gauge. Cassie kept her eyes darting around the road, easily seen in the night's glow. Despite her path being lit, the forest to each side of her was black as pitch. Her ears were trained for any noise, not just the raspy growl of the dead, but any noise at all. All it would take is zombie to see her in the light, and she'd be done.

Cassie wasn't sure when the adrenaline faded, and tiredness took over. She shambled along the road, using most of her concentration on keeping her steps quiet. When she first saw the light through the trees, she thought her mind was playing tricks on her. She stood, stock-still in the road, watching it. She counted her heartbeats, waiting for the light to move. It didn't.

Two options warred in her mind. Run or go to it. One foot moved hesitantly forward, then the other. There was a dirt road headed towards the light. A little green sign with a house number indicated the road was a driveway. Cassie stayed in the shadows at the edge of the drive as she slowly walked towards the light. Once near the house, she ducked all the way into the trees. The illumination came from a porch light.

The power had gone out weeks ago. How was it still on? Cassie watched the light, thoughts pushing their way through all the defences she had created. For the first time in weeks, real hope bloomed in her.

Could it be diesel power? Solar? How the hell is that light working? Could someone be living there somehow?

As she stood there, watching the porch light, she noticed that the details of the house were becoming more clear. Sunlight was showing in the sky to the east. Cassie ducked further into the bushes. If someone was in the house, she didn't want them to see her. At least, she didn't want them to see her until she chose to let them.

Then the light flicked out. Cassie froze again.

Did someone turn it out?

With daylight helping her see, Cassie was able to make out the wind tower on the rooftop of the house, and the solar panels covering the garage.

Could the light have been on a timer? No one in their right mind would have just turned the porch light on all night for no reason. Could the house be...vacant?

She slipped out of her hiding spot and slowly stepped towards the house. When she reached the door, she stood there looking at it. She had no idea what to do next. Finally, she reached forward, and calling herself crazy, she rang the doorbell.

The *bing-bong* of the bell felt nostalgic like childhood cartoons, a normalcy that couldn't exist anymore. She rushed back around the garage, ducking away from the door in case she was wrong, and the house was occupied.

Always be extra-careful, and you might live.

It was her dad's voice ringing in her head. She had never trusted his advice more.

No one came to the door. Cassie crept towards the entrance a second time. There were windows on either side of the door, the same height as the door itself, but only six inches wide. She peeked in. Hardwood floors ran the length of a hallway, cherry red that lined grey walls. A bench sat near the door with a coat rack above it. There were no shoes under the bench or jackets on the rack. There seemed to be no people, living or dead, in the house. Cassie couldn't see any signs of habitation.

She rang the bell again, but this time stayed at the door, staring into the window for any signs of movement in the house. Minutes passed, and nothing changed. She tried the door handle. As she expected, it was locked. Feverishly, Cassie started searching around the door.

There's got to be a spare key, everyone hides a spare somewhere!

There was nothing under the planters nor under the rug. She ran her hand on the top of the door frame. Nothing there either. She turned to look for another way in when she saw it. She had run right past it after ringing the doorbell the first time. On the side of the garage was a lock, like the one on apartment buildings, or used by real estate agents, to put keys in.

It had to have a key in it, the question was how to get it. Cassie knew a fair bit about locks. Her dad had taught her every trick he knew, from getting out of handcuffs to breaking into cars - in case she ever locked her keys in her car, he had admonished strictly. Despite all those lessons, she had no experience with this type of lock. It took a round key of some sort. The lock's door had a seam but she'd need something to use to pry it open. She thought again of the knife stuck in the body of that little girl. She pulled out her utility knife and flipped the blade out. It looked so thin, not at all up to the job of breaking open the little safe, but what choice did she have.

The blade was thin enough to slip in the tiny slit between the frame and door of the key safe. Cassie pried on the door once the knife was as deep as it would go. The blade bent and the plastic housing for the blade also started to separate from the strain as Cassie leaned her weight in. The door on the safe didn't budge. It didn't even bend.

This isn't going to work. I'm just going to break my knife if I don't stop. A rock maybe? I could bash the lock open. How many hits would it take, how much noise would it make?

That idea wasn't attractive at all. Survival had become all about risk and reward. There was no way to know if bashing the lock would work, so limited chance of reward, but a fair amount of risk.

She could just break a window to gain entry to the house, but that also came with its own risks. Whoever had owned this house had put a lot of effort into making the house a self-sustaining sanctuary. Thinking of the timer for the lights, she wondered what other features might be still functioning, like a security alarm. The house wouldn't do her any good if she bashed a window in, only to have an alarm start ringing.

What about shooting the lock open?

This thought was much more appealing, assuming she didn't waste all her bullets trying to hit the lock, and assuming she didn't destroy the key in the attempt. The truth was, she needed this house, needed a place to feel safe, needed it to be as intact as possible because she needed something to feel normal. Anything that could feel at all like what the world was before the sickness was something to be cherished. Cassie wasn't sure how much more of this world she could handle. She needed to get in.

The knife is the quietest and safest option, but the least likely to succeed. One way or the other I'm getting in, so let's start with that anyway. If it breaks, it breaks.

It did break. Cassie stuck the blade into the slit again and gave it a hard shove. The cheap blade snapped in two, and the plastic casing split apart, ruining the tool completely.

"That's okay," she whispered to herself. She didn't believe a word of it.

"Move on. Bullet, rock, or window?"

Risk versus reward. I want to live here long-term if I can, so the window is the last resort. So rock or bullet? Bullet.

Cassie pulled the handgun out. There was no hesitation, she pointed the gun directly at the lock and pulled the trigger. Pain shot through her arm and she screamed. Blood oozed out of it, soaking her jacket. Her hand gripped the wound on her arm as she looked at the lock. The bullet had hit the side of the lock, carving out some of the metal, but exploding the wood siding next to it. She had only been a few feet away from the lock when she shot. The wood had exploded, and some of the shrapnel had hit her arm.

It hurt like hell. She moved her hand and inspected the wound. It wasn't too bad, a shallow cut, but she needed to bandage it up. She didn't have anything to sterilize it with, but she pulled a tank top out her pack and tied it around the wound.

Cassie looked at the lock again. She moved closer and examined the damage. The lock was damaged, but still completely sealed.

Great. What now? Chance wasting another bullet? And injure yourself again, maybe worse next time?

She wasn't sure that was a good idea, but what other choice did she have? She was not going to leave this house.

As she thought, she kept out a sharp ear. Noise attracted the dead, and gunshots were like homing beacons. If she was going to do something, anything, more to get into the house, she needed to do it soon. If she waited too long, she was either going to garner attention she didn't want, or she would lose her nerve.

Maybe I should just use a rock and smash a window. Risk versus reward, right? It's the simplest way in.

Her mind made up, she pulled Mark's rifle over her shoulder, then dropped her pack. She could smash her way in, then unlock the front door and get her stuff. A couple of swift kicks loosened one of the river rocks that had been used for landscaping. Boulder in hand, she walked around the house. From the west side, Cassie saw for the first time that the house was an A-frame set on a hill. What was the basement level from the front had a walkout into the backyard. There were lots of windows, many at ground level.

She looked at the windows with trepidation. Sure, she could knock out a window, but the basement was a huge open space. There was likely a door from the basement to the upstairs of the house, but breaking a basement window would open up that entire area to the elements and intrusion.

You can't help that, she chided herself. She hefted the rock with both hands, testing the weight. She wouldn't be able to throw it very far. That meant she had to be fairly close to the window. Lifting the rock caused a sharp stabbing pain in her injured arm. She'd have to step back right away, to make sure she didn't get cut by the glass. The last thing she needed was another injury. Cassie could feel the tank top she had used as a bandage soaking up her blood.

Come on, just get this done, go unlock the door and get your pack.

She hoped there would be something in the house she could use to clean up her arm. Then, as she thought about her pack, she realized what she had to do.

The emergency bullet!

Cassie dropped the rock and ran back around the house. The rifle was the perfect answer, but it only offered one shot. The rifle had more force than her little handgun. With the scope, she could stand far enough back to ensure she didn't get hurt and she'd have a much better chance at making the shot.

Rounding the corner of the house, she saw three dead shambling up the drive. Her first shot must have attracted them. Cassie didn't even have to think about it, she pulled the handgun out. She took the familiar stance and raised the weapon. In the month since all the dead the sickness had killed rose from the grave, Cassie had never defended a location, had never stood her ground. Until today, survival had always meant running. She would only engage if she was back into a corner. If she spent time killing any of the dead she found, more would just come. There were always more. This was different. She was in the middle of the country, hours away from the millions of dead walking around Vancouver. This house represented safety and security. Cassie needed both.

Just like the firing range, just like dad taught you.

Three shots and all three zombies fell. She scanned the driveway and surrounding woods for more, the whole time repeating the number of bullets left in the gun.

Five. Five left. Five bullets.

If she ran out, and there were still more dead coming at her, the house would have to be abandoned. Seconds passed, then a minute. Cassie didn't see any more of the dead. No growls emanated from the woods. Everything was silent, even whatever wildlife was around had been scared off by the four reports from the handgun.

Cassie holstered her weapon and rushed to her small pile of belongings. Once she was a safe distance away, she dropped the pack in the grass. Cassie was much more comfortable with handguns. She had gone to the range regularly, but she had never owned a rifle. Still, she remembered the basics, and the .22 she held was as basic as a rifle could get.

The grass was damp with dew, but Cassie knelt in it anyway. She pulled the single round out of her pocket and loaded it into the barrel. The pack made a decent mount, and she lined up the shot easily. Once the key safe was in the scope's crosshairs, she flicked off the safety.

Please work.

She pulled the trigger. The key safe exploded in a spray of dust. Cassie dropped the now useless rifle, tossed her pack on her back and pulled out her handgun again.

Between the two weapons, she had fired five shots around the house at different intervals. If there were any swarms around, she was helping point the way to her with every shot. She hurried to the destroyed safe but the key was obviously not in the remains of the small metal safe. Cassie scanned the ground, her eyes shooting from one mangled piece of metal to another. Then she saw it, a bronze key with a little green plastic cover around the handle.

It was in the deadbolt as quickly as she could manage, and the door opened. The air inside was still but fresh. Cassie walked in, closed the door and latched the deadbolt.

Despite not seeing signs of life - or unlife for that matter - when she rang the bell, she couldn't help but call out.

"Hello? Is anyone home?"

She waited, not for the answer of a living person, but the growl of the dead. She couldn't believe that the house was actually unoccupied. Inside her chest, her heart *chunked* with each beat, rattling her ribs. Her stomach flopped, roiling like a storm.

When no answer came, Cassie dropped the pack on the rug at the front door. The gun was in her hands. She had to use both hands to keep them steady. For the first time since the end of the world, she felt like she had something tangible to lose, but the truth was, she didn't know if it was even hers yet. There could be death waiting behind any or every door in the house. There was no doubt that she would rather die in this house than give it up.

Slowly, she made her way into the first room off the main door. It was an office, a massive hardwood desk and shelves lined with books. Cassie entered the room and double-checked the lock on the window. Finding it secured, she went on to the next room. It was a powder room, empty. Then on to the living room. It was open-concept to the kitchen and dining room. The huge windows climbed all the way up to the twenty-foot vaulted ceiling. Nothing stirred in the open space.

Another door stood ajar off to the living space, and another short hall off the kitchen led to more doors. Cassie started with the door off the living space. She entered a massive bedroom. A king-size bed on an enormous wood frame sat in the middle of the room. She checked the bathroom off the master and checked the locks on the window. Her eye kept going to the alarm clock next to the bed, flashing red light, burning into her vision.

12:00 12:00 12:00 12:00 12:00

Every time her eyes returned to the clock, her heart would skip a beat. She wanted to believe the house was empty, safe, but she had been running for what felt like a lifetime. Always running, always in danger.

The prospect of safety felt so foreign. It was like a memory of childhood, distant and indistinct. It felt like a lie. She wanted to believe that lie so badly that tears leaked down her face as she checked each room. Everyone was empty. The locks on each window secured.

A door off the hallway led to the basement. Again she found each room empty. All the windows and the double doors to the outside world were also securely locked.

Cassie made her way back upstairs. Her heart was slowing, but her hands couldn't stop shaking. The house was empty, locked, clean... safe. She sat down on the sofa and looked out the window. She watched the clouds float by over the horizon and tried to take all of this in. She had a safe place to be, a haven surrounded by hell.

Then she remembered the door in the kitchen. She shot up from the sofa and grabbed the gun from its holster again. Slowly she crept towards the closed door in the kitchen, the only door in the house that was actually closed. Sure something was behind the door, something ready to jump out to attack, her heart pounded again.

When she reached the door, both hands were trembling uncontrollably. She held the gun out with one hand and turned the knob with the other. A pantry. It was a pantry. Although Cassie found no threat in the small room, it also wasn't empty. Cans and jars lined the wall. She flicked the light, to get a better look, and gasped. The shelves were full all the way to the ceiling. Pasta and rice, fruit cups, soups, canned vegetables, and beans.

A sound, hoarse and desperate, issued out of Cassie's throat. Relief flooded in with such a rush it brought her to her knees. She collapsed on the floor of the pantry and cried until she slept. Safe.

More Books by D.G.R.

Vancity Vampires

Newborn

Paranoia

Rex's Diner (free short-story)

Hunter

Night Things

Bender's Cough

Day 9

The Horde (coming soon)

Manufactured by Amazon.ca
Bolton, ON

33013649R00127